I stared into the water, willing the memory to surface. As I did so, something white caught my eye. It was tangled in the lily pads, just at the edge of my vision. At first, I thought I was simply remembering—that the glassy eyes staring up at me through the murky water weren't really there. I blinked, hoping to shake free of the ghastly image.

But the picture would not go away.

I had found another body.

Praise for Leslie Rule's
WHISPERS FROM THE GRAVE

D0556934

KILL ME AGAIN

LESLIE RULE

JOVE BOOKS, NEW YORK

KILL ME AGAIN

A Jove Book / published by arrangement with
the author

PRINTING HISTORY
Jove edition / September 1996

The Putnam Berkley World Wide Web site address is
http://www.berkley.com

ISBN: 0-515-11939-3

A JOVE BOOK®
Jove Books are published by The Berkley Publishing Group,
200 Madison Avenue, New York, New York 10016.
JOVE and the "J" design are trademarks
belonging to Jove Publications, Inc.

PRINTED IN THE UNITED STATES OF AMERICA

10 9 8 7 6 5 4 3 2 1

For Kevin Wagner, my soul mate.

I'd like to thank the following people for their friendship and support over the years:

My editor, Gary Goldstein; Doris Bruner, Bill Baker, Millie Yoacham, Eilene Schultz, Janet Loughrey, Gail Jeidy, Harmonie Rose Keene, Anne Jaeger, Donna Anders, Cyndie Douglas, Maureen Woodcock, Le Ann Reardon, Ann Rule, Mike Rule, Andy Rule, Laura Harris, Rebecca Harris, Matthew Harris, Celia Sadlou, Teresa Grandon-Garcia, Jamie Thorstad, Daniel Thorstad, Jeanne Muchnick, Nancy Meyer, and Wendy Dennis. Special thanks to Amy Dennis who set aside her homework to carefully read my manuscript and caught a mistake that several pairs of more practiced eyes had missed.

I am grateful to my agents, Mary Alice Kier and Anna Cottle, for their enthusiasm, professionalism and friendship.

1

Insane.

Crazy.

Deeply disturbed.

There was a time when people I loved described me that way. Of course, they didn't realize I overheard them—that I was sneaking around, my eye to the keyhole or my ear to the door, desperately trying to piece together the odd puzzle my life had become.

My mom, my grandparents, my brother and sister, and even my boyfriend all thought I had lost my mind. They didn't believe me when I told them my life was in danger. And they *especially* didn't believe my theory on why it was so.

Sometimes I wondered if I *was* going crazy. That happens to artists sometimes. We are sensitive souls with restless imaginations. (My mother has always said I'm high-strung.) But the very fact I considered I might be going insane precluded the possibility. Crazy people seldom question their own sanity.

There was no time to sit around pondering the impossibleness of my situation. I needed to find answers to save my own life.

I can pinpoint the exact moment I knew something was wrong. I was stuffed in the backseat of our car, squished between my little sister, True, and a pile of suitcases. Toby, my ten-year-old brother, sat in front beside my mother and he exclaimed loudly as we drove over the bridge that led to Oxford, "Wow! Look, a giant clown head!"

"That's the Big Top Restaurant," Mom said. "It was owned in the forties by a retired clown. He had it built in the shape of a clown's head."

I peered over the top of True's curly hair at the strange-looking restaurant. The building *was* shaped like a clown's head, its bright red lips stretched into a wide "O" to form the front door.

Suddenly a long, blue convertible with its top down began to pass us, and Mom leaned on her horn. "Stupid jerks!" she yelled, as if the people in the other car could hear her. "You're not supposed to pass us on the bridge!"

As the car shot past, the driver turned and smirked at us. She was a striking girl about sixteen, and her shiny brown hair whipped wildly about her head. In the front seat beside her, two others laughed in our direction. My gaze shifted past the frizzy-haired girl in the middle to the guy next to her. His face was as finely chiseled as a statue of a Greek god—high cheekbones, smooth, broad forehead, and full, sensuous lips. A mass of chocolately curls bounced about his head. If this was a sampling of Oxford boys, I liked it here already.

The car sped ahead and the three kids glanced over their shoulders at us, apparently amused by my mother, who was shaking her fist at them. At that moment, all I wanted to do was slink under the seat and hide in embarrassment as I realized I'd probably be going to school with them. I had no inkling I'd just looked into the eyes of death—that one of those three laughing people would soon stop smiling forever.

I watched the car veer off the Oxford exit ahead of us and pull into the Big Top Restaurant. For the moment, I forgot the blue convertible and its snickering occupants as my attention was riveted on the strange restaurant.

"Can we eat in the giant clown head?" Toby asked excitedly. "I'm hungry!"

"We're almost to Grandma's and she's probably got lunch waiting for us," Mom said. "We'll go there another time. The Big Top is famous for its milk shakes—or at least it was when I lived here."

It had been years since Mom had visited her hometown. Our father had died of cancer five years earlier, and Mom had just lost her job as a cake decorator when the small bakery she'd worked for went out of business. So she'd decided to take her parents up on their invitation for us to live with them. She was hoping to start her own business, baking and decorating cakes for weddings.

"Oxford is a lovely little town," she had told us. "And Washington is a pretty state—not as warm as California like you're used to, but it's got more trees. Oxford is in the foothills of Mount Rainier and it gets snow every winter. I know you'll just love it!"

At first I'd grumbled at the idea of moving. It's not easy changing schools and saying good-bye to all of your friends. Then my adventuresome spirit took over and I got excited about the idea of a new place and new people.

But the instant I glimpsed the Big Top Restaurant, a shiver crept through me. It was so oddly familiar—the giant clown head's pointed red nose, his almost maniacal wide green eyes, the thick shrubbery growing from the top of the building to resemble wild hair. Why did I feel as if I'd seen it before?

It was as if the clown's eyes followed us as we drove past. I felt a chill that went all the way to my toes.

"Inside the clown's head there's a mural of the town of Oxford," I heard myself say. "It covers a whole wall."

"Did I tell you about that?" Mom asked absently. "Nan painted it."

Had she told me about the mural? I searched my memory, shuffling through the many stories she'd told us about her sister, Nan, but I could not recall hearing about a mural.

I'd never met my only aunt because she'd left home years ago at age seventeen. She'd sent a postcard from Hawaii shortly after she left but had been out of touch with the family since. I wished she would visit, because I thought I would like her. She was an artist like I was, and everyone said we looked alike.

"Are Grandma and Grandpa sad because Nan ran away?" True asked.

"Of course they are," Mom said. "Just think how I'd feel if one of you kids ran away."

"Why doesn't she come home?" True asked.

"Because Grandpa Eric told her to never come back!" Toby said.

"Toby!" Mom said sharply. "Where did you hear that?"

"From you," he replied smugly. "I heard you on the phone talking about it."

"You shouldn't have been eavesdropping," she scolded. "Now, I want you kids to drop the subject. Nan left home a long time ago but Grandpa still gets very upset if anyone mentions her, so I don't want you asking questions about her."

I guess every family has their secrets, and ours is no exception. Most of the time when Mom talks about her younger sister, a sad smile twists her mouth and her eyes brim bright with memories. "We used to have so much fun together. She was always thinking up crazy schemes—like the time we were teenagers and she talked me into dressing up like old ladies with her. Nan was really good at applying makeup and we actually fooled the clerk into thinking we were old. He gave us the senior citizen discount!"

It was hard to imagine my humorless mother with her deep-set serious eyes and bland manner actually setting out to do something silly. It must have been Nan's influence. "She always was a free spirit," Mom was fond of saying. "I could never quite guess what was going on behind those nutty green eyes of hers. It doesn't really surprise me she wanted to spread her wings and fly away."

But if the conversation turns to the night Nan left, Mom's eyes go dark and she changes the subject.

I've often wondered what drove my aunt away. What could make a teenage girl walk away from her family *forever*? What could have been so awful that she would never even phone home again?

Those are questions my mother would not—or *could* not—answer. "She'll get herself straightened out and come back someday," Mom says with a forced cheerfulness whenever I try to get answers from her. "And I know she'll love you, Alex! You're the spitting image of her and you've inherited her talent, too."

Toby's remark about Grandpa Eric seemed to have really rattled her. Her hands clamped tight on the steering wheel, her knuckles cresting white.

Had Grandpa actually ordered his daughter to leave? Is that why Nan never came home? I shuddered, imagining his face twisted in anger as he towered over his daughter. I've always thought he looks a little like Frankenstein. He is a big man of monstrous proportions. His feet are so huge he has to order shoes from a special catalog, and when he visited us in our apartment he bumped his head three times in the kitchen doorway because he forgot to duck. His head is sort of square-shaped, he rarely smiles, and he has gray shadows under sunken eyes. If he slicked his hair down and painted a jagged scar on his forehead, people would probably run away screaming.

Maybe that's a mean way for a girl to describe her grandfather, but I've never been very close to Grandpa. He doesn't really acknowledge us kids except at Christmas when he gives us each a card with five bucks inside. It's been the same every year as long as I can remember, with no adjustment for inflation. I don't mean to sound ungrateful. I'm very grateful. I'm grateful I didn't inherit Grandpa Eric's looks.

I suppose I should confess right now that sometimes I make jokes about things that make me sad. Grandpa has always made me sad. I can't explain why. All I know is that from the time I was a tiny girl and he came to visit, I'd look into his moist gray eyes and a wave of sadness would splash over me with such force I thought it would knock me down.

Maybe it was because Grandpa never smiled. Mom said it was because of what happened to his hand—but that was something *else* we weren't supposed to ask him about.

A missing daughter.

A missing hand.

Which one was it that made his eyes so heavy with bitterness?

We turned onto a quiet street and I experienced that odd pang of familiarity again.

Déjà vu.

That peculiar sensation of having been somewhere before.

"I've dreamed about this place!" I exclaimed. I somehow knew the wide street would curve gently, that knotted oaks would flank each driveway, and that a forested hill would rise in the distance.

I held my breath as the scene unfolded before us.

Exactly as I knew it would.

"There's your great-aunt Sidney's house," Mom said, pointing to a tall, green Victorian house, perched on a hill, overlooking a grassy park.

I *knew* it was my aunt's house almost before the words were out of my mother's mouth. Trimmed with pale gold gingerbread lace and encircled by a broad porch, the house was snuggled against a grove of fir trees.

My grandparents' house, at the end of the street, was big, boxy, and yellow. A short picket fence bordered a tulip bed around the front porch.

"I *have*!" I breathed. "I *have* dreamed about this place!"

"You must have seen a picture of it," Mom said.

That, of course, was the most logical explanation. I'd probably seen photographs of my grandparents' and my great-aunt's houses in our family album. And Mom had told us lots of stories about growing up here. No wonder it was familiar!

"You've only been here once before and you were so little that I doubt you'd remember it," Mom said.

"When?"

"You were about a year old," she said. "You'd just started walking. We went to the Oxford High faculty picnic with Grandma and you were toddling all around trying to catch the ducks. You were so adorable you got your picture in the paper."

"I was in the *newspaper*?" I asked, as we pulled into the driveway. "You never told me that! Did Grandma save a copy of the paper?"

"I'm sure she did. She has boxes of scrapbooks full of mementos. Actually, the Saturday of the picnic was a pretty eventful day in Oxford. It was a faculty picnic, but almost everyone in town ended up going to it. That's the way small towns are. A reporter from the *Oxford Journal* was there covering it, and he ended up writing a very sad story."

"Why?"

"A girl drowned."

A spiky chill went through me. I have always been afraid of the water. When our family visits the lake everyone else leaps right in, but I don't even like to go wading.

"How old was the girl?" I asked.

"Sixteen or seventeen. It was tragic—*just* tragic! Oh, look! There's Grandma!"

Grandma Thelma popped out the front door, clutching her squirming gray poodle, Edward, in one hand as she enthusiastically waved with her other. Grandma was as bubbly as Grandpa was dour. Her blue eyes sparkled merrily, her brightly painted purple lips were forever turned up into a cheery smile; and she could chatter endlessly about the most mundane topic. Grandma Thelma had a kind of nervous energy—much like her little dog, Edward, who peed on the rug when he got overly excited. When you stopped to think about it, Grandma and Edward were quite a bit alike. They both had poofy gray hair, they both loved strawberry ice cream, and they both made instant friends of everyone they met. (But, as far as I knew, Grandma never peed on the rug.)

"We're so glad to see you!" Grandma gushed and blew us a kiss. She moved Edward's paw so he appeared to be waving and blowing kisses, too. "Edward's glad to see you also!"

Please don't do stuff like that when we're at school! I silently pleaded. Grandma was a secretary at Oxford High where I'd be enrolling. I had a sudden mortifying vision of her blowing me kisses in the school halls. At least I knew Edward wouldn't be blowing me kisses because last time I checked, they didn't allow dogs in school.

A moment later, Grandma was all over us, her enthusiastic wet kisses smudging our cheeks with purple lipstick. "Alexis!" she exclaimed, her eyes registering something close to shock. "You look more like your aunt Nan every time I see you. It's uncanny!"

I, too, had noticed my resemblance to Nan when I studied the family photo album. We shared the same heart-shaped face, softly pointed chin, and long golden hair. Unfortunately, my nose was a little too long like Nan's, and I didn't like to wear my hair pulled back because my ears stuck out like hers. Everyone said she had a nice smile and that I dimpled just like she did when I laughed. We also shared the same slightly slanted green eyes. Cat's eyes, my mother called them.

"She's the spitting image!" Grandma said, shaking her head in amazement.

Mom nodded in agreement. "The last photos of the kids I sent you were from a year ago," she said. "Since Alexis lost twenty pounds and grew her hair out, you can really see the resemblance to Nan."

I'd struggled with my weight since seventh grade but when I started jogging a few months earlier, the pounds finally began to fall off. I was slender now, though I still had a weakness for chocolate chip mint ice cream.

Grandpa lumbered out the door, awkwardly hugging everyone as Grandma ushered us into the house. He stepped back, startled, when he focused on me. He did not mention my resemblance to his daughter, but he was obviously rattled as he gave me a quick hug and turned away.

We weren't to so much as mention Nan. According to my mother, all pictures of her had been put away. Now, here I was looking exactly like her. Would Grandpa hold that against me?

"How's Aunt Sidney?" Mom asked him. Sidney was Grandpa's older sister and everyone said she was senile.

"Still kicking," he said. "I told her we'd all come visit as soon as you're settled in."

Edward hopped around our feet, yipping sharply as we spilled into the living room.

Orange shag carpet. A fat tan couch. Silly knickknacks everywhere. My grandparents' wedding picture hanging over the fireplace.

So, so familiar!

My stomach stirred strangely.

I was just a baby last time I'd been here. Somehow, I remembered this house, yet there was so much more I could not recall. Though I could not label them, I *felt* memories, stirring urgently just below the surface of my consciousness. It was like staring down into murky water at a school of nervous fish. The water quivered and rippled with their movements, but the fish themselves were hidden.

Goose bumps rose on my neck and I knew instinctively my forgotten memories were not happy ones. In fact, they *terrified* me. I shuddered, disturbed.

"Are you cold, Alexis?" Grandma asked. "Your grandfather is always turning down the heat to save on the electric bill. Would you like to wear one of my sweaters?"

"I'm fine," I said. "But I would like to see the old photo albums."

I reasoned if I studied old pictures, I could put a name to this odd feeling in the pit of my stomach. Maybe I would recall what was troubling me.

While Grandma made lunch and Toby plopped down in front of the television, True and I pawed through the boxes of mementos my grandmother had stored in the hall closet. We lugged them into the living room and spread the scrapbooks out on the shag carpet. They were packed with keepsakes from my mother's and aunt's childhoods. Girl Scout badges Grandma had never gotten around to sewing onto sashes, prize ribbons from school relay races, report cards with the same boring comments from teachers: *Suzie is a pleasure to have in class*, and *Nan needs to work on her penmanship*.

It was interesting leafing through the remnants of my mother's childhood, but I was especially eager to see my picture in the paper.

I found it halfway through the second box. The fading newspaper photograph was neatly taped into a bright, red album. I was dressed in a flowered sunsuit and tiny white sneakers. My hair was a fluff of gold, combed straight up into a point. My chubby arms were stretched in front of me, as I laughed gleefully and toddled toward a duck.

"Is that you?" True asked. "You were a cute baby! Did you really think you could catch the ducks?"

"I guess so," I said. "But I don't remember that far back." With a sense of disappointment, I realized it was true. I might remember some things about this house and this town, but I had no tangible recollections of any of the early events in my life.

"How come you don't remember?" she asked.

"You can't remember being a baby, can you?"

"I *can*," she insisted. "The day I got borned the nurses put a little Santa hat on me because it was Christmas Eve."

"Mom hung the photograph of you in the Santa hat on the hall wall," I explained. "That's why you *think* you remember that day. You can't really remember that. *Nobody* remembers *that* far back!"

"I *do* so remember!" True said. "I was playing on the clouds with the angels and then God told me to go down and get in Mommy's stomach because you wanted a little sister!"

"You have a better memory than I do," I said, humoring her as I stared at the old photograph of me. It's strange to think the child in the picture was me, yet I could not recall that time. Why *do* we forget our baby days? It should be such a memorable time with the world so new and exciting.

I remembered life at three clearly, but the years before were nothing but vague shadows.

True turned the page in the scrapbook and I was surprised to see another newspaper photo of me in my mother's arms.

"What do all these words say?" she asked, pointing a chubby finger at the newspaper. My sister impatiently tugged on my arm, but I could only sit there, staring wide-eyed at the article.

"*Alex*, what's wrong?" she asked. "Does it say something bad?"

"Yes, True," I whispered. "It does. It says something *awful*!"

2

If the article had been about someone else, I would have found it interesting. I'd have sat riveted, shuddering and picturing the macabre scenario. Then I would have turned to the comics or the advice columns, soon forgetting the peculiar story. But this story was about *me*, not a faraway stranger I could forget in an instant. The article contained facts so shocking, I could hardly breathe.

A cold breeze seemed to blow through my bones as the tall black letters of the headline stared up at me: TODDLER DISCOVERS BODY.

I quickly read the article.

A thirteen-month-old child discovered the body of Judy Fitzwater, a senior at Oxford High, Saturday morning at Pioneer Park. The child and her mother,

Suzie Baxter, were attending the Oxford High Annual Faculty Picnic with Suzie's mother, Thelma Sorenson.

"I guess I'm still not used to the fact that Alexis is walking," said Baxter. "I wasn't watching her as closely as I should have. One moment she was chasing the ducks, and then she was gone. I heard her screaming and we all rushed over to the pond. My baby was sitting on the bank and crying. She had her little hand in the water and she was patting something. At first I thought she had found a big doll. But then I saw it was a girl!"

Judy Fitzwater was floating facedown in the duck pond. Pete Cline, Oxford High principal, pulled Judy from the water but was unable to resuscitate her.

Why hadn't anyone told me I'd found a body? My stomach churned queasily and a cold wave of shock flowed over me. With growing horror, I read the rest of the article.

"Alexis is just a year old, but I could tell she was upset," said her mother. "She was white as a sheet and she fell asleep in my arms, and didn't wake up until after dinner. It looked like Alexis was trying to pull the girl out of the water, but I don't think she really understood what had happened."

Picnickers reacted with shock to the tragedy. "Things like this don't happen in Oxford," said Patsy Sims, a recent graduate of Oxford High, and a volunteer for the event.

The coroner's office concluded Judy had been dead less than an hour, and police have not ruled out foul play. They are conducting interviews with everyone attending the picnic to see if someone may have witnessed something.

"The little girl who found the body may have seen something, but she's too young to talk," said Officer Bryer. "It's quite possible a baby may be our only witness to the tragedy. According to her mother, she was focused on that duck pond all morning. It's very frustrating for all of us involved in this investigation. The only person who knows what happened probably doesn't understand it herself, and if she does, she certainly can't verbalize it."

I snatched up the scrapbook and raced into the kitchen, sending a trail of Christmas cards and prize ribbons fluttering behind me.

"Mom!" I shrieked. "You never told me I witnessed a murder!"

My mother and grandparents turned to stare at me, their mouths dropping open. "What are you talking about?" Grandma asked as she ladled pea soup into a green porcelain bowl.

"The dead body in the pond! The one *I* found. And the police said I probably witnessed the whole thing!"

"Nobody was murdered," my grandfather said flatly. He was seated at the kitchen table, across from my mother, and as he shifted his large form, the chair creaked with his weight. "That poor girl drowned. She was walking on the slippery embankment and fell and hit her head on a rock."

"But the article says—" I began.

"That was the first article and the reporter was jumping to conclusions," my mother said. "Not much happens in a small town like Oxford and I'm afraid when something *does* happen, everyone milks it for all the excitement they can."

"Bruce Wingate, the reporter who wrote the article, was once a neighbor of ours," Grandma added. "I knew him as little Brucey. I used to bake him cookies when he was small, and he'd tell me all kinds of wild stories. He always did have a tendency to exaggerate."

"He wanted to grow up to be a journalist so he could be in the middle of the excitement," Mom said.

"Why didn't you tell me about the body?" I demanded.

"I didn't want to upset you," she said. "I didn't think you'd want to picture yourself—"

"Touching a dead person!" I finished her sentence. "The article said I was *patting* her!" A chill zipped through me. The sight of the bowls of pea soup lined up on the counter made my stomach turn.

"You used to pat me when I was napping," Mom said. "You probably thought she was asleep and you were trying to wake her up."

"It's so *awful*!" I sunk into a chair, numb with shock.

"Oh, honey!" Mom said. "I'm sorry. I should never have mentioned your picture in the paper. I didn't stop to think or I'd have realized you'd want to see it and you'd find the article. I should have known this would upset you."

"I—I wasn't expecting something so creepy," I said.

"I know," she said gently. "That was a bad day for all of us. It started out so happy! You were so adorable and the photographer took that first picture of you early in the day before that poor girl drowned."

I could not remember that day, yet I could imagine it. A happy day. A *picnic*! The sun was shining and people were eating chicken and blackberry pie and telling each other jokes. Children were laughing and shrieking and running in breathless circles, and the grown-ups were complimenting each other's potato salad and saying how lucky it was it hadn't rained.

How could someone die at a picnic?

It wasn't as if somebody's great-great-uncle of ninety-five had leaned back in his lawn chair after a satisfying meal, and with the sunshine heavy on his face had shut his eyes forever.

A young girl had walked out into the morning's golden light and died.

Young people can't die.

At least that is the way it *should* be. Death should be for the old, for those who have spent so many years alive they're bored with the whole routine.

What is the point of dying young? Why be born only to turn around and die before we're grown?

It was a question I found myself asking again and again in the next weeks as death reached out a shadowy paw and took another of Oxford's young.

I felt things in the following weeks with an intensity I had not known before. There was, of course, the great sense of indignity over the unfairness of death's choices. And there was *fear*—a vague fear I could not yet put a finger on. There was anguish and despair and a strange hollow sorrow.

But I would not trade those weeks or my suffering for anything in the world. For in the midst of all the turmoil, I fell in love. A great, golden cleansing love that made my heart light and the air taste sweet.

I know I'm jumping way ahead of things, yet when I tell this story, that is the part I like best. It was the love, after all, that got me through it. But on my first night in Oxford, I was not dreaming of falling in love or any of the other things yet to come. All I could think of was the past.

True and I shared Nan's old room, a remodeled attic with sloping ceilings and small dusty windows that peered out over the eaves.

We were tired from a day of traveling, and True fell asleep instantly in the twin bed across from mine.

I lay awake for a long time. The sheets were stiff and scratchy and smelled too flowery, and True was snoring loudly. But worse than that, my thoughts were alive with the terrible facts of the old article. I strained my mind, trying to remember the girl in the pond. I groped back into the depths of my memory files for a glimpse of my past.

You don't want to know.

That is what I finally told myself. After all, what good could it do to remember?

The thought set me free and I felt my hands unclench at my sides. The first layer of sleep gently flowed over me and I was just about to give into sweet slumber when something occurred to me. Wrenched awake, I sat up in bed and reached blindly for the string to the ceiling light. I yanked it, filling the room with light.

I huddled under the blankets and shivered as I watched True stir in her sleep.

What if Judy was *murdered?*

I reached under my bed, where I liked to stash things, and pulled out the scrapbook containing the newspaper clipping about the girl in the pond.

Her killer could still be out there! Does he live here in Oxford? What if he finds out I'm back?

I reread the article, searching for something to spark a memory. I still could not remember what happened to Judy Fitzwater. But her killer did not know that. If he thought I remembered the murder, it would make him very nervous.

Would he try to kill me, too?

3

It *was at the breakfast table that True broke one of the rules*. When you're six years old, it's hard to keep track of all the impolite questions not to ask adults, and my little sister seems to have a special knack for picking the very worst thing to ask at the very worst moment.

Grandpa was glowering behind his newspaper as he slurped his coffee, obviously trying to ignore the fact his normally peaceful table was suddenly bursting with the chaos my sister and brother brought to it.

"Grandpa's not a morning person," Grandma chirped cheerfully as she set a pitcher of orange juice on the table. "It's best if you kids don't talk to him until he's had his second cup of coffee."

True chose that instant to ask him to pass the sugar. He reached clumsily for the sugar bowl and swore under his breath as he tipped it over, spilling sugar on the table.

"That's okay, Grandpa," she said. "It's hard to pick things up with a plastic hand."

Grandma rushed over to clean up the sugar and Grandpa remained hidden behind his newspaper.

"What happened to your hand, Grandpa?" True asked innocently.

"*True!*" Grandma cried.

True looked bewildered, her blue eyes huge and glistening with approaching tears as Grandpa stomped from the room.

Grandma's tone softened. "You must *never* ask Grandpa about his hand." She patted True's shoulder. "It's a sensitive subject for him."

"That's because he used to be an artist," Toby said knowingly. "Now he can't draw anymore. How come he doesn't use his other hand? Or his feet? I read about some artists who didn't have hands who drew pictures with their toes."

"That's wonderful for them," Grandma said. "But your grandfather isn't like those other people. It's been hard for him to adjust."

"It's not like it just happened," Toby scoffed. "He's had a fake hand as long as I've known him!"

"*Toby!*" Mom appeared in the doorway in her fluffy blue bathrobe. Her cinnamon-red hair had not been combed and wild strands poked out in all directions. "Remember what I told you about that topic?"

"I know," he muttered. "Don't ask about Grandpa's hand and don't ask about Nan. What's with this family anyway? How come there are so many damn secrets?"

"Watch your mouth," Mom snapped, squinting her eyes warningly as she shook her head at my brother.

But Grandma said, "Toby, it's all the same story. Grandpa's hand and . . ." Her words trailed off and she swallowed hard before uttering her daughter's name. "Nan. Grandpa's hand and Nan! This used to be a happy family, but everything bad that happened is tied to the same tragedy."

For a moment, I hoped she would say more, that she'd finally let the proverbial skeleton come dancing from the closet. But True broke the spell by loudly griping, "I'm *sick* of secrets!"

"That's too bad, missy!" Mom said. "Now drink your orange juice and find your shoes before you miss the bus." She frowned at the kitchen clock and turned to me. "Your classes start in five minutes, Alex."

"You'll be late!" Grandma said. "Sue, you'll have to drive her. Normally, she could ride with me, but I have the morning off."

Mom threw an overcoat on over her bathrobe. I followed her out to the car. She opened the door and screamed.

"What's the matter?" I cried, running around to her side of the car where she stood frozen. Her gray eyes were wide with terror and I followed her gaze to the steering wheel.

"Oh, it's just a little spider," I said. The car was still a mess from our trip, and I picked up one of the crumpled napkins from the floor and gently plucked up the little brown creature and deposited him on a low branch of the apple tree.

Mom's appearance makes her look fearless. She wears little makeup, her jaw is square and strong, and she has her father's stature. But despite her height and sturdy build, she acts like a tiny frightened child whenever an insect crosses her path.

"What's so funny?" she asked. "That guy was *huge*!"

"He was more scared of you than you were of him," I said, giggling at the nervous way she surveyed the car seat before she sat down. "It's okay, Mom. I don't think he had his friends with him."

"I don't laugh at you because you're claustrophobic and afraid of the water," she said.

For the most part, I consider myself brave. I got my driver's license before any of my friends. I pick up garter snakes with my bare hands, and I looked right at the needle without wincing when I got my flu shot. But I actually panic when confined in small spaces. Once, when my brother locked me in a closet, I tore off my little fingernail trying to claw my way out. But nothing frightens me more than water.

"I'm sorry," I said. "I guess everybody's afraid of something."

We got in the car and headed for Oxford High.

I had wanted to walk to school on that first Monday in Oxford. The school was only a half mile from my new home, and I have to admit I'm a little embarrassed by my mother at times. She doesn't seem to have any awareness of the people around us and she'll ask me things in public in a loud voice like, "Do you still have diarrhea?"

But I was so engrossed by the scene at the breakfast table I'd lost track of time.

I was tempted to ask Mom about what Grandma had started to tell us. But she was in a sour mood and I sensed it wasn't the time. Still, I wondered. What did Nan's leaving have to do with Grandpa losing his hand? Did Nan somehow *cause* him to have an accident?

There was so much to think about!

With a little persistence, I hoped to get answers to those questions. Yet, my family did not have the answers for the questions that nagged me the most. *What* really *happened to the girl in the pond? Was she murdered? Did her killer know about* me?

We drove along the peaceful Oxford streets, and soft morning sunlight filtered gently through the branches of the magnificent old maple trees. As I glanced around at the sweet little houses with their blooming rose gardens and neatly trimmed yards, my terror of last night suddenly seemed like an overreaction.

Oxford simply did not look like a place a killer would live. True, I had witnessed a sad thing here—a *horribly* sad thing. And though I could not remember the day I found the girl in the pond, it was natural I'd be disturbed to learn about it. And it was natural my imagination would dash away with me. My friends have always told me I have a wild imagination.

By the time we got to the school, it was after nine and only a couple of kids were hanging around outside. "It hasn't changed at all since I went here," said Mom as she pulled up along the curb.

Oxford High was a big, brick building at the top of a steeply sloping hill. Maple trees circled the school, their long, strong branches reaching out to each other as if they were trying to join hands.

I was late for my first class, typing. The teacher was young and snippy with dyed red hair and did not hide her annoyance when I walked in late. I decided to get off to a good start in my second class and hurried down the hall so fast I slipped on a wet spot. My feet flew out from under me and I landed hard on my back.

"Whoa! Girlie, are you okay?"

I looked up into the bloodshot eyes of the janitor, who was staring lecherously at my legs.

I quickly smoothed down my skirt. "I'm fine," I said coolly.

"I just got done mopping. I guess the floor's still a little wet." He grinned broadly through a mouth of missing teeth. He was fortyish with a scraggly black mustache and greasy hair. I shuddered as his eyes swept my figure.

Shakily, I stood up, ignoring his outstretched hand.

"Independent woman," he said, smirking. "You're one of

those who gets riled if a guy opens a door for you, aren't you?"

I felt my face flush. How dare he mock me? If I were him, I'd be apologizing all over the place. He'd slopped water on the floor and made me fall. He was lucky I didn't break a bone! I could have sued him.

I was still shaking when I found my psychology class. As it turned out, it was just down the hall from my typing class, much closer than I thought. I was the first one there. The teacher was an attractive man with a neatly trimmed blond beard. When I walked in, he glanced up from his desk and his mouth dropped open. His small brown eyes widened behind steel-framed glasses.

"Hi," I said, squirming slightly at his intense gaze. "If you're Mr. Stetson, I'm supposed to be in this class," I added awkwardly as he continued to stare.

What was he staring at? I glanced down at my blouse, afraid for a moment the buttons had come undone when I fell. I looked back up at him and asked, "Is something wrong?"

"Who are you?" he asked hoarsely.

"I'm Alexis Baxter. I just moved here."

"Baxter!" He tossed back his head with relieved laughter. "*That* explains it! You're Suzie's daughter."

"You know my mother?"

"I know Suzie and I was very good friends with your aunt Nan. You look so much like her, it startled me. I thought for a moment you *were* her!"

"Nope." I giggled self-consciously. "I'm not her. She probably looks a lot different than I do now."

"Well, yes," he acknowledged. "I guess she would. It's been a long time since I've seen her. Has your family heard anything from her lately?"

"No. My mom feels real bad about that. It's really weird how she left like that and never even came back for a visit."

"Nan was always stubborn," he said, shaking his head.

"You knew her really well?"

A faint smile crept over his mouth as his eyes lit with a memory.

"Did you date her?" I asked boldly.

"Well, not exactly. Your aunt always had a little crush on me, but we were just friends."

"Oh." I could see why my aunt had been attracted to him. His voice was low and silky and when he leaned back in his chair, his crisp blue shirt stretched tautly across his muscular chest. His sandy hair swept away from his tan face in soft waves. He was probably a real hunk back in high school.

"Nan and I hung around together a lot," he said. "She was a great girl, but she had some problems. I feel bad I wasn't more supportive of her. Maybe she wouldn't have run off like that if I had been. I still worry about how her life turned out." Suddenly, he cleared his throat and began shuffling papers on his desk. His round face flushed with embarrassment, as if he realized he'd said too much. It was the most personal conversation I'd ever had with a teacher and I stood there for a moment, staring, not sure what to say.

"Were you enrolled in a psychology class at your last school?" he asked suddenly, obviously eager to change the subject.

"No, I've never had a psychology class before, but it sounds really interesting."

"I do my best," he said. "In fact, I encourage my students' input on what they'd like to learn about. Is there anything you're especially curious about?"

"You mean about how our minds work?"

"Precisely."

"Well, I *was* wondering about memory," I said. "Why do

we forget some things and remember others? And how come we can't remember when we were babies?"

"And how come I forgot to do my homework again?" said a girl, walking up behind me.

"It's either because your brain is the size of a walnut, or you're so busy thinking about boys you can't think of anything else, Tawny," said Mr. Stetson.

"Tom!" She giggled. It was the girl from the convertible. I recognized her, though her hair was no longer flying wildly. It fell past her shoulders in neat, shimmering locks. Her big eyes were layered with frosty, blue shadow, and she wore a tight pink dress that showed off her slender build. "Is that any way to talk to a student?" She tossed a scrunched up wad of paper at him.

"That's how I talk to students who don't do their homework, Tawny," he said.

"Hi, Tom," yelled a tall, athletic-looking boy from the doorway. "What boring thing do you have planned for us today?"

"Can't I get any respect from you, Mark?" Tom Stetson asked, smiling and apparently enjoying the banter.

I'd had a couple of teachers like him before, youngish and fun who liked students to call them by their first names. Tom looked about twenty-five. But he'd gone to school with my aunt so he must be closer to thirty-five, I realized.

The teacher grabbed a fat, blue mug from his desk and headed toward the door. "I've got to get caffeinated so I won't fall asleep in the middle of my *boring* lecture," he said pointedly, looking at Mark.

"Bring me back a double espresso," Mark shot back.

"Yeah, *right*," Tom said sarcastically. "Whatever you want. I'm here to wait on you."

"Hey, *I* pay your salary," Mark said flippantly. "You *should* wait on me."

"Your *parents'* taxes pay my salary. And fetching

espressos for students is not in my job description." He
turned to me before he ducked out the door. "Sit anywhere
you like, Alexis. We're pretty informal around here."

I slid into a seat in the second row, in front of Tawny, as
kids began to pour through the door.

"Got any gum?" Tawny tapped my shoulder with a sharp
fingernail.

"Sorry," I said. "I'm trying to quit."

She stared at me blankly, missing my attempt at humor.
"You're the girl in that car," she said suddenly. "You're the
one who tried to run us off the bridge."

I shrugged. "That was my mom, and she didn't try to run
you off the bridge. *You* cut in front of *us*." The words
rushed out before I could stop them. Her pouty mouth flattened into a straight line and I knew I had antagonized her.
The last thing I wanted was to make an enemy on my first
day of school. I forced a smile and said quickly, "I hate riding with my mom. I never know what she's going to do."

She grinned. "My mom is the same way. She gets tickets
for driving too *slow*."

"Who were those other people in the car with you?" I
asked.

She regarded me slyly. "Those other *people*? You want
to know about Kelly, or do you want to know about *Josh*?"

A warm flush crept up my cheeks.

Tawny laughed. "Girls notice Josh Shelldrick everyplace
we go," she said possessively. "Kelly—that's my cousin—
just about melts into a puddle when he's around. I think
that's why she's been hanging around me lately, so she can
be near Josh."

"He's your boyfriend?"

She stared at her desk and began doodling daisies around
the holes in the cover of her notebook. She ignored my
question and said, "Kelly's kind of crazy. Well, the whole

Sims family is kind of nuts, but she is *really* crazy. I mean sometimes she actually seems *insane*."

"Really?"

"Yeah. She's always flipping out over little things. She might have to come live with us because her mom can't handle her. I told my mom that if Kelly moves into our house, then *I'm* moving into the guest house."

"Why?"

"She's unpredictable," Tawny said. "She skipped fifth grade, so she's really smart. But now she hates school and is flunking a couple of her classes. I think the only reason she comes to school is so she can be near Josh. She might try to murder me in my sleep so she could get to him. Oh! Here she comes."

Kelly, a skinny girl in tight jeans, bounced into the room. Her coarse black hair was pulled into a high ponytail that bobbed with each step. She grinned a huge gummy grin at her cousin as she headed toward us.

"At least she's in a good mood today," Tawny mumbled.

"There better not be a test today," Kelly said, sliding into the seat next to Tawny. "Because I didn't study for it and I think I'm already flunking this class." The prospect of failing didn't really seem to concern her. She appeared amused at the idea, but Tawny gave her advice anyway.

"You just have to know how to talk to Tom. Flirt with him a little and he won't flunk you."

"Eyuck!" she said. "I'm not flirting with a *teacher*! He's old enough to be my father!"

"He's a *guy*," Tawny said simply. "So what if he's a little older than we are. All guys are flattered when girls flirt with them."

"Tawny!" Kelly rolled her eyes. "You've got the morals of an alley cat."

Tawny reddened and let out a dry laugh. "I'm just talking about a little flirting. I didn't suggest you go *out* with him or anything."

Their discussion ended abruptly as Tom entered, carrying a steaming mug. He kicked off his shoes and sat on the edge of his desk in his stocking feet as he balanced the coffee cup on one knee. "Who studied for the test?" he asked and was answered with several groans.

"Those of you who haven't studied are off the hook," he said. "I've decided to scrap the test."

"*What?*" a chubby girl in the front row cried. "I stayed up until *midnight* cramming!"

He took a sip of coffee. "My apologies to you, Courtney, and all the rest of you who studied. I'm sorry if you think it was a waste of time, but at least you learned something. Now, today we're going to talk about memory."

I felt pleased as I realized he'd chosen the very topic I'd asked him about. He noticed me smiling and winked at me. Embarrassed, I looked down at my desk. The top was worn and scratched and covered with carved initials and names. *Kilroy was here, 1976. Jill loves Jason. F.G. and C.C. Forever. N.S. + S.D. = Love.*

N.S.? Could that be my aunt? I ran my finger around the carving, thinking how strange it was to attend the same school my mother and aunt had, strolling down the same halls, staring out the same windows, maybe even sitting in the same desks. It was hard to imagine Mom as a teenager, scrunched and uncomfortable in one of these confining desks, waiting patiently for the teachers to call on her when she raised her hand. She tended to blurt things out when she got the urge and didn't like people telling her what to do.

"Take a look at the picture on the wall," Tom instructed. Thirty pairs of eyes shifted to the seascape.

"Now, look back at me," he said. "Who can tell me how many boats are in the painting?"

"Seven?" Tawny ventured.

"Good guess. There are eight boats there. But you *knew* that, Tawny," he said.

"I *did*?"

"Yes, and you also may know exactly how many waves are splashing by the boats."

"I *do*?"

"Memory varies from person to person. Facts are locked away in a part of our brains we can't easily access. Our minds record everything we see, hear, smell, and taste. In short, *everything* we experience. But we edit out the unimportant things and recall only what is pertinent and useful to us."

It was incredible to ponder. Somewhere in the shadows of my mind, I *remembered* the girl in the pond.

I raised my hand. "Is there a way to remember something you forgot—like the details of a crime you witnessed?"

"Hypnosis has proved useful for retrieving forgotten memories," said Tom.

A voice came from the doorway. "I've got a message from the office for you, Tom."

Glancing up, I nearly gasped at the sight of the gorgeous guy. It was Josh, Tawny's friend. He strode across the tile floor, long and lean and gracefully masculine in snug, faded blue jeans. Under the fluorescent lights, his springy, dark curls held a hint of red. His startling blue eyes were a pleasing contrast to his brown hair. As he smiled at the teacher, I found myself thinking Josh's full, sensuous lips were designed for kissing.

He handed a folded slip of pink paper to Tom, who thanked him, unfolded the note, and read it silently before tossing it into the recycling bin.

Josh turned to leave and then—suddenly—stopped and stared back at me. It was as if he'd *felt* my eyes on him, *felt* the intensity of my gaze.

I could not look away.

His eyes were fringed with long, inky lashes and he watched me, unblinking. I was lost at sea in the blue of his eyes. I wanted to drown in his gaze, to be pulled into the depths of him and stay there forever.

Then he looked away.

Was it an instant we stared at each other? A minute? Or an eternity? It is really hard to say, because what we exchanged was unlike anything I'd felt before. It did not know the boundaries of time or place. For a fractured moment, I had the sense I'd known that beautiful boy forever.

The spell was broken as Josh slipped back into the hallway, and I glanced about, expecting to see everyone gawking at me. I was sure they'd noticed the odd thing that had passed between us. But the others were talking to each other or scribbling notes or staring blankly at the teacher.

"Can anyone describe the boy who just left?" asked Tom.

Courtney, the girl in the front, groaned. "No fair!" she squealed indignantly. "I didn't know you were *testing* us on that. Did you tell him to come here so you could quiz us on what he looked like?"

Tom grinned and pulled the slip of pink paper from the recycling bin. He smoothed out the creases and held it up. It was blank. "That's right, Courtney. I asked Josh to pop in here to see what you'd remember about him."

"I didn't even *look* at him," she protested. "I was looking at my math homework."

"Relax." Tom rolled his eyes at the ceiling. "I'm not grading you on this. Who can tell me what Josh was wearing?"

"A blue coat and jeans?" asked a boy in the front.

"He wasn't wearing a coat," blurted Kelly. "Josh was wearing a green T-shirt and *tight* jeans."

"I think he had a watch on," Mark said.

I raised my hand and cleared my throat when Tom called

on me. "He wasn't wearing a watch," I said certainly. "But he had a silver ring on the little finger of his left hand. Kelly's right. He was wearing a green shirt. It had a pocket in it, and his tennis shoes were supposed to be white but they were kind of gray because they were dirty. His shirt was tucked in, and he had on a thin, brown leather belt."

"*Well, well.*" Tom was amused. "We know what Alex's favorite subject is. It seems you take your education seriously when it comes to studying boys."

The class tittered and a hot rush of embarrassment flowed through me.

"You take after your aunt," Tom added quietly, and I blushed some more.

A cold voice spoke behind me. "I *knew* you were interested in him."

I did not turn around to look at Tawny. I could not deny what she was saying. I *was* interested. And I had foolishly just let a whole classroom of people in on it. Before the day was over, I would come to regret it.

4

I *saw him again that afternoon. It was right before lunch when* I stopped by my locker to dump my armload of books. My head was bent in concentration as I swirled the lock for the dozenth time. I was just beginning to think I had the wrong combination when the door popped open. I shoved in my books and when I looked up, there he was, at the locker next to mine.

His locker was open and he was scooping a handful of change from the coat of a jean jacket hanging inside. "Lunch money," he said and smiled at me.

"Oh," I said, for lack of anything better to say.

Suddenly a pair of slender white arms slithered around his neck. *Tawny!*

"Gotcha!" She giggled as she let him go. Then she saw me. "This is the girl everyone's been teasing you about,

Josh," she said. "She's the one who described you right down to your underwear size."

I blushed madly. Josh's smile tightened and his cheeks reddened, too.

"Hey, Shelldrick!" Mark, from class, yelled. "There she is!" He made his voice squeaky in an unflattering imitation of me as he added, "And he has a silver ring on the little finger of his left hand!"

Josh punched Mark in the arm and said, "What can I say, Kelborne, old buddy? She must be hot for me. I have that effect on girls everyplace I go."

I slammed my locker shut and whirled away. I rushed down the hall, stinging with the sound of Josh's laughter. *Of all the arrogant boys!* How could I possibly have thought he was attractive? I chided myself. How could I have thought something special had actually passed between us?

Humiliated, I decided not to risk running into him in the cafeteria. Instead, I got an apple and some chips from the vending machine and went back to my locker for my books. I ate outside in the sun, sitting on a boulder and leafing through *Beowulf*, my book from English literature, *not* because I was particularly interested in it, but because I wanted to look busy. Although I had no friends at Oxford High, I did not want to appear lonely.

My book looked ancient. Its spine was soft and loose, and hundreds of kids had doodled in the margins of its pages. "Sorry this isn't in better shape," Mr. Higgins, my English lit. teacher, had said. "That's what happens when you start school late. All the books in good shape are already taken."

This book was probably around when my mom went to school here, I realized as I leafed through the weathered pages. My name had been added to the long list of names on the front jacket—the names of all the students who had been assigned the book before me. I scanned the list, wondering if my mother may have had this very same book. I gasped when I spotted the familiar name. It was second from the top, a neat, flowing signature. *Judy Fitzwater.*

It really wasn't such a shock to discover I had the same book as the drowned girl, though it *was* an eerie coincidence. It was the ugly scrawl beside the name that made me swallow hard. Someone had circled Judy's name and written "Die Bitch" in red letters beside it.

Sick, I thought. What a sick joke! The red ink had faded to a weak pink, so it must have been written long ago, perhaps shortly after her death when people at the school would have still remembered her.

It made me sad that people could be so ugly.

I set aside my chips, sick to my stomach. *I wish we'd never moved here!* I thought, as I pulled out my class schedule: *4th period: History, Jacobbi; 5th period: P.E., Hamill; 6th period: Art, Barnes.*

I usually found history classes boring, and P.E. wasn't much fun either because teachers were always forcing us to climb ropes or do sit-ups, and there was never enough time for showers to pull yourself back together for the rest of the day. But I felt a surge of hope at the thought of art class.

I've always loved art. My parents said I found a crayon when I was eleven months old and tried to draw with it, so I must take to art naturally. I still remember the time when I was three and scribbled a "mural" on my mother's freshly painted dining room wall.

I proudly led my parents into the dining room and said, "See. *I* drew that!"

"Alexis!" they cried in unison, color draining from their faces. I could see they were upset as they scolded me, but I remember thinking, *I'm a good artist!*

I guess true artists don't let anyone discourage them.

Someday, I would go to art school and study nothing but

art all day long. But now I had to wade through mostly boring classes. In history, Mr. Jacobbi, a thin, bald man who looked about ninety-five, showed a film and I dozed through most of it.

P.E. was the first day of a water safety program, so all we did was sit in folding chairs around the twenty-five-yard pool and watch as Mrs. Hamill, a square-faced woman who never smiled, demonstrated how to save people from drowning.

"Next week we'll be taking turns feigning drowning and rescuing each other," Mrs. Hamill told us, her hands on her thick, sturdy hips.

How am I going to get out of that? I worried, squirming inwardly. I didn't want to admit to the teacher that I'd never learned to swim. I was afraid she'd embarrass me by saying something about it in front of the class. Not too many sixteen-year-olds can't swim, but the school I just moved from didn't have a pool so I'd managed to keep my embarrassing secret.

Finally, sixth period rolled around and I headed for art class. All day I'd thought of this last class of the day as a reward. I'd looked forward to it like a sugary dessert after a tasteless meal.

Anita Barnes, the teacher, was a pretty, bubbly woman in her mid-twenties with fine blond hair that fluffed out like chicken feathers around her oval face. She wore a yellow, cotton dress, cinched at her slim waist by a red belt.

"I'm so excited you're in my class," she exclaimed when I walked in. "Your aunt Nan used to baby-sit me."

"Really?" I asked, smiling back at her. "It seems like everyone here knows each other."

"Oxford is a small town. It's like one big family. I grew up down the street from your grandparents. Nan baby-sat me every Saturday. In fact, she taught me how to draw! She's the one who inspired me to love art."

The warmth in Anita's voice touched her eyes—soft gray eyes, brimming with a childlike excitement unexpected in a teacher. I liked her immediately. "Rumor has it that you're quite the artist," she said. "If you're half as good as your aunt, we're going to have a lot of fun."

Anita was still chattering about my aunt when Josh came in. After his rude comment at the lockers, I had vowed to ignore him—to never so much as *look* his way again. But I was dizzy at the sight of him, striding purposefully across the room with a large sketch pad under his arm.

He's an egotistical ass! I told myself. Still, I watched from the corner of my eye as he took a seat by the window. He flipped open the sketch pad, and when he bent his head and concentrated on his drawing, his long, springy curls fell over his face.

I forced myself to look back at Anita, who was shaking her head in amazement. "Your resemblance to Nan is so striking," she said. "Tom told me you really startled him the first time he saw you."

"He looked at me like he'd seen a ghost."

"Genes are a funny thing," she said. "I don't resemble anybody in my family, but my sister is a perfect mix between my mother and my father. And here you are, looking exactly like your aunt!"

"I wonder what she looks like now."

"If you could see her, you'd know what you'll look like in twenty years," she said. "Maybe she'll come back someday. I think about her a lot. I always figured she'd become a famous cartoonist. Someday we'll probably pick up the newspaper and find a comic strip by her. Wherever she is, I hope she's still drawing."

As Anita began setting tall jars of tempera paint on a round table near her desk, I selected a seat near the front of the room and a safe distance from Josh.

I tried not to look at him, but my eyes would not behave.

He'd crossed his legs, with his right ankle resting on his left knee, and had propped his drawing tablet up on his lap. His hand moved gracefully over the page as he sketched. I wondered if he was a good artist. Maybe we had something in common.

Anita smacked her hands together to get the class's attention. "Okay, you guys! Listen up!" she yelled. "I know some of you are going to give me a hard time about this, but today we're going to do something you probably haven't done since kindergarten. We're going to finger-paint."

The class stared at her, stony-faced, as she continued. "I've noticed this is an uptight class," she said with an apologetic smile. "You people seem to be afraid to get into the art. So today we're going to throw away all the rules and go back to basics. I want you to *feel* the paint on your fingers. I want you to get in touch with the little child you once were and find that creative place inside of you. If you're worried about your clothes, the smocks are in the front closet."

While most of the class sauntered to the front of the room for paint and smocks, Josh continued to sketch. He seemed lost in his drawing, and—despite my resolve—I was lost in *him*. What was it about him that fascinated me?

His forehead was high and smooth, and as he looked down on his drawing, his long, dark lashes occasionally flickered against his cheeks as if he was closing his eyes to picture the thing he was drawing.

His full lips curled beautifully as he smiled to himself.

I was captivated.

He was gorgeous, but there was something more. There was just something about him . . .

Suddenly, he glanced up and caught me staring. I could feel my cheeks burning as I turned away and smiled at the girl who sat beside me. It was Courtney, the chubby girl from psychology class.

She had set several jars of paint on our table and poked a pointed, pink nail into the blue paint. "Yuck," she said. "I hope this doesn't ruin my nails!"

I dipped my fingers into the orange paint. It felt awkward and messy. I was definitely more comfortable with a paintbrush. Tentatively, I smeared a fiery arc across the top of the paper.

"Get in touch with the little child you once were," Anita had said.

The little child I once was.

Could I get in touch with that part of me?

Somewhere inside of me, she was still there. A funny-faced baby with round, green eyes and a gurgling laugh. If I got in touch with her, would I *be* her, with all her thoughts and memories? Would I recall a sunny picnic and a dead girl in the water?

Would I remember a *murder*?

I shuddered as I dipped into the red paint. My hand trembled, bumping the jar.

I reached to steady it, but it was too late. Courtney squealed as it skidded to the edge of the desk and tipped over, unleashing a wave of brilliant red paint.

It splattered everywhere—across the floor in the front of the room, up the side of Anita's desk, and onto the shoe of a boy who happened to be walking by.

"Shit!" he said, grimacing at his now red tennis shoe.

"Cool," another boy said. "It looks like blood."

Everyone was staring. I prickled with embarrassment as Anita rushed over and handed me a roll of paper towels.

My first day of school and I'd humiliated myself in front of *two* classes.

I dropped a paper towel onto the nearest puddle where it was instantly soaked. As I knelt to clean up the mess, everyone but Josh went back to painting. I glimpsed his oversized basketball shoes plodding toward me as I ineffectively swiped at a lake of red paint.

"Wow," he said. "Looks like a major mess."

"Thanks for the brilliant observation!" I snapped. I glanced up at him, steeling myself for the arrogant smirk I was sure I would see. But he looked bewildered. He shrugged and awkwardly turned away.

I felt a sudden stab of regret.

Had he been trying to be friendly?

"Those paper towels aren't going to do the job," Anita told me. "You better get Deke, the janitor, and have him bring his mop."

I followed her directions and headed down the long hallway which led past the office, where my grandmother leaned on the counter, chattering on the phone. She waved and blew me a kiss, and I silently thanked God no one was around to see it. I passed a dozen classrooms. Some had their doors propped open and the droning voices of teachers poured into the hall, punctuated by the occasional sound of chairs scraping along the floor as restless students fidgeted in their seats, eager for school to end so they could burst out into the sunshine.

At the end of the hall, a wide staircase led down to a dimly lit basement. The ceiling was low and thick with cobwebs. Unnamed machinery hummed and buzzed and clicked and coughed. I moved deeper along the shadowy hallway, searching for the door with CUSTODIAN stenciled on it that Anita said I would find.

Raucous laughter flowed through an open doorway. I peered in. The janitor and a fat, bearded man hunched over a desk, playing cards. Behind them, a monsterlike furnace dominated the big, boxy room. It breathed and belched, its fiery tongue flicking in and out of view through the little door that looked to me like a grimacing mouth.

An odd assortment of objects crowded a tall bookcase in the corner. A child's tricycle. Several nonmatching boots. A twisted license plate, a flat basketball, and a broken umbrella. A headless doll.

What kind of collection was *that*? It was creepy.

I'd been waiting for the janitor to acknowledge me. I had the feeling he'd seen me in the doorway and was deliberately ignoring me. I cleared my throat and said, "Excuse me."

"Yeah?" he asked. He set his cards down and stretched. "Somebody throw up or are the toilets overflowing again?"

"I spilled paint," I said meekly.

"Shit. Every time we get into a real good game some kid loses his lunch or a little prima donna spills paint."

"It was an accident," I said lamely.

"Yeah, yeah. Where did it happen?"

"Anita's class. I tried to wipe it up with paper towels but there was just too much."

He waved me away. "I'll be there in a minute, sweetheart," he said. The bearded man was staring at me blankly, his mouth hanging open. I turned and hurried up the hall and felt a great wave of relief when I crested the stairs.

It was another twenty minutes before the janitor arrived, grumbling to himself as he slopped his mop through the paint.

"Sorry about the mess, Deke," Anita smiled at him. "I've got some things to take care of down the hall, so I probably won't be back until you're done. Make sure you get the puddle of paint that dribbled under my desk."

"Whatever you say, your highness. You've taken an unusual interest in the newspaper business lately. While you're off playing games, I'll be here cleaning up your messes." He spoke so softly I didn't think she heard.

But she *did* and obviously took offense because her fine,

blond eyebrows leapt into arches and her voice lost its sweetness as she said, "*What* did you say?"

His lips curled away from stained teeth as he grinned at her, amused. "I *said* I'll be sure to get the puddle under your desk."

She stared at him a moment, unsure what to do. They both knew what he had said. Apparently, half the front row had also heard because we were all listening intently.

Anita became aware of this, and, flustered, she picked up her purse and quickly left the room, her yellow skirt swishing crisply.

"I wonder what he meant by that?" I said.

"Oh, everyone knows she's dating Tom, the psychology teacher," said Courtney. "She's always finding excuses to sneak down to the teacher's lounge when he's there."

"What did he mean about the newspaper?" I asked.

"Who knows?" Courtney said. "That Deke is a strange guy. He hangs around with that slow man who lives in the park. Neither of them makes much sense. Anita is kind of embarrassed when Tom puts his arm around her in front of us. She's always trying to act like there's nothing going on, but everyone knows there is."

Anita's eyes were sparkling a few minutes later when she returned to class.

"Looks like Deke got the place all cleaned up," she said when I passed her desk on the way to get more paint.

"I feel awful about spilling the paint," I said. "I'm really sorry."

"It was an accident. Everyone makes mistakes. Once when Nan was baby-sitting me, I spilled orange pop all over her sketchbook and ruined half her drawings. I started crying because I felt so bad, but she was so sweet about it. She said the orange coloring made the drawing better. She was the nicest baby-sitter I ever had. I can't get over how much you remind me of her." Anita's face glowed and her words tilted with a happy lilt as her eyes met mine.

I felt a sudden closeness with her, as if we were going to be friends.

I was happy to know she and Tom were dating. They made such a cute couple. I didn't spend too much time thinking about my teachers' love life. My mind was still on Josh.

Class ended and I felt a twinge of disappointment as he slipped out with the crowd. I'd wanted to make eye contact with him, to let him know I was receptive if he ever wanted to be friendly again.

As it turned out, I did not have to wait long for a chance to talk to him. I saw him after school, as I cut through the park on my way home.

His back to me, he sat on a bench with his drawing tablet on his lap. His hand moved deftly over the paper as his head bent in concentration. Curious, I crept up behind him and peered over his shoulder. I recognized the girl in the picture immediately.

The high cheekbones, the full lower lip, and the slightly slanted eyes. I recognized those features because I saw them every time I looked in the mirror.

5

"That's me," I said quietly and Josh jumped.

He turned around and regarded me with an embarrassed smile. "She sure looks like you, doesn't she?"

"I guess so."

He set his pencil down and scooted over. "Have a seat."

Gingerly, I sat down beside him.

"I'm glad you're here. I've been wanting to talk to you."

"Yeah?"

"Yeah. Hey, I'm really sorry for being such a jerk today. I didn't mean what I said about you. You must have thought I was an arrogant ass when I said that about you being hot for me."

I smiled. "Well, as a matter of fact, I did."

"But not anymore?"

"You just apologized, didn't you?"

Our eyes locked. Suddenly, I was breathless. He was so

near, I could reach out and touch him. But of course I didn't.

"Why are you drawing me?" I asked.

"It's really weird. I've been drawing the girl in this picture for a couple of years now. Lots of times I start out to draw something else and I end up drawing her. I call her my mystery girl."

He flipped through the tablet and showed me several more pictures. "Even her profile is like yours," he said in awe as he pointed to a drawing of the girl smelling a rose. He lightly placed his thumb under my chin, turning my face so he could study my profile.

His touch sent shivers through me.

"What does it mean?" I asked. "Are you psychic or something?"

He shook his head. "I don't know what's going on. But I think I like it."

For a moment it was as if we were the only two people in the world—until a deep voice interrupted. "Can I have this?"

We turned to see a big, stooping man in old, soiled clothes. It was the strange, bearded man who had been playing cards with the janitor. He held up one of Josh's drawings of the girl who looked like me. It was apparently half-finished and discarded. "Did you mean to throw this away?" he asked.

"Yes, Burrel," Josh said. "That one didn't turn out right. The eyes are funny. You can have it."

He grinned at us through a mouth devoid of teeth and folded up the picture. He jammed it into one of the big pockets in his coat.

"That's Burrel," Josh said as we watched the raggedy bulk disappear into the trees. "He collects garbage. Don't ask me why."

"He's weird. He kind of scared me."

"He's harmless. He's about fifty and still lives with his mother. He had an accident when he was a kid and has never been normal since. But he's never hurt anybody."

I loved listening to Josh tell me about the interesting characters in Oxford. He'd lived here all of his life and seemed to know something about everybody. "My house is about half a mile from here," he explained. "It's toward Kettleburg, near the Ackerman's berry fields."

"There're my two favorite artists!" a cheerful voice called out. It was Anita, the art teacher, pedaling by ferociously on a shiny blue bicycle.

"Hi, Speedy," Josh said as she whizzed by. "We call her that because she's always racing around on that thing."

That hour I spent with Josh changed me forever. Just knowing he existed on the same planet with me made everything more vivid. The crisp maple leaves drifting from the trees were no longer an everyday orange. They were the orange of fire—a fire so brilliant it hurt to look at them.

The sky was bluer and the clouds snuggled on the horizon were whiter and fluffier than ever before.

The shouts and laughter of children playing nearby rang with extra excitement.

Everything was more of what it had been before.

Josh made me feel vibrant with life. And, strangely, suddenly, *everyone* seemed more alive. When the old man walking his Scottie dog in the park smiled at us, his blue eyes shined as brightly as if two light bulbs were burning behind them. His little dog wagged his whole body at us, his coal-black fur shimmering in the sunshine.

The ground under my feet sent surges of energy through my being so I seemed to bounce with each step. I had the sense that with a little effort I could spread my arms and fly into the sweet, smoky autumn sky.

And it was all because of Josh.

His gaze was electric. His laugh—deep and rolling and rich with soul—was perfect.

Everything about Josh was perfect. The squared slope of his shoulders. His long muscular legs. The way he tilted his head when he was trying to follow one of my long-winded stories.

Josh Shelldrick was the perfect boy. And I knew if I lived ten thousand years, I'd never meet another boy who could compare to him. *I'm falling in love*, I realized when I arrived home and my mother asked me if I was on drugs.

"I've told you three times I have some good news for you," she said. "But you're just staring into space with a weird smile on your face like you don't hear me."

"I'm sorry. What's the news?"

"Get out your paintbrushes," she said. "A friend of Grandma's has a job for you."

"A window job?" I asked. I'd painted store windows over the holidays when we lived back in Milltown. I'd made over five hundred bucks painting elves and reindeer and snow people in the shop windows along Main Street.

"Roger Wainsworth owns the Big Top. He wants you to touch up the mural. Grandma told him how good you are, and she says he'll pay you a fair price. Maybe you can start saving for a car of your own. I won't be able to let you drive mine very often because I'll need it for my bakery business. I've got an ad going in the paper next week, so I expect to start getting calls soon."

"I don't have any money to buy paint."

"Roger already bought the paint, so all you need to do is bring your brushes."

"I don't know about touching up someone else's work," I said, suddenly nervous. "What if their style is totally different from mine?"

Mom beamed. "My sister painted the original mural! Remember? You have the same whimsical style that Nan does and I know you'll do a great job."

Style is a rather personal thing. The only art Mom attempts is in her cake decorating, and the truth is, she is rather unimaginative. So I figured she couldn't really understand. Still, Nan wasn't here and the mural apparently needed touching up. And *I* needed some money. Things were tight since Mom lost her job, and there was all kinds of stuff I'd like to buy.

"Roger says you can start tonight if you like," she said. "I'll drop you off, but first I'm going to swing by and see Aunt Sidney."

Dusty and musty and eerily timeless.

That was my first impression when we stepped into the parlor of Aunt Sidney's Victorian house.

Sequoia, a stocky girl with a wide, pleasant smile, let us in. Mom explained that Sequoia was attending the nearby community college and she and another student lived in two of the downstairs rooms and looked after Aunt Sidney in exchange for room and board.

"I'm glad you're here," Sequoia said and ran her fingers through her long frizzy dark hair. She wore a yellow T-shirt and flowing turquoise skirt. Her wide, sturdy feet were strapped into sandals. "Cassie's not here yet," she said as she stuffed books into a backpack. "She was supposed to get home fifteen minutes ago. I'm going to miss my bus and be late for class if I don't leave soon, but I didn't want to leave Sidney alone."

"What classes are you taking?" Mom asked.

"Diesel Mechanics, Introduction to Eastern Philosophy, and pottery," said Sequoia.

"How interesting," Mom said politely.

Sequoia laughed, a full burbling sound. "I know it's a weird combination. My parents owned a gas station so I'm used to working on engines, and I like pottery because it helps me relax, but I'm struggling with Eastern philosophy. I'm not much of a writer and I've got to produce a fifteen-page paper by the end of next week."

As Sequoia glanced at her watch, Mom said, "You run along. We'll wait here until Cassie gets home."

Aunt Sidney had trouble remembering to turn off the stove and sometimes she forgot her parents were dead. "But other than that, Daddy says she manages quite well as long as someone's here to look after her," Mom told me. "She's got a television in her room and sits glued to it all day. The girls make her soup and toast and help her keep track of when her favorite shows are on."

I wandered around the parlor, running my fingers over the dust-laden furniture. An antique velvety red sofa was positioned at the edge of a sun-faded Oriental rug. With its arched back and doily-covered carved wooden arms, it looked rather grand as if it were a queen holding court over the room full of empty chairs.

"It would be nice if the girls would vacuum in here." Mom punched an overstuffed chair. A cloud of dust rose and hovered like a gray ghost. "But I suppose they're busy with their studies and we aren't paying them anything. Nobody really comes in here anymore, so I guess it doesn't matter."

Though the antiques were lovely, the room did not feel like a place where a person could get comfortable. A stifling thickness hung in the air, punctuated by the dulled ticking of the grandfather clock.

"Mom, have I ever been here before?" I asked.

From the outside, the Victorian house had seemed familiar. Yet I did not recognize the inside.

Mom frowned in concentration. "I think I brought you here when you were a baby," she said. "Why, is this familiar to you, too?"

"No. Not at all."

"Now I remember! I *did* bring you here," she said, laughing as she picked up a cherub-faced figurine. She traced her finger along a dark crack down the middle of the body. "I remember because Aunt Sidney finally had the whole place to herself and she got out all her parents'—*my* grandparents'—knickknacks and placed them all over. This was my grandparents' house and they died when I was really little. When I was growing up, Aunt Sidney lived in the upstairs. It has a separate entrance so it was kind of like she lived in an apartment," she explained. "Right after you were born, the old man who rented the downstairs passed away. Aunt Sidney decided she wanted the whole house to herself, so she quit leasing the downstairs and has lived here alone until recently. She wasn't used to little children and she almost swallowed her dentures when you broke this Hummel."

I grimaced. "I know a girl whose mom collects Hummels," I said. "Those things are expensive!"

"You were so cute, she forgave you." She set down the figurine. "Let's go up and see if she remembers us!"

A wide, curving staircase led to the upstairs. As soon as I stepped off the thickly carpeted steps onto the polished wooden floor of the upper level, I felt that familiar pang of recognition again.

I gazed around the hallway, my eyes captured by the crystal chandelier that swayed from the ceiling. Afternoon sunlight reached its airy fingers through the tall window at the end of the hall and played a silent tune on the prisms. Where sunlight caressed them, a melody of colors burst forth and spilled rainbows on the walls.

The gentle yellow light strumming the hanging fixture made me think of angels playing harps. The rays of light were graceful golden hands of angels playing tunes so softly that only those in heaven could hear.

"Isn't that pretty?" Mom said, pausing beside me to admire the effect. "Aunt Sidney used to tell us that when the light hit the chandelier like that it was angels playing a tune on the prisms that only other angels could hear."

Stunned, I stared at her. "Have you told me that before? I was just thinking that exact same thing!"

"I must have. How else would you know? Unless you're psychic."

Psychic! Was it possible I was? Was that what was going on? Was I having premonitions?

"Knock, knock!" Mom said, opening a door on our left.

"Who is that?" a creaky voice called.

"It's Suzie, Aunt Sidney. And Alex. Remember Alex?"

"What do you want?" the old lady asked suspiciously.

I followed Mom into the room where a shriveled being with bright red hair sat hunched under a fuzzy green blanket in a rocking chair by the window. On closer inspection, I realized her hair was actually a wig, resting slightly askew atop the pink head.

The shades were drawn and the room was cluttered and gloomy. Stacks of magazines dominated the corners and out-of-style flowered blouses hung from a clothesline strung across one side of the room. "Garage sale finds," Mom whispered when she saw me looking at them. "Aunt Sidney can't pass up a bargain and she ran out of room in her closets."

"Daisies for you!" Mom said, thrusting a handful of flowers at her.

"Did you pick those from my yard?" she said, her spotted hand closing around the stems. "That's stealing, you know."

"No, Aunt Sidney," Mom said, laughing. "I got them from Gertie Olson next door to Dad's house. I told her we were coming to see you and she insisted we take you some fresh daisies because they're your favorite."

Her brow creased, creating a rippling effect of more

wrinkles. "Gertie Olson," she said slowly. "She has the worst taste in men. Every one of her husbands dies."

"She has had some bad luck," Mom agreed.

"Not bad *luck*," she said so vehemently a spray of spittle flew from her dry lips. "Just bad *judgment*, if you ask me."

The conversation didn't make much sense, but Mom rolled with it, barely missing a beat as she responded to her aunt's strange comments. I stood in the corner, disturbed by the sights and sounds and smells around me.

Decay.

That's what this was—this musty old room with its dried-up occupant. I was witnessing the crumbling of a life. Is this what the future holds for us? I wondered. If we live long enough do we all become like Aunt Sidney? Stale and confused and annoying to our relatives? I could see by Mom's strained pink smile she was holding tight to her patience.

"You didn't steal these from my yard, did you?" Aunt Sidney asked again as she let the daises fall into her lap.

"No, Aunt Sidney," Mom said. "Gertie Olson gave them to me. Remember? I just told you that and you said she had bad judgment in men because all of her husbands died."

"I wouldn't be surprised if Gertie killed them," she said. "Poisoned them probably. And buried them out behind that little garden shed in her backyard. I saw something like that on one of my programs."

"Oh, Aunt Sidney," Mom said, a ripple of irritation flowing into her voice, "I don't think Gertie would do that. That kind of thing doesn't happen very often and when it does they always show it on television so it just seems like it happens all the time."

"Television? Did you say you wanted to watch television? Go ahead and turn it on if you like."

The television was already on, two feet away from her. It sat on a little wooden table and at the moment it blared with a commercial depicting a woman parachuting from an airplane as she shampooed her hair.

"What's got into people nowadays?" Aunt Sidney said, shaking her head as she focused on the TV. "That looks just plain dangerous to me. What if she gets shampoo in her eyes? How is she going to rinse it out up there in the sky?"

"It's a *commercial*." Mom's voice flattened in exasperation.

In that instant, I felt a stirring of compassion for Aunt Sidney as her eyes sprung wide open at Mom's tone. She sounded hurt as she said, "I *knew* it was a commercial. Of course I knew that!"

"Yes, yes. I know you did." Mom patted her arm and rolled her eyes at me. Neither of us believed the old lady. But she looked so chagrined I found myself moving to her side.

"I think it's a pretty stupid commercial, too," I told her.

She beamed, her smile spreading like honey on warm toast. "*Nan!*" she cried and reached for my hand. Her fingers felt dry and papery as they closed over mine. "You were always my favorite niece!"

"Yes, Aunt Sidney, Nan was *obviously* your favorite," Mom said resignedly. "But this is *Alex*. She's my daughter."

"*Nan!*" Aunt Sidney said again, pure joy radiating from her face.

As our eyes touched, I felt a great wave of love coming from her and I knelt to hug her. Bony arms wrapped around me, holding me with surprising strength. The scent of her perfume, heavy and tropical, rolled over me. It was somehow comforting. "We always understood each other," she whispered.

"Yes, we did," I agreed because it seemed like a nice thing to do.

As we pulled apart, her smile withered. "I'm going to

miss you," she said. "But I want what's best for you, so take the money and *run!*"

"Money?"

"You got the money I gave you, didn't you? There was six hundred dollars in that envelope. I don't care what your daddy says, honey. True love only comes along once in a lifetime and sometimes not at all."

As I stared into her hazy gray eyes, they suddenly grew clear and bright—like fog-filled skies burned clean with sunshine.

Startled, I realized that though she appeared to chatter mindlessly, Aunt Sidney was actually reliving a conversation she'd had long ago. And I knew with unquestionable certainty she had loved Nan. She'd loved her so much she'd helped her run away.

6

I *turned to see my mother's reaction, but she had moved to* the hallway where she was straightening a painting on the wall.

A sad and secret smile tiptoed over my great-aunt's mouth.

I had so many questions. Where had Nan gone? Why had she left? Had she kept in touch with her?

I feared a straightforward question would shake the old woman back to reality, to the here and now where she existed beneath layers of confusion and probably would barely remember Nan. So I simply stared at her, holding my tongue as I silently urged her to tell me more.

"He is your true love, isn't he?" she asked.

"Yes," I whispered, though I did not know what she was talking about. I assumed she was referring to a boyfriend of Nan's.

True love.

Was there really such a thing?

My mind flew to Josh. I shivered, remembering the delicious thrill of his touch. We'd walked to the edge of the park, our fingers laced together, our hands swinging between us. *Is he going to kiss me?* I'd wondered as we stood at the park entrance, preparing to go our separate ways.

His pepperminty breath was warm on my neck as he bent and kissed my cheek. Short and sweet. It was enough to make me feel as if my knees were dissolving. I had floated on a cloud the rest of the way home.

"I see in your eyes you are in love," Aunt Sidney said. "Don't let a love like yours slip through your fingers," she warned. "You'll regret it. It's hard to live with a heart full of regret. I kissed my true love good-bye in his soldier uniform. If I had it to do over, I'd never have let him go. He didn't come back to me, Nanny."

"That's sad."

She blinked away old tears. "It doesn't have to be like that for you. You can be happy."

Though puzzled, I smiled and nodded, encouraging her to keep talking.

"Oh, your daddy's not going to like it," she said. "But he's too stubborn to know what's good for his own daughter. He thinks Scott's no good just because—"

"I just heard Cassie come in," Mom called out, interrupting from the hallway.

"*Why?*" I asked Aunt Sidney. "Why doesn't he like Scott?" I could not contain myself any longer. I was desperately curious about the secrets of my aunt Nan, the aunt who was so much like I was.

But as Mom bustled into the room, Aunt Sidney clammed up.

"We better get going, Alex," Mom said.

As we drove to the Big Top, I opened my mouth a dozen times, wanting to tell my mother about my strange conver-

sation with Aunt Sidney. Yet, somehow—oddly—I felt as
if I'd be betraying the old woman. She and Nan had shared
a secret that I was privy to only because I resembled Nan.
Aunt Sidney had spilled the beans because she believed I
was her beloved Nan.

I felt as if I was a link in a chain of a secret so old it had
a special power. I could not bring myself to break the
chain, to tell the long kept secret.

What good could it possibly do to tell?

Surely it would hurt the family to know Aunt Sidney had
aided her seventeen-year-old niece in fleeing her home.

I could imagine the shock skirting through their eyes
when they heard the truth. I did not want to hurt my mother
and grandparents.

I silently rolled the words around in my mouth, carefully
tasting them: *Mom, Aunt Sidney gave Nan the money to run
away.*

I suppose it sounds strange to say words have a taste, but
these did, even silent on my tongue. They were sharp and
bitter and held the flavor of betrayal.

I silently vowed to visit Aunt Sidney again, to learn
more about what had transpired between her and Nan. For
now, I decided to ask a few questions without giving away
what I had learned. "Mom, did you like Nan's boyfriend?"
I asked.

"No," she said flatly. Then she asked suspiciously,
"What do you know about him?"

"Not much. Just that she had one. How did they meet?"

"Nan stole him away from one of her friends. Poor Patsy
didn't get over it for years. Scott was no prize. My sister
actually did her a favor."

"How come you didn't like him?"

She shrugged. "He seemed okay at first, but Dad didn't
like him. He worked for Scott's father and detested the

man. Dad nearly blew a gasket when Nan took up with Scott."

"Grandpa shouldn't have judged Scott because he didn't like Scott's father."

"You sound like Nan," she said with a laugh. "She used to say the exact same thing."

"She was right," I said.

"No," she said bitterly. "Nan turned out to be wrong."

"Why? What happened?"

"It's all water under the bridge now." She took a sharp turn into the Big Top parking lot.

I hesitated, my fingers curled lightly on the door handle, waiting for her to say more.

"You better get going," she said, "Roger's waiting for you."

As she drove off, I stood for a moment, staring up at the giant clown head gazing back at me. A curved mouth formed the front door, and high up in the building, two round windows made eyes. Long, curled eyelashes and steeply arched eyebrows had been painted on, giving the clown a wide-awake effect.

Inside, it was brightly lit. I glanced around at the worn red vinyl booths that lined one wall. The tables were covered with balloon-patterned tablecloths, and the salt and pepper shakers were shaped like circus animals—lions, elephants, and monkeys.

"Can I help you?" someone asked, and I turned to see Tawny, standing behind the counter. She wore a baggy uniform, covered with huge, blue dots, and a tall, pointy hat with a pom-pom on the end. She looked so ridiculous, I couldn't help smiling.

She glared at me. "You have a *problem*?"

"I'm just surprised to see you here," I said quickly.

"I'm surprised to see me here, too," she muttered. "Believe me, I'm not here because I *want* to be!"

A skinny, grinning girl, carrying a tray of plastic mustard containers, burst through a pair of swinging doors, and the soft clink of dishes rang from the kitchen behind her. "Tawny's working here *only* because her father got her the job. He thought she should learn how to be 'responsible,'" she said, shaking her head so the little pom-pom on the top of her hat jiggled. "We all hate these uniforms, but it's worse for Tawny because she's never worn anything but designer clothes."

Tawny took off her hat and slammed it on the counter. "It was a sick and twisted mind who came up with these uniforms."

"It sure was," the other girl said. "I call him 'Dad.'"

"Oh, you must be Rachel," I said. "I'm Alex. I'm here to work on the mural."

"I'll get my dad," she said. "He's in the kitchen making chili for the chili dogs."

A moment later a burly blond man with ruddy cheeks was vigorously shaking my hand. "I'm Roger Wainsworth," he said. "I hear you're quite the artist. Customers are always complimenting us on your aunt's mural. It's one of the things that makes this place unique. That's why we were so upset when the roof leaked on it."

I followed him over to the wall, where the rolling hills of Oxford were immediately recognizable in the faded mural.

"Your aunt painted both the old and new parts of Oxford." He pointed a thick finger at the corner of the wall. "That's the part of town that's underwater now. When they built the hydroelectric project and put in the dam, they had to back the river up several miles. This mural is a real conversation piece because new folks in town like to know what Oxford looked like twenty years ago before it was flooded, and the old-timers like it for the memories."

The mural had an almost cartoon quality, yet the detail was meticulous. Nan had painted a group of townspeople, gathered around the fountain in Pioneer Park. My eyes swept over the crowd, mothers pushing strollers, a helpful-looking policeman, a chubby, laughing barber with a pair of scissors in his hands. Each figure was painted with a loving and careful hand. An inexplicable rush of pride flowed over me.

"It really should be hanging in a gallery somewhere," Roger said.

"Thank you." My face tingled and I knew I was blushing. I hadn't meant to take credit for the mural, but for an instant I felt as if *I* had painted it. "I'm proud of my aunt," I said quickly. "She's really talented."

"Yes, and, according to your grandmother, you have inherited your aunt's talent."

"I hope so," I said modestly. The truth was, I *knew* I had Nan's talent. And I was stunned by the similarity in our styles. It was the first time I'd seen my aunt's work and I stared in amazement. Her faces all had the big round eyes I'd long considered *my* trademark. And she used the same carefree, exaggerated strokes I did for the hair and grass.

"Well, what do you think?" Roger asked. "Can you fix her up?"

"I think so. My style resembles my aunt's. I've always thought of myself as a cartoonist and I like to paint the same kinds of whimsical scenes as she does."

"Apparently, you *look* like her, too," he said and pointed to a figure in the bottom of the picture. Nan had painted herself in the foreground, larger than the other figures. She held a dripping paintbrush and winked one eye. Her fluff of gold hair swept away from her face, showing off high cheekbones just like mine.

"Everyone says that," I said.

Customers began filing in and Roger lumbered back to the kitchen. I stared at the mural for a long moment, afraid to get started. What if I *ruined* it? I worried. What if I botched the whole thing and Nan came home and saw what I'd done?

A large hand suddenly curled around my shoulder and I jumped. "Sorry, Alexis Arlene," a gravelly voice said. "I didn't mean to startle you."

I turned to see my grandfather, an unaccustomed gentleness in his eyes. His gaze roamed slowly over the wall. "It's something, isn't it?"

"It's wonderful," I agreed, surprised to see him. This, after all, was the mural his "evil" daughter had painted— the daughter he had banished, the daughter no one was ever supposed to mention! So why was he standing here admiring her work?

"Artistic talent runs in our family," Grandpa said. "My grandmother was an artist and she passed it on to my father who passed it on to me and now you have it."

I noticed he didn't mention Nan. He'd carefully avoided mentioning her name. He'd skipped over her as if she'd never existed, although we were standing there admiring *her* work. Apparently, his sudden show of emotion was not about Nan, but simply about the artistic genes in the Sorenson family.

He held up his left hand and nodded at his prosthesis. "I'd hoped to have a career as an artist," he confided. "Unfortunately, I'm left-handed. After the accident I tried to paint with my right hand, but it never felt comfortable to me."

I stared at him, shocked he'd brought up the very thing we weren't ever supposed to mention. "That's too bad," I said awkwardly. "I don't know what I'd do if I couldn't paint."

"It's *awful*!" he said, bitterness creeping into his tone. His eyes narrowed in anger. "It's like being a bird who can no longer fly!"

His fury frightened me and I took a step back.

"But that's history." He forced a smile. "You can't change the past."

"I'm left-handed, too," I said. I couldn't think of anything else to say.

"I brought something that might help you in the restoration process of the mural." He turned to the table behind him and picked up an instant camera. "I know you're going to have to scrape away some of the paint where it's flaked," he said. "You can photograph those areas first so you can duplicate the original while you're repainting."

I got busy snapping pictures, and Grandpa said he was ordering something to go. He told me good-bye a few minutes later and headed out the door carrying a large white bag of steaming food. Ten minutes later he was back, an impatient scowl on his face as he headed for the counter. "This isn't what I ordered!" He slid the bag over the counter toward Tawny.

She slowly turned it upside down and shook out its contents. "Three chili dogs and three cheeseburgers," she said flatly.

"That's not what I asked for."

"Yes it is." Tawny began riffling through the tickets stuck on the little nail behind the counter. With a satisfied smile she ripped one off and thrust it at him. "*See!*"

"That's not *my* order," he said. "You must have got it mixed up with someone else's."

"I remember *you* ordering this."

"Look here, young lady," he said harshly. "I know what I ordered! You must have had dozens of people in here tonight. Why can't you admit you've made a mistake?"

Tawny folded her arms in front of her and thrust out her chin. The clown uniform did not help her position. She looked sillier than ever. To make matters worse, a group of popular girls from school were in line behind Grandpa. They giggled and whispered, relishing the confrontation.

But Tawny, obviously embarrassed, was not about to back down.

A moment later Roger emerged from the back, wiping his hands on his apron. "What's the problem?" he asked.

"I ordered a small pizza and four chili dogs, and your girl here gave me three cheeseburgers and three chili dogs," Grandpa barked.

"We're so sorry about that, Mr. Sorenson. Have a coke on me while I fix that order up."

"He's lying," Tawny said. "He must have changed his mind about what he wanted to eat. He didn't order any pizza!"

Grandpa's eyes widened in shock and his lined face flushed.

"Tawny!" Roger said. "The customer is *always* right. If you talk to my customers like that again, you're out of a job!"

"Fine!" Tawny threw her hat on the counter. "I didn't want to work here anyway!"

I ran into her a couple of minutes later as she was changing in the rest room. She yanked her uniform off, ripping the front of it. A large orange button popped off and bounced in the sink.

"That was your grandpa who got me in trouble, wasn't it?" she asked.

"Afraid so," I said. "Sorry he got you fired."

She smirked and rolled her eyes. "Who cares? I told you it wasn't my choice to work here. Now I don't have to wear that ridiculous clown suit."

I watched her flounce out, with a defiant flip of her long hair. Though she made the whole thing sound like a joke, an angry edge lined her voice. I grimaced as she slammed the bathroom door.

I wished it didn't have to be *my* grandfather of all people who had confronted her. First my mom yelled at her from our car and now my grandpa got in an argument with her. I hoped Tawny wouldn't hate me now. I didn't really want to be pals with her, but I didn't want to be enemies either. I sensed she could make trouble for me. What would I say the next time we met?

That turned out to be the least of my concerns, because the next time I saw her, words could make no difference. The next time I saw Tawny Ferrel it was the most frightening experience of my life.

7

"*How is it coming?*" *Roger asked. His face was still flushed* from the confrontation with Tawny, but he smiled good-naturedly.

"I'm taking photos of the mural first, before I scrape away the old flaked paint," I explained. "That way I can reproduce it as closely as possible."

"I know it's hard to work around here with all the commotion." He nodded toward the counter where his daughter had taken Tawny's place waiting on customers. "There's a pretty big turnover of employees here, but I've never had one leave that fast—or that *loudly*."

"She was really mad," I agreed.

Roger went back to the kitchen and soon Tawny was forgotten as I focused on the mural.

The wispy lines of the colorful images took my eyes on a

pleasing journey. As I studied it, new whimsical details popped out at me.

I was thoroughly enjoying this job. I just hoped I'd be able to restore it to its original form.

The paint on Nan's self-portrait caricature was beginning to crack around the face. It was just a matter of time before it flaked off on its own, so I pulled out my razor blade and carefully began to chip away at it. I had hoped to leave the eyes intact. She'd taken great care with the long, wispy eyelashes and I was nervous about botching them. As I began to scratch at the paint, it splintered into huge pieces that sprinkled down around my feet.

The paint was especially thick on the Nan part of the mural, and at first I couldn't figure out why. But as I continued to chisel, another Nan emerged from beneath the top layer.

I smiled to myself. She must not have liked her first self-portrait. It was the only part of the mural she'd actually painted over. Apparently my aunt is vain, I thought. But my smile disappeared an instant later as a grotesque image of Nan materialized. Her face was contorted in agony, her tongue hanging out as she clutched at her throat. Her body was slashed with red streaks—*bloody streaks*.

This, obviously, was *not* Nan's work. She wouldn't have done something like this and the style wasn't hers. The person who painted this awful image couldn't have been an artist. It was painted by someone about as skillful as the average fifth grader.

Horrified, I continued to chip away the paint. Beneath Nan's figure were the words "Die Bitch."

"What a sick act of vandalism," said a raspy voice.

I jumped and swung around. It was the janitor from school. He was seated at a nearby booth, eating a chili dog as he watched me intently.

"Who could have done this?" I said. I didn't really want

his opinion. But I was so shocked by my discovery and he was the only one around.

He shrugged and said slowly, "Maybe someone who was jealous of her."

"*Jealous?* What do you mean?"

He smirked. A smudge of mustard streaked his chin, and he took a big chomp of chili dog and said through a full mouth, "You know what I'm talking about. You look just like your aunt. You're both blond and pretty and don't care about anyone else's feelings."

"That's not true! I'm not like that and neither was my aunt!"

He took another bite of chili dog. "You've never met her. How do *you* know what she's like?"

"I-I just do." I hadn't gotten over the shock of finding the ugly picture on the mural and now someone was attacking me and my family. Anger bubbled up inside me. "How do *you* know what I'm like? How can you say I don't care about people's feelings?"

A slow smile spread over his face. His lips made me think of two fat pink earthworms. "I know your type," he said. "And girls like you always get what's coming to them."

8

---

*There is a kind of nightmare that strikes in the blackest shad-*ows of sleep. Within this dream is an instant so terrifying it is accompanied by a furious drumbeat. When I awake the pounding continues and I freeze in the darkness too fright-ened to breathe as I listen to the frenzied thumping. Perhaps it is *not* a drum, but the sound of footsteps. Something is coming to get me! A faceless monster headed straight for my room. But even as the thought forms, I realize the sound is neither footsteps or drumbeat. It is the sound of my own heart.

The evil of my nightmare has set my heart to hammering so ferociously it beats itself to a crescendo that wakes me.

The darkness is a close place, confining me so I cannot kick or lash out. Wildly, I thrash around on the bed. Fi-nally, I realize I *can* move. The ceiling and walls are far away. I stretch my arms and legs and draw deep breaths.

As my heartbeat quiets, the nightmare shadows melt into the darkness. In a while I am asleep again with the reassuring thought bouncing about my mind—just a dream. Just a dream. Just a dream . . .

Sometimes in the morning I remember wisps of the horror. Yet when the day splashes so brightly, and people are laughing and dishes are clinking, and coffee is pungently brewing, how can I hold on to elusive shreds of a nightmare? Why would I *want* to?

Friday morning I awoke in a fog.

"Wake up, Alex!" True tugged on my arm.

I opened my eyes, groaning in protest.

"I thought you were dead," she said.

"I'm just really tired. I didn't sleep very well. I had dreams all night."

"Bad dreams?"

"Yeah."

"I hate that," she said sympathetically. "You should have crawled in bed with me."

I smiled at her serious expression. Her soft little face was crinkled in concern, making her look, for an instant, old and wise. I remembered waking up frightened in the night. I'd felt reassured by her snoring in the bed across from mine. I would not, however, have considered crawling in with her. She still wet the bed, and believe me, I learned the hard way it is not very pleasant to wake up beside a bed wetter.

It's funny how children can sometimes seem so wise but then do something to remind you they were just babies not long ago.

I can so remember when I was baby! True had said. I wondered now if it was possible. When *do* we forget our baby days?

I found myself mulling this over in psychology class,

when we heard Tom had invited an expert on memory regression to speak to the class.

"Her name is Ona Trollen," Josh told me. "I saw her on a local talk show. She asked for a volunteer from the audience and then hypnotized him and got him to remember stuff about his past that he'd forgotten."

Could Dr. Trollen do that for me? I wondered. Could she help me recall Judy Fitzwater's death?

"Dr. Trollen teaches at the community college," he said. "My sister took her class and she said she was eccentric but really interesting." He was in the seat behind me—Tawny's usual spot. "I *did* have study hall this period," he told me, "but Tom let me transfer to this class because I was getting bored. He's a great guy. He's always doing favors for me. When I told him I wanted into this class, he fixed it with the office."

I was deliriously happy. The smile in his eyes told me *I* had something to do with his decision—that he'd given up his easiest period of the day so he could be near me.

"If you're not doing anything after school, I'd like to show you around town," he said.

"Sounds good," I said quickly. I hoped Tawny wouldn't be too angry when she realized something special had sparked between Josh and me. She obviously believed she had dibs on him. But she wasn't here today. For a moment, as we sat grinning at each other, it seemed that Josh and I were the only two people on the planet.

"I hope you like boats," he said. "The *Seabird* isn't exactly a yacht, but it'll take you to parts of Oxford you can't see from the street."

A boat ride! He wanted to take me out on a boat. I'd been on one only once in my life. It was a huge ferryboat. While my family stood on the deck watching the vast, rippling view, I'd stayed inside, sitting in the middle of the row of plastic seats that faced the snack bar, because I was too nervous to look out at the water.

Of course I couldn't tell Josh. He'd just asked me on our first official date and I was not about to ruin it.

I've got to come to terms with my fear of water, I told myself. Josh was the best incentive imaginable. *I will not be afraid!* I vowed and was filled with sudden, inexplicable confidence.

At the moment, of course, I was miles from any water, sitting in a straight-backed chair with my feet planted on a solid floor. It's easy to say you won't be scared of something when you're not directly confronting it.

As I gazed into Josh's wonderful blue eyes, I became so sure of myself I was almost smug. How could I have guessed that the very source of my fear was about to be up-rooted? That before this class was over, I'd feel terror like I'd never felt before?

"I'm going to visit my great-aunt after school," I said. "Maybe you can come by there. She lives in the green Victorian by the park."

"I know Sidney," he said. "Can I pick you up about four-thirty?"

Suddenly, the principal's voice burst through the P.A. system. "Attention students and faculty," he said, his words crackling with static.

Josh grimaced. "This P.A. system is ancient. Sometimes you can't even understand the announcements."

"One of our students has run away from home and her parents are quite concerned," Mr. Cline continued. "If any-one knows anything about the whereabouts of Tawny Fer-rel, please contact this office immediately."

"I can't believe she really did it!" Josh said, and every-one started chattering at once.

"She's been talking about this practically *forever*!" Kelly said, scurrying over to Josh's desk. She plopped herself on top of it. "She's always saying she wants to go to California!"

Josh shook his head. "It's not going to be as easy as she thinks. Tawny's had a soft life. When she hits the limit on her daddy's charge card, she'll come crawling back."

"She was really mad because her dad made her go to work at the Big Top," Kelly said. "I can't believe she didn't even say good-bye to me!"

"She got fired," I volunteered.

"*Really?*" she squealed, practically salivating over this piece of gossip.

"Well, she kind of got fired and she kind of quit," I said and described the scene between Tawny and Roger, deliberately leaving out the fact that it was my grandfather who got in the argument with her.

Kelly grinned gleefully. "I knew she wouldn't last three days at that job!" She seemed to be really enjoying her cousin's troubles. *That's not very nice*, I thought. But who was I to judge? The truth is, I, too, was glad Tawny was gone. Now I didn't have to worry about her making trouble for me over Josh.

By the time she got back I hoped we would be a solid couple and Tawny couldn't interfere.

"Settle down, people," Tom said. "I'd like you to welcome Dr. Ona Trollen." He nodded toward a tall, white-haired woman about fifty in a crisp red suit. "Dr. Trollen is an expert on memory regression and has graciously agreed to come here today and share some of her vast knowledge."

She smiled and nodded at the class, her clear hazel eyes roaming deliberately over our faces. Her eyebrows were plucked to thin lines and finely arched. Her cheekbones were high and elegant and sprinkled with unexpected freckles. "It's a pleasure to be here," she said in a husky Russian accent. "I am a professor at Oxford Community College and also the author of a book, *Unlocking Our Secret Pasts*. Perhaps some of you have seen me on television."

A titter of recognition ran through the class. "I saw you on that television show, *City Hall Up Front*, last week," said Kelly. "You hypnotized an old woman and got her to remember the house she lived in when she was three. Are you going to hypnotize us?"

"If any of you would like to volunteer, I'd be glad to do a demonstration."

"Hold it," said Tom. "This isn't going to get me in trouble with the school board, is it?"

"The school board?" Dr. Trollen laughed caustically. "How do you spell that, b-o-r-e-d? If I sound bitter it's because in my experience the school 'bored' is not dedicated to learning. It is only interested in stifling creative minds."

"I told you she was eccentric," Josh whispered to me.

"The mind is a fascinating mechanism," Dr. Trollen continued. "It gives us the information we need to function on a daily basis, while simultaneously storing superfluous data in what I like to describe as 'inaccessible files.' Hypnosis is a key to unlocking these files, sifting through useless information and getting to the crux of what makes us tick."

Kelly raised her hand. "My grandmother died when I was three. I don't remember her when I'm awake, but sometimes I dream about her. I dreamed she came to see me on a big, white horse and sprinkled salt all over my room. What does that mean?"

"Dreams are the language of the unconscious," said Dr. Trollen. "The unconscious is much like water. In fact, the symbol of the unconscious is water. At times it is clear, and at times it is murky. Perhaps you are trying to remember something about your grandmother that you have pushed away in your waking hours."

"She was sick for a long time," said Kelly. "She lived with us and died at our house."

"It must have been traumatic for you to see your grandmother so ill," said Dr. Trollen. "It is understandable that your conscious mind blocks out this memory. It is important to listen to your dreams. That is how your subconscious communicates with your waking self."

Is that true for me? I wondered, as I remembered my nightmare. *Was my unconscious trying to remind me of something I'd forgotten—something like a girl in a pond?*

"Listen to your inner voice," Dr. Trollen continued, "for it is the subconscious that sustains us in our daily lives. Much like a boat, floating on the surface of the water, our awareness rides upon the rippled ocean of the inner mind, oblivious to the motion and activity below. Like that boat, we must beware of things just below the surface—things that may damage or harm us.

"We use techniques such as hypnosis to learn more about this other world so closely interwoven with ours."

Mark Kelborne raised his hand. "If you're ready to hypnotize someone, I'll be your first guinea pig."

Dr. Trollen invited him to the front of the class. "Sit comfortably in a relaxed position," she said. "Fold your hands in your lap. Close your eyes and feel a sense of warmth and heaviness through your entire body—beginning in your toes."

Mark shut his eyes. A couple of girls giggled as his head rolled limply onto his chest.

"Feel the warmth and heaviness flowing up through your legs and into your hips and pelvis so that your entire lower body is perfectly relaxed." Dr. Trollen's soothing voice covered every inch of the body. "You are wonderfully and perfectly relaxed," she said.

He slumped forward.

"Can you hear me, Mark?" asked Dr. Trollen.

"Yes."

"Where are you?"

"I'm in Burgess General Hospital," he said in a zombielike tone.

"Where in the hospital?" She sounded surprised.

"I'm in the nursery with a bunch of other screaming brats. I'd say I'm about three hours old. Whoa! There goes a cute nurse. I'm pinching her behind now and—wham!— she slapped me."

The class laughed as Mark hammed it up, pretending to be a crying baby.

Dr. Trollen appeared unruffled as she said, "It seems I've been had. Would anyone else like to volunteer?"

My hand shot up before I could stop it. I was a little self-conscious as I settled into the chair in front of the class and Dr. Trollen asked me, "Why would you like to be regressed?"

"Something frightened me when I was a baby," I said. "I'd like to remember it."

I was deliberately vague. I did not want to let the whole class in on my private thoughts. The truth is, I did not think I could be hypnotized. I figured that when Dr. Trollen spoke to me as she had to Mark, my mind would relax a little and perhaps later I would begin to remember.

"Feel the warmth and heaviness flowing up through your legs . . ."

As she spun her calming words, my body felt light.

"You are wonderfully and perfectly relaxed," she said.

Amazingly, I *was*. My eyelids shut and my head rolled forward.

"Let us go back to the time when you are afraid. You are drifting along peacefully. What do you see?"

Shimmering colors flashed through my mind. A brilliant gold sparkling against a beautiful deep blue—like sun against the sky. "Sunshine," I mumbled.

"What else?" she asked. "What else do you see?"

"Trees."

"Where are you?"

"Picnic."

Suddenly, I was no longer hearing Dr. Trollen's voice—simply *feeling* her words. It was as if she were leading me along a path.

Soft, warm sunshine falls on me. Everything is golden. I grab on to a leg and when I look up, I see it belongs to my mommy. "Cookie?" she asks. "Do you want a cookie?"

My fat little hand reaches out and I clumsily grab the cookie from her. I sway a little, unsteady on my legs. Then I am running across the grassy lawn, giggling as the tall blades of grass tickle my bare knees.

A squeaking gray squirrel runs down the trunk of a tree. He looks like the squirrel in the storybook my mommy reads to me. He chatters at me, and I toddle toward him.

Does he want my cookie? I take a bite, then throw it at him. But he scampers back up the tree.

"Cookie!" I yell. "Cookie!" I point at the cookie but the squirrel is far over my head now, in the branches of the glowing green leaves.

The pond is glistening at me. I bolt toward it. It reflects the trees above and this makes me laugh. It is so pretty. But then I feel scared. Why do I feel scared? I want Mommy.

Something floats in the water. A big dolly. Hello, big dolly. I want the big dolly!

I hear a high-pitched ringing. It overpowers all other sound. I am numb. My body is so light it feels as if I'm made of air. Gold light swirls around me—so beautiful it makes my eyes ache. The ground vibrates. I feel as if I am being shaken free from a trap.

My world spins around like a tornado. I am screaming. Someone has my leg. "No!" I yell. "God, no!" He is pulling me down. Water closes over my face, it fills my mouth. Horror. Explosion. Darkness.

"Alex, are you okay?" Josh's voice was alarmed.

I was on the cold, tile floor, staring up into a circle of concerned faces.

"She looked like she had a seizure!" Kelly said.

Dr. Trollen helped me sit up. "Tell me what happened, dear."

"It was like I was someplace else," I said. "I was in the water."

"Okay, everybody!" Tom said. "Back off and give Alexis room to breathe."

As Dr. Trollen led me back to the chair, Tom dismissed the class. "I knew this wasn't a good idea," he said.

9

"It was like I was Judy," I said.

Sequoia sat across from me, her eyes huge and absorbed as she nibbled on a peanut butter cookie. We were in Aunt Sidney's kitchen, at the big, round maple table. I had come to see my old aunt but she was sound asleep. So instead I visited with Sequoia, who seemed to know something was wrong the moment she saw my face. She'd urged me to sit and listened intently as I described my frightening experience.

"Somebody killed Judy!" I said. "It was like I was in her body and *I* felt it!"

"Wow," Sequoia said. "*Wow!*" Her thick, wiry hair was twisted into two braids and wound up in snakelike coils on the sides of her head. Her earrings, strings of tiny silver bells, jingled tunelessly each time she turned her head.

"It was awful. Oh, Sequoia, it was so awful!"

"What did Dr. Trollen say about it?"

"I didn't tell anybody the details of what happened. I was so embarrassed to find myself lying on the floor. I wanted to get out of the classroom fast."

"You're green. You look like you're going to throw up."

"I just need to sit here for a while. I'll be okay. It's so weird. I've always been scared of water and now I know why."

She nodded. "Even though you didn't remember seeing Judy get killed, it was in your subconscious all these years. It's kind of like you stored the memory of what happened to Judy and then you made it into your own experience."

"It felt like *I* was dying."

"You must be a really sensitive person to feel someone else's pain like that. Did you scream?"

"I tried. When I opened my mouth it filled with water. He pulled me under. He was so strong and I was so tired. It was like I'd been swimming for hours, trying to get away from him."

"In the pond?"

"I know it doesn't make sense, but that's what it felt like—like I was in a big body of water."

"Maybe when you were a baby the pond seemed that big to you."

"It probably did. My mom always said I was scared of the water and she was really surprised that I even went near the pond that day."

"It is the oddest thing," Mom had told me. "Most babies love to splash in the bath with their little ducks and boats, but you'd start shrieking the minute your toes touched the water."

Sequoia got up from her chair and poked her head into the refrigerator. "You want some milk?" she asked, as she refilled her own glass. "It might make you feel better."

I wrapped my hands around the red, porcelain mug she handed me and sipped the cold milk.

Sequoia sat in the carved, wooden chair across from mine. "Take a deep breath," she instructed. "It will help you relax."

Inhaling the warm, cinnamon-flavored air, I felt comforted as I glanced about the sunny yellow kitchen. The stove was huge and old-fashioned and had probably baked many miles of sweet-smelling pies and thousands of warm, chewy cookies.

A fat cookie jar in the shape of a smiling, pink pig sat on the counter beside a row of worn, tin canisters that were marked "Flour," "Sugar," and "Salt." The lettering was nearly worn away, probably by loving hands, reaching for them again and again over the years.

Lacy curtains fringed the bay windows, and I pulled back a piece of the frilly material and peered out at the grassy scape of the park.

Sequoia followed my gaze. "The pond is in that park, isn't it?" she asked.

"Somewhere in there. I don't remember where."

"Do you remember anything about the killer?"

"He was strong. He kept grabbing my legs and pulling me under."

"Did you see his face?"

"I don't remember." When I shut my eyes, I could still feel the horror of the water closing over my face, squeezing the breath from me as my world turned black. I could still feel the viselike grip of the angry hand wrapped around my ankle and the violent tugs as he pulled me to my death.

But I could not see his face.

"I'm trying to remember," I said. "But I can't. All I've got is that terrible image of drowning and my fear of water."

"Did you ever learn to swim?" Sequoia asked.

"No. I can't stand to put my head under the water. I can barely stand to *look* at water. I was enrolled in a P.E. class and then I found out we had to swim. So I dropped it today and switched to science instead." I buried my face in my arms and groaned. "I need to get over this quick, because Josh will be here to pick me up in half an hour. Guess where we're going?"

"Surfing?" she asked with a laugh.

"Almost that bad. He's taking me for a ride in his boat."

"Why don't you tell him you're scared?"

"We made the date before I got regressed. I thought I'd be able to handle it. I don't want to back out of it now. I really like this guy, Sequoia. What if I cancel and he never asks me out again?"

"If *he* likes *you* then he'll take you out for a pizza or something."

I suppose if I'd explained the situation to Josh, he would have. But I was embarrassed by my water phobia. People usually found it very strange. What would Josh think? He was an accomplished swimmer who belonged to the scuba club.

Would he want to date a girl who didn't share his interests?

I was encouraged by the fact we were both artists. At least we had that in common. I hoped it was enough.

For now, I vowed to be brave, so I smiled and tried to appear enthusiastic as I shakily climbed into Josh's blue wooden rowboat. He untied it from the dock, sat opposite of me, and began rowing, his strong arms guiding the paddles so they cut through the water like knives through warm butter.

The lake reflected the deep blue of the afternoon sky. And I knew it was pretty as it rippled and twinkled and sparkled under the sun. It was exactly the kind of picture that should be framed on a wall—a couple in a rowboat, gliding over a glimmering lake as fluffy, white clouds scud across the sky above them.

It *was* a pretty picture. But not to me. Though my eyes could appreciate the glassy shimmer of the water, my heart turned to ice at the sight of it.

"Are you cold?" Josh asked when he noticed me shivering. "Would you like to wear my jacket?"

"I'm fine." I looked away from the water, training my gaze on the hill rising in the distance. A charming little white church with a steeple sat at the top. I'd been awakened this morning by the sweet pealing of a bell and now I wondered aloud if the old church had been the source.

"It rings every Sunday," he said. "It's the only church for miles around with a bell. That church has an interesting history. It used to be where the lake is now."

"Oh!" I gasped. "This is the old part of Oxford! It's in the mural I'm touching up."

"This is called Forgotten Lake, because of the forgotten town beneath it." He pointed over the edge of the boat. "The church was right about here. They moved it just before they flooded the town."

"Are there any houses under there?" I peered hesitantly into the water.

"The old theater is the only building under the lake."

"The old Oxy Roxy!"

"Yeah. The Oxy Roxy Theater. How did you know?"

A chill blew through me. "I must have heard my mother mention it."

"Most of the year the water's murky because of the runoff from the glaciers," said Josh. "But the water is low and clear this time of year. We might be able to look down into the lake and see the theater. I'll head over that way."

"Why did they move everything else and leave the theater?"

"It was too much of a hassle to move. They tore down a

lot of the houses, but the EPA said the theater could stay because it was made mostly out of concrete and masonry and didn't contain any environmentally hazardous materials."

As we headed further from shore, a dank, earthy smell emanated from the water. It was hard to imagine that birds once flew where fish now swam—that this dark place beneath us was once filled with sunlight.

I nervously glanced at the shore. The large homes on the softly curved hills had shrunk to dollhouse size.

If the boat were to tip over, how far could Josh swim with me in tow?

"Are you okay?" he asked.

I forced a smile. "Sure. This is great. Just think, my mom used to walk along the streets that are under us now."

"Do you scuba dive? We could dive down there sometime and get a close up look." He set down the oars and the boat rocked softly. Waves slapped at the sides with a wet hollow sound as if the lake were slurping its supper—as if it wanted to swallow us whole.

"Here we are," he said. "We're right above the old Oxy Roxy."

As the water calmed, the waves melted into lazy ripples and the building below came slowly into focus. I shuddered as I gazed down at the old theater. The rippling effect made it look as if it were writhing in anger, its black windows stretching and shrinking and winking menacingly. It looked like an alive thing!

"It's kind of creepy," I said.

"Why?" Josh asked, an amused smile tugging on his lips.

"The whole idea of a town underwater gives me a weird feeling," I admitted. "It almost seems like people are still down there—trapped in that building."

"That's a creepy image." He raised one eyebrow, regarding me quizzically.

I laughed self-consciously. "Sorry. I have sort of a weird imagination."

"That's a good thing in an artist," he said. "You didn't answer my question about scuba diving. Do you know how?"

"No. I've never tried it."

"Tom is a certified instructor and I'm his assistant. Why don't you take lessons?"

"Sounds interesting," I said, neglecting to mention the fact I could not swim.

At the moment, I figured there would be plenty of time to break it to him. It never occurred to me my very life hinged on my secret.

10

Relationships, they say, should be built on trust. Does that mean you have to divulge all of your embarrassing secrets the moment you meet someone?

Of course not, I told myself as Josh rowed toward shore. It really wasn't anyone's business but my own that I couldn't swim.

"Who's that on the dock?" I asked.

He looked over his shoulder and grinned.

A wiry figure with a mop of dark hair danced around on the dock, kicking her legs and hamming it up as she waved at us.

"That crazy girl," he said. "That's Kelly."

As the boat drew closer, I recognized her. A thin-limbed, rosy-complected, chipmunk-cheeked girl.

Josh said, "Every time I turn around, there she is!"

He did not sound unhappy about this and I felt a flash of jealousy.

Girls notice Josh everyplace we go.

I remembered when Tawny had spoken those words, possessively, as if she had permanent dibs on him. Is that the way girls felt around him—as if he were special to them and they to him? Was I just another girl in a long string of admiring females?

As the boat thudded against the dock, Kelly shouted, "*Where* were you, Josh? I've been riding around on my bike, looking *everywhere* for you!"

"Was I supposed to be somewhere?" he asked with a dazzling grin.

"I wanted you to help me pick out my scuba equipment." She poked her lower lip out into a pout.

"Well, *tell* me next time," he said good-naturedly. "You can't expect me to sit around at home waiting to do favors for you."

She stared down at us, a goofy grin pasted on her face. She wore a red T-shirt and baggy shorts, and I noted with satisfaction that her legs were bowed and too skinny.

Josh climbed onto the dock, the boat's rope in his hand.

"See if I got the right mask," Kelly said, pointing to a canvas bag at her feet.

He squatted to examine her mask. "What's this for?" he asked, pulling an instant camera from the bag.

"That's Alex's." She placed one foot in the boat. "Alex, you left that in the cafeteria today so I picked it up for you. I was going to give it to you tomorrow, then I heard you were here with Josh. Hey, Josh, how come you never take *me* for a boat ride?" she asked and unexpectedly leapt into the boat. It wobbled dangerously.

"Sit down, Kelly!" I gasped.

She smirked at me, her eyes two bright spots of jealousy. "Are you scared you'll get wet?" she asked, and began swaying from side to side. Her sneakered feet were spread wide, one planted on each side of the boat. It began to rock wildly and she laughed, an annoying shriek of a laugh.

"Kelly, *please*—"

My words were ripped away as I was plunged into black iciness. Instinctively—thankfully—I'd filled my lungs with air an instant before the boat tipped. As the water closed over me, I thrashed around wildly, eyes bulging.

It was as if the cold, dark world had reached up a wet hand and wrenched me below. I did not know up from down, and if I did, I certainly did not know how to get there.

Help! I silently screamed the word.

It was so quiet here. So deathly quiet. Why couldn't I see? I bumped against something hard. I clawed at it. The boat! I was trapped under the boat. My lungs burned. I needed air.

This is it. This is the end. I knew it all along.

An evil cackle seemed to echo silently in my ears. Someone, somewhere was laughing at me. Suddenly, I was angry.

I will not let you do this again. I will not die! With that thought I summoned a strength from deep within. Kicking my legs, I swam downward, free of the boat.

The bottom of the lake was clear. I could easily see the shards of broken green glass sprinkled among the rocks. I looked up, amazed to see the cottony clouds floating above me in the blue sky.

Lack of oxygen seared my lungs, yet I was no longer afraid.

My arms fluttered out in front of me and I paddled upward, moving as swiftly as a monkey on a ladder.

I popped from the water, gasping and coughing. Josh reached out a hand and it closed over mine, warm and strong. "Are you okay?" he asked.

Kelly surfaced a moment later, her hair plastered against the side of her head, mascara squiggling down her cheeks.

"Didn't anyone ever tell you not to stand up in a boat, girl?" Josh asked her.

"She did that on purpose!" I cried between gulps of fresh air. Neither of them seemed to realize I had nearly drowned. I couldn't blame Josh for that, for I had not told him I couldn't swim.

But I can swim!

The realization was exhilarating. I could swim. Alexis Arlene Baxter could swim!

This is not to say I was anxious to do it again or that I was no longer afraid of the water.

I was grateful to be on land again, and I stretched out on the grass beside the dock, tasting sweet air and slowly drying in the weak autumn sun.

Josh sat beside me, his fingers laced in mine. Kelly glanced at our hands and then quickly looked away. She pretended to be fascinated with her battered, red ten-speed bicycle which lay on its side next to her. Her fingers danced over the front wheel as she spun it in circles. "Not much tread left on my tires," she said. And then she began chattering endlessly, making stupid jokes and generally trying to be the center of attention.

"Will you look at that!" she said suddenly, and we turned our heads to follow her gaze. There, across the parking lot on a grassy knoll, was Anita, the art teacher, and a man, snuggled close on a bench.

"I can't believe she's with Mr. Wingate!" Kelly giggled with delight.

"I wonder if Tom knows," said Josh.

"Who's Mr. Wingate?" I asked.

Why did that name sound familiar?

"He's the journalism teacher at Oxford High," said Kelly. "He got divorced last year."

"I can't believe she'd do this to Tom." Josh shook his head. "He's such a nice guy."

"Were they getting married or something?" I asked.

He shrugged. "I just know he really likes her."

"I think this is great!" said Kelly. "Going to Oxford High is like watching a soap opera!"

"I wonder if anyone else knows," said Josh.

"I think the janitor knows," I said, as suddenly that strange comment he made began to make sense.

"Deke the Creep?" asked Kelly.

"Yeah," I said. "He told her he knew she was playing games and he'd noticed she'd taken an unusual interest in the newspaper business."

"He must have seen her down at the *Weekly Scoop* office flirting with Mr. Wingate," said Josh. "That's the school newspaper. What an awful thing for Anita to do to Tom! She's sneaking around behind his back. Somebody should teach her a lesson."

"I can't wait to tell everybody!" Kelly said.

"Nobody will believe you," said Josh.

"They will if all three of us say we saw them," said Kelly. "Those two are *definitely* having an affair!"

"Why don't you take a picture?" I asked.

If I had known she'd take me seriously, I'd never have suggested it.

"Great idea!" She hopped to her feet. "How much film is in your camera?"

"I was just kidding, Kelly! They'll see you!" I protested as she grabbed my camera.

"There's two pictures left," she said gleefully, and before I could protest any further, she crept up the hill, lay down on her stomach, and aimed the camera at Anita and Mr. Wingate.

Josh laughed as we watched her. "Kelly's got guts. I'll say that much for her."

I couldn't help but laugh, too. She looked so silly, with her bottom in the air as she tentatively raised her head and snapped a picture. A moment later she was back with the instant photo tucked under her shirt as it developed.

"I should blow this up into poster size," she said, handing the photo to Josh.

"That would sure teach Anita," he said. "You could put it up on the bulletin board in the 900 hall where everyone would see it."

I peered over his shoulder at the photograph. The unmistakable profile of Anita's pretty face leaned on Mr. Wingate's shoulder. Their arms encircled each other as he stroked her hair.

"If they do this in public, just think what they must do in private," said Kelly.

"She'll think twice before she goes out on Tom again," Josh said.

Later I would wish I had protested. Why didn't I speak up to say we had no right to punish Anita? Who were we to flaunt her personal life for all the school to see? Perhaps it was the light in Josh's eyes as they held mine. Or maybe it was the way he squeezed my hand while the three of us joked about what everyone would think when Kelly passed the picture around.

At the time, it *was* humorous. I've never really thought of teachers as people. It's always been hard to picture them doing normal things like eating dinner or going to the movies. And here was not one, but *two* teachers stuck to each other like a couple of globs of gum.

We ended up behind them on Swing-Low Street, the old bumpy road that winds along the lake. Kelly had ridden off on her bicycle and I hopped on the back of Josh's motorcycle, my arms wrapped around his waist as we roared along.

My clothes were still damp and the brisk breeze brought

goose bumps to my skin. I closed my eyes and pressed my cheek against Josh's back. It felt wonderful to hug him.

As we came around a bend in the road, we had to slow because the squat purple car in front of us was inching along. "Women always drive too slow!" Josh yelled to me over his shoulder.

The road straightened and we passed the purple car. As we did so, I saw that Anita was driving and Mr. Wingate sat beside her.

Anita's window was down and she smiled and waved. But the smile did not reach her eyes. They were small and red and smudged with mascara. I was startled to realize she'd been crying. I waved back, a sick feeling in the pit of my stomach as I thought of the photo Kelly had taken with my camera.

When Josh pulled up in front of our house, Toby popped out the front door. "Wow!" he yelled. "A motorcycle! Can I have a ride?"

His shouts brought my mother and grandmother outside. I climbed off the motorcycle and Josh followed me up the walk for an awkward introduction. "This is Josh," I told them.

"I know Josh," Grandma said crisply.

Mom nodded at him curtly and turned to me. "What were you doing on that thing?" she demanded. "You know I don't want you riding around on a motorcycle!"

As far as I remembered, the subject had never come up before.

"It's really cool!" said Toby. "If Alex gets to ride it, I want to, too."

"You're wet, Alex!" Grandma exclaimed. "What on earth happened to you?"

"She had a little accident in my boat," said Josh. "It tipped over and Alex fell in the lake."

."*What?*" said Mom. "I hope you were wearing a life jacket!"

"It was no big deal." I squirmed with embarrassment as I glanced at Josh. He wore a confused grin, but was obviously trying to be polite as my strange family closed in on us, grilling me as if I were a criminal. They were making a terrible first impression. I glared at my mother, hoping she'd get the hint and back off.

"You know better than to get in a boat," she said. "I thought you were afraid of the water."

"Alex can't swim," Toby announced. "Did you have to jump in and save her, Josh? Maybe we should call the paper and you could be on the front page for being a hero."

"I can so swim," I said quickly, my cheeks burning as I felt Josh's eyes on me. "I saved myself!"

Josh left a few minutes later, his long curls flowing behind him as his motorcycle sputtered and thundered. I could still hear it as he turned the corner, humming in the distance like the buzz of an angry bumblebee.

I whirled to face my mother, furious she had embarrassed me. But before I could say anything, she shouted, "You used very poor judgment! What did you think you were doing? You went out with a boy you hardly know and nearly got yourself drowned! Then you rode that awful motorcycle! And without a helmet!"

"I didn't drown," I said defensively. "We didn't get in a wreck. I'm *fine*. I'm home in one piece. You embarrassed me in front of Josh. Now he probably won't want to see me again."

"That's good, because I don't want you going out with him again."

"*What?*" I cried.

"Grandma was shocked when she looked out the window and saw you with him," she said. "That boy has a very bad reputation."

"He's a nice guy," I said. "*I* like him."

"He's been in trouble," said Grandma. "Everybody knows about it."

"What did he do?" I asked sarcastically. "Rob a bank?"

"Don't take that tone with Grandma," Mom warned.

"Please just tell me what Josh did that was so horrible?" I asked, trying to keep my voice calm. He was the most beautiful boy I'd ever met. I couldn't believe my mother didn't want me to date him.

"He stole a car and wrecked it," Grandma said. "Not only that, he was drunk at the time."

I hadn't noticed my grandfather in the doorway, but apparently he'd been standing there, watching everything. "I should have known," he said, his voice so quiet it was nearly a whisper. "I should have known our problems would begin all over again. This is how it started with Nan."

11

I *have never been the perfect daughter*. My room is usually a mess and I sometimes argue with my mother and complain when I don't get my way.

I very rarely disobey Mom. Of course there was the time when I was twelve and she forbade me to get my ears pierced. I was the only girl in my seventh grade class who couldn't wear earrings, so I let my best friend, Brittany, pierce my ears for me.

That was four years earlier and we have had few conflicts since.

Except for the earrings, Mom has never told me I couldn't have something I really wanted.

Now there was Josh.

My stomach flipped at the thought of him. When his gaze met mine it sent delicious shivers through me.

I was falling in love.

I wanted to be with Josh more than anything I'd ever wanted before.

He was not just another boy. He was *Josh*! My mother and grandparents were terribly unfair to tell me I couldn't love him.

When I woke up Saturday morning, I knew I was in for a fight.

I did not want to face my mother and grandparents, so I skipped breakfast and headed over to Aunt Sidney's. "I'm feeling chipper today," she said and nodded at Sequoia. "Mary Jane, here, brought me downstairs to sit in the parlor."

Sequoia smiled as she poured me some tea. "She's really lucid today," she whispered. "But I don't know why she calls me Mary Jane."

"Maybe you remind her of someone she used to know."

The thin morning sunshine filtered through the window and pooled on the Oriental rug like melted butter. "It's going to be a beautiful day," said Aunt Sidney. She looked younger than usual. Sequoia had fixed her silver hair, sweeping it up into a neat bun with soft tendrils curling about her face. She wore a crisp, blue dress with fine white polka dots. Sitting up straight in the rocking chair, she daintily sipped her tea. "So how are you today, Nan, dear?" she asked.

"Okay," I said.

"Just okay? I sense something is wrong. You know I've always been able to read your face, dear."

It was strange because in some ways Aunt Sidney was so sharp. She did not know who I was, yet she spotted the sadness in me. Today she reminded me of an alert little bird, her head cocked to one side, her eyes bright and watching.

"Tell me what's troubling you, dear," she said warmly.

I sighed and said, "I'm in love. But Mom and Grandma and Grandpa don't want me to see him."

She clucked her tongue. "Why do people think they can make such important decisions for other people?"

I wanted to leap up and hug her for understanding. "I'm old enough to make my own decisions. I'm nearly seventeen—almost a legal adult!"

"How come they don't want you to date Josh?" asked Sequoia.

"He got in trouble last year," I said. "He got drunk and stole a car and smashed it through the window of Peachman's Hardware Store."

"Good heavens!" Aunt Sidney's eyes popped wide open. "Was anyone hurt?"

"I don't think so," I said. "I didn't want to ask Grandma too many questions about it. I'd like to talk to Josh myself and find out what happened."

"People make mistakes," said Aunt Sidney as she picked a ball of fuzz off her sweater.

Sequoia loudly slurped her tea. "Karma," she said as her eyebrows shot up.

"What?" I asked.

"I was just thinking that if Josh did something awful, he'll pay for it. That's the way karma works. We're rewarded for our good deeds and punished for our bad ones. I'm writing a paper on it for my Eastern Philosophy class. You know the saying, 'what goes around comes around'? Everything we do in life eventually comes back to us—if not in this life, then in the next one."

"That's right," said Aunt Sidney. "We get our just desserts."

"Are you saying Josh is going to be punished?" I asked.

Sequoia shrugged. "I'm not the one to say. Maybe he's already made up for what happened."

"Don't let true love slip away," Aunt Sidney said, repeating the advice she'd given the day we met.

"Believe me, I don't *want* to, but what am I supposed to

do if my true love calls and Grandpa won't even let me talk to him?"

With a rush of prickly frustration, I remembered Friday evening when I'd been up in my room, flopped across the bed as True sat on the floor and colored a picture of autumn leaves—her very first homework assignment. She was so excited she couldn't wait to get to it and eagerly asked my advice on which crayons to choose. I smiled as her stubby fingers squeezed the orange crayon so tightly it nearly snapped in two. Fiery curls bounced across her eyes as she bent her head in concentration and pressed the crayon to the paper. I, of course, was not as excited about my history homework and was saving it for 10 p.m. Sunday night.

My ears were pricked for the phone because Josh and I had made a tentative date to see a late movie, and when the shrill ring finally came around seven, I flew off the bed and raced down the stairs.

"No, she can't come to the phone," Grandpa was saying as I skidded into the hallway.

"Is that for me?" I asked.

"No, I don't think so," he barked into the receiver, ignoring me. "She won't be returning your call. Please don't call here again."

Helplessly, I'd watched him hang up.

"You heard your mother," he said sternly as he towered over me. "She doesn't want you to see that boy again."

I'd opened my mouth to protest, but when I looked up into his steely eyes the words died on my tongue. It was obvious that arguing would get me nowhere. Enraged, I'd stomped up the stairs without a word.

Now, sitting sipping tea with Sequoia and Aunt Sidney, I was grateful for their support.

"Grandpa's wrong, isn't he?" I said. "He doesn't have the right to choose my friends!"

"Of course not," said Sequoia.

"What am I going to do?" I groaned.

"You could start by apologizing to Josh for the way your family treated him." She pointed to the bay window. "I just saw him walking toward the park."

I found him at the bench where we'd talked that first day. His sketch pad and pencils lay on the seat beside him as he stared at the fountain. He looked up at me with a startled smile that danced into his eyes.

Electrical.

That is the best way to describe Josh's eyes. They are electrical blue and seem to ignite the air with invisible sparks each time he looks at me.

"I'm sorry my grandfather wouldn't let me talk to you," I said.

"Did he tell you I'm a criminal?"

"My grandma mentioned something about a stolen car."

"I've had a hard time living that night down. I was afraid when you found out, you wouldn't want to see me again either."

I sat beside him, quietly listening as he told me about the strange night he still struggled to understand. "It happened a year ago. I don't know why I did it." His voice was low and bewildered. "I was drunk, but I know that's not an excuse.

"The thing is, I don't usually drink. I'm an athlete and try to stay in top form for the swim meets. But that night, I was out with some of my friends and we kind of cut loose. Mark Kelborne's older sister bought us a case of beer, and we were all sitting around behind the library when Kelly and Tawny started guzzling it. They dared the rest of us to keep up with them and, before I knew it, I was having a hard time standing.

"Most of the night is unclear. I guess I blacked out for a lot of it. But I remember when I first spotted the car. I'd said good-bye to my friends and took a shortcut through the alley just off of Malone Street. I fell down and when I got up, there it was. A '55 Ford Fairlane. *Beautiful* car. I'd seen it before, chugging down Main Street, and I always stopped and watched it go. I wished I had a car like that."

"So you took it?"

"It wasn't like that. I wasn't planning on stealing it. I was feeling sick to my stomach and just wanted to sit down for a while. The car was unlocked so I got in and sat behind the wheel. I noticed the keys in the ignition. Something just came over me." He stared at his knees, his voice faltering as he continued. "All of a sudden I was living a nightmare. This panicky feeling came over me and I started the car. Next thing you know, I was roaring out of the alley with the tires squealing and gravel spraying everywhere."

"Where were you going?"

He laughed, a dry humorless laugh. "Nobody believes this, but I was going to the police station."

"To turn yourself in?"

He laughed again and this time it was closer to a happy sound. "Nope. I didn't think I'd done anything wrong. I had this idea something was in the trunk and I had to bring it to the police station."

"What did you think was in the trunk?"

He closed his eyes. I stared at his long dark lashes as he shook his head. "I wish I knew. I remember thinking it was something precious."

"Like jewels or treasure?"

He shrugged. "Maybe. But I never made it to the police station. Peachman's Hardware Store is right next to the police. I passed out and drove right through their front window."

"You must have got in bad trouble."

"It could have been worse. It was Tom's car I stole that night. That's how I got to know him. He came down to the police station and told the cops he wasn't going to press charges. When he saw me sitting there, he said I reminded him of himself when he was a teenager and he didn't want to see my life ruined over one mistake. He let me work off the damage to the car. That's when I started assisting him in scuba lessons. We fixed the car together. I'm buying the Fairlane. Tom's giving me a good deal and I've almost paid it off."

"So you got off the hook?"

"Not completely. I got cited for drunk driving and had to attend alcohol classes. Harry Peachman was really angry about the window. But Tom talked to him for me and I worked off the damage by painting the store. I'm just glad I didn't hurt anybody. Everything worked out, except now I have this reputation as a really wild kid who's headed straight for the penitentiary."

"That's stupid. Everyone makes mistakes."

"Not like this. I see the way people look at me. Your mom and grandma looked at me like I was an ax murderer. And your grandfather hung up on me last night."

"They're kind of uptight," I said apologetically.

He shrugged. "Yeah, well there are a few people around here who are pretty cool about it. Tom's been really great and Kelly's mom is always having me over for dinner. I guess they feel sorry for me because my mom works in computer sales and she's traveling half the time. My parents split up when I was three and we don't know where my dad is. That's one of the reasons Tom said I reminded him of himself. He grew up without a dad, too."

"I'm sure when I explain things to my mother, she'll understand."

A wry smile twisted Josh's mouth. "Yeah, right," he said sarcastically. "She's not going to let you spend five minutes alone with me. I couldn't believe the big deal she made because you took a little spill in the lake."

"There's a reason for that," I said. "Yesterday was the first time I ever swam." Suddenly, I was telling him all about my water phobia. He had shared something personal with me and I felt more comfortable about divulging my embarrassing secret. "I know it sounds funny," I said. "It's just that I've always had this thing about water. I'm embarrassed to admit this. But I'm terrified of water. I, um, can't even take baths."

He laughed and edged away from me in mock repulsion.

"I take *showers*," I said.

"So before yesterday you couldn't swim?"

"No."

"I'm surprised you got in the boat with me. I'd have thought you'd be afraid."

I smiled weakly.

"I wish you'd said something. I would have made sure you had a life jacket."

"There probably aren't a lot of sixteen-year-olds who can't swim."

"But you *can* swim, Alex. You proved that yesterday."

"That's right! I *can*. I guess I could all along. I just didn't know it."

We sat quietly for a minute, watching each other's eyes. I saw a gentle soul in his; I'm not sure what he saw in mine.

Our first kiss surprised us both. His lips were as soft as ripe berries and tasted as sweet. I nestled in his arms as they closed around me, and I felt the quick thump of his heartbeat. Warm and safe. Ecstatically happy. That is what I felt for the short moment we held each other. It was a moment, I sensed, that we both would have liked to go on forever.

But suddenly strong fingers squeezed my arm and I felt myself yanked from the bench, lifted to my feet and out of Josh's embrace.

12

"*You little sneak!*" *my grandfather yelled.*

"Let go of me!" I cried as I twisted from his grasp.

Josh leapt up. "You don't have any right—"

"*You* listen to *me*!" Grandpa jabbed his finger into Josh's chest. "I told you to stay away from her!"

"Grandpa, *please!*"

My grandfather fixed his eyes on me and I was startled to find no anger in them. Only sorrow. "Your mother told you not to see him again," he said evenly.

"We were just—"

"I saw what you were 'just' doing." He whirled back to Josh. "You run along home now. Don't make any more trouble."

"Sir—" Josh began helplessly, and then with shoulders sagging, he picked up his sketch pad from the bench.

Humiliated, I turned and fled.

"Alexis!" Grandpa called after me. "You get back here!"

His words were lost in the rush of wind that blew through my hair as I sprinted over the grass, heart pounding, fists pumping at my sides.

I ran for perhaps ten minutes, then collapsed under a pine tree on the other side of the park. Unwelcome tears escaped my eyes and squiggled uncomfortably down my face and neck. At least my grandfather had not seen my tears. I would not give him the satisfaction of seeing me cry.

How dare he? I thought angrily. How *dare* he embarrass me like that? I barely knew my grandfather. I'd seen him just twice a year for my entire life. He had had nothing to do with my upbringing. And now, because my mother had lost her job and I was forced to live in his house, he thought he had the right to follow me around like a policeman after a fugitive.

I shut my eyes and allowed a special memory to overtake me. I recalled the sensation as my father's powerful arms encircled me. The scent of his spicy after-shave filled my nostrils as a tuft of his curly chest hair tickled my nose. I was four years old and perched atop his sleeping form as we swayed in the old back porch hammock. I listened to the rumbling snore echo through his body. Warm and safe. Warm and safe, he seemed to promise with each gentle rise and fall of his chest. Life was unfair. Now, when I needed him the most, my father was only a memory.

I wiped my nose on the sleeve of my jacket and picked up a pinecone, oddly fascinated with its tiny, intricate beauty. I did not want to replay the awful scene I had just lived through, so I counted the little sheaths encircling the cone. I tried to pretend the pinecone was the only thing in the world that mattered. "One, two, three, four," I counted.

The shock in Josh's eyes!

"Five, six, seven, eight."

You little sneak!

"Nine, ten, eleven—" I angrily hurled the pinecone into

the air as the full-blown memory of being wrenched out of my first kiss with Josh descended upon me.

The cone skidded across the grass and bounced to a stop on the sidewalk. A shabby finger bent and picked it up. It was Burrel, the janitor's friend. His gray overcoat was stained and torn and missing most of its buttons. He wore a tennis shoe on one foot and a brown loafer on the other.

I tensed, then remembered what Josh had said.

He's harmless.

The man before me, with the bulbous nose and quivering smile, had never hurt anybody. He held the pinecone in his grubby fingers, scrutinizing it closely, then slowly shifted his gaze to me, peering at me from beneath his matted, dirty blond bangs.

"You can have it," I said gently.

He dropped it into a burlap bag and shuffled off.

My tears dried and I breathed deeply, inhaling the earthy scent of damp grass. Soon I would have to go home and face my problems. Grandpa was very angry and by now he had probably told my mother what I had done.

How was I ever going to convince my family to let me see Josh?

We had something special between us. I had felt it when he kissed me. I sensed he felt it, too. He was a good person, and I was just going to have to convince my family of that.

Though Grandpa would be hard to persuade, he wasn't really in charge of me. My mother was the one who would have the final say on whether or not I could see Josh. If she got to know him, I was sure she would realize he was not a troublemaker.

I might not have been so confident had I known what would be waiting for me Monday morning.

At first I didn't think much of it when I saw the cluster of kids gathered around the bulletin board outside the school office. When Mr. Cline burst from the office and pushed his way through the crowd, I knew something was wrong.

"Okay, everybody!" he snapped. "Get what you need from your lockers and go to your classes."

As the kids moved away from the bulletin board, I saw the poster. It was the blowup of the picture Kelly had taken of Anita and Mr. Wingate in each other's arms.

I spotted it at almost the same moment Anita did. She was bustling down the hallway, a box of brightly colored paper in her arms, and her fluffy golden hair bouncing as she approached the office. "What's all the excitement about?" she asked Mr. Cline. Her smile vanished. "Oh, no!"

"I was just taking it down," said Mr. Cline.

"Who would do something like this?" Her eyes were those of a wounded rabbit, bright with pain and wide with shock.

I fell numbly into the stream of students rushing toward class.

Why had I suggested Kelly take a picture? I wished I could turn back time and relive that moment. If *only* I had it to do all over again, I would swallow my words.

Why don't you take a picture? I had asked. I winced at the memory. I saw myself laughing along with Josh as Kelly carried out her plan.

If only I had it to do over again . . .

If *only*!

But we only get one chance. Just one chance to do the right thing. And when we hurt somebody, we can *never* take it back.

By the time psychology class rolled around, everyone was gossiping about the photograph of Anita and Mr. Wingate.

I cringed each time I heard it mentioned. The fact that Anita did not know about my part in the scheme did not make me feel any better.

"Can you *believe* it?" a curly-haired girl in a pink dress called out to her friend across the room. "They were actually making out in the park!"

"Hey, Tom," said Mark Kelborne, who was always ribbing him. "I hear you have some competition."

Tom sat calmly at his desk and took a long sip of coffee from the ever-present bright blue mug. He seemed composed, but the distinct spark of humiliation lit his small brown eyes. "Are you telling me you want to take a surprise test today?"

"Is that a threat?" said Mark, who never seemed to know when to keep his mouth shut. "That art teacher really gets around."

"Don't believe everything you hear," said Tom.

"I *saw* the picture. And I talked to the girl who took it." He winked at Kelly. "She said they were really going at it."

It seemed to be common knowledge that Kelly had taken the picture. Apparently, her desire to be the center of attention outweighed her discretion. She had bragged openly to a number of people about the fact she'd arranged the morning's excitement.

"Hi," Josh said softly as he slipped into the seat behind me. His raised eyebrows punctuated the questions in his eyes.

I had not seen him since Grandpa interrupted our kiss. "Sorry about Saturday," I mumbled. "That was really embarrassing."

"You don't need to be embarrassed. It wasn't your fault your grandfather showed up and acted like a maniac."

"He was terrible! I'm not used to having someone trying to control me like that. My mom's usually pretty cool."

"Did you get in a lot of trouble?"

"My mom and grandpa both yelled at me when I got home."

"I didn't mean to cause you any problems."

"Look, it wasn't any more your fault than it was mine," I said. "Can we just forget about it?"

"Sure. Did you hear about the poster Kelly made? I can't believe she really did it."

"I *saw* it. Kelly posted it right in the middle of the bulletin board outside the office. Anita was there and she looked like she was going to cry."

"Wow. That's too bad. It wasn't very nice of Anita to go behind Tom's back, but I didn't want this to happen."

"You said someone should teach her a lesson," I reminded him.

"You were the one who suggested it. I wasn't any more serious than you were. I was mad because Tom's my friend, but Kelly shouldn't have done that."

"She's been the center of attention all morning," I said. "Just what she wanted!"

"Where is she?" Josh asked, and I followed his glance to her empty desk.

"I don't know. She was here a minute ago. Maybe she went to the rest room."

Josh shook his head. "I wish I'd discouraged her. It seemed so funny at the time, but I didn't think she'd really do it."

"Tom looks like he's shaken up about it, too."

"What a mess." Josh's full mouth flattened into a straight line as he watched Tom quietly shuffling through a pile of papers.

I thought that would be the end of it—that Josh and I were simply guilty bystanders whose worst crime was we had not stopped a cruel joke.

I was wrong.

A skinny boy slipped through the doorway and delivered a message to Tom, who scrutinized it a moment and then looked in our direction. "Alexis and Joshua, it says here that you've been summoned to the principal's office."

13

Kelly, Josh and I sat in a row on three straight-backed chairs facing the principal's desk.

"What did you kids think you were doing?" he demanded as he held up the poster.

"We didn't—I mean, it was Kelly—" I began.

"It was *your* idea!" she snapped. "It was *your* idea and *your* camera!"

Mr. Cline's cool blue eyes roamed over our faces. "Is that true, Alexis?"

"Well, it *was* my camera, but I was just kidding when I told Kelly she should take a picture."

"You thought the whole thing was hilarious." Her voice twisted into an angry whine. "You didn't exactly try to stop me, Alex!"

"Alex was just kidding around," Josh said in my defense.

"We were all joking about it. We didn't mean it. Alex shouldn't be punished for this."

"All I know is that Ms. Barnes is in tears right now," said Mr. Cline. "Somebody invaded her privacy with a very cruel prank. I want to know who was behind it."

"I admitted *my* part," said Kelly, glaring at me.

"Would you have come forward and confessed if I hadn't confronted you, Kelly?" asked Mr. Cline. "What if your homeroom teacher hadn't overheard you bragging about it? Would you be sitting here right now trying to make amends?"

"I don't know. Probably." Her pale, skinny arms were crossed defiantly over her chest. "It's not fair if I'm the only one in trouble when everybody else was planning it, too."

"Alex?" Mr. Cline said. "Is Kelly telling the truth? Did you suggest she take that picture and did you provide the camera and film?"

"Yes," I said simply. "But I didn't think—"

"That's right," he snapped. "You didn't *think*!"

His gaze settled on Josh. "What about you? Were you in on this, too?"

He shrugged. "I was there," he said evenly.

"It wasn't your fault, Josh!" I said. "You didn't think Kelly was serious."

"I'm in this as much as you are, Alex," he said.

He was being so noble, the protests died in my throat. Josh was willing to sit there and take the blame, yet he was no more involved in Kelly's awful backfiring joke than I was.

We all received the same punishment. We were ordered to pick up garbage on the school grounds during the second half of our lunch hours for a month, stay for an hour after school for one week, and apologize to Mr. Wingate and Anita.

Facing Anita was the hardest part.

Mr. Cline called her into his office, and, one by one, we sat down alone with her.

"You remind me so much of your aunt Nan," said Anita as she blew her nose on a yellow tissue. "I think that's one of the things that hurts the most. I was ready to be your friend, Alex. Then you did this to me."

"I'm sorry. You don't know how sorry I am. We didn't think Kelly was really going to do it."

Anita's normally rosy face was powdery white. A pained smile twisted her mouth. "My life is very complicated now, Alex. You could not even begin to understand. This horrible joke—or whatever you want to call it—has made things even worse."

I must have apologized a dozen times as we sat there, staring at each other across the vast oak desk. But it was clear that all the "I'm sorry's" in the world would not put the twinkle back in her eyes.

Grandma, of course, was privy to the whole scenario. As the principal's secretary, she knew the details of all that had transpired. Her voice lacked its usual warmth when she said, "I'm writing you up a hall pass to go see Bruce, Alex. He has this period free so now would be a good time to apologize to him."

"Bruce?"

"Bruce Wingate. He was once our neighbor. He's a *friend* of the family's, Alex! And you've got to tell him how sorry you are."

"Oh!" I said, as realization crept over me. "I knew the name was familiar. He's the one who wrote the article about the body in the pond! He wrote about *me!*"

"That's right. This is a small town. Everybody in Oxford is connected to everybody else in some way. People care about each other here. We don't play unkind tricks on each other, Alexis."

"I'm sorry," I said quietly. "It wasn't me, it was—"

"It was that *Josh*!" Her blue eyes flashed.

"No," I protested. "It was Kelly's fault."

Grandma signed the green hall pass and said, "I know your mother will want you home right after school tonight—as soon as you've finished your detention."

She obviously thought her warning about Josh was correct. I could already hear her, triumphantly announcing, "I told you that boy would get Alex in trouble!"

And my grandfather would answer, "I knew it. This is how it started with Nan."

"I'll be home by five," I said. "I told Mom I was going to visit Aunt Sidney after school and she said it was a good idea."

"All right. Now run along and see Bruce. He should be in his classroom."

I turned away and found myself face-to-face with Deke, who was grinning broadly. "So you got in a little trouble, eh?" he asked and chuckled—a full, nasty chuckle that set his eyes aglow with an irritating mixture of spite and humor. He set the large box he was carrying on the floor. "Here's the paper for the copy machine," he called out to my grandmother, who had crossed the room and was fishing for something in the filing cabinet.

Anita exited the principal's office and briskly pushed past Deke.

"In a hurry?" he asked. He turned back to me as she disappeared into the hallway.

"We played some good pranks when I was going to this school," he said in a conspiring whisper. "Our principal back then drove a Volkswagen bug. A bunch of us guys got together and carried it right through the front door one morning and parked it outside his office."

"He must have been mad." I tried to edge past his greasy bulk, but the box was in my way.

"I've got to admire that joke of yours," he said. "Wish I'd have thought up something that good. Of course we didn't have any teachers like Anita when I was in high school. Have you seen the way she shows off on that bike of hers, in that tight riding outfit?"

"She's a nice person," I said. "I'm sorry I let Kelly use my camera."

"I guess birds of a feather flock together, as the old saying goes."

"Your roses are looking beautiful, Deke," Grandma said, interrupting our conversation as she appeared at the counter again.

"Thank you, Thelma. I'll cut you some for your vase."

"That would be lovely," she gushed.

Deke walked away, whistling as he went.

"Deke has a garden?" I asked her. "He doesn't seem like the type."

"Oh, yes. It's behind the school and it's just charming. I remember when he started it. It was just a patch of dry dirt, but he turned it into a work of art. He seems like a rough character and he does have his problems, but deep down he's a kind soul. He planted his garden around the time Nan ran away. He knew how bad I felt about her, and as soon as he got something to bloom he'd bring me bouquets."

"I guess you never know about people," I said.

Grandma cleared her throat. "Shouldn't you be somewhere, Alexis?" she asked pointedly.

"Okay," I said. "I'll go see Mr. Wingate."

I was unable to apologize to him. I found his classroom empty, and later that day I learned he'd gone home sick.

"I wish we could have just gotten it over with," I said to Josh as we walked home from school. "Now all night long I'm going to be thinking about what I'm going to say to Mr. Wingate tomorrow."

Josh had fallen into step beside me as I exited the school,

and I was not about to tell him he could not walk with me. My mother and grandparents would certainly object if they saw us together. But I liked Josh. In fact, I not only *liked* him, I loved him.

I suppose that sounds strange because I hadn't known him long. Yet it felt as if I'd known him forever. His sweet smile touched something at the crux of my soul, stirring a forgotten memory I could not name.

"I'm not looking forward to apologizing to Mr. Wingate either," he said. "But it won't be as bad as facing Anita was." His eyes were disturbed, distant sapphires. "She's really not a bad person. And she's a good teacher. She's been supportive of my drawing. She doesn't make me do all the silly assignments like finger painting that everyone else has to do."

"You're a great artist," I said. "She knows you're way beyond that stuff. Did you take drawing lessons when you were a kid?"

"I've always drawn. No one ever showed me how."

"It's the same with me," I said. "I guess I inherited my drawing talent from my aunt Nan. My cartoons look almost exactly like hers."

"Does she make her living as an artist?"

"I don't know. Nobody's heard from her in nearly twenty years. She got in a fight with my grandpa one night. He told her to leave and she never came back."

"I wouldn't want to tangle with him either. But it's weird she stayed away for all this time."

"I know. I guess there's more to the story because everybody is so secretive about it. We're not ever supposed to mention Nan. My grandma let it slip that Nan had something to do with Grandpa's accident."

"What happened?"

I shrugged. "Nobody will tell me. All I know is that I look like I could be Nan's twin. Sometimes I think my grandfather picks on me because I remind him of his daughter."

"That's not fair."

"I wish she'd come home and work stuff out with him. And I'd love to meet her. I guess we're alike in a lot of ways. I think that's one of the reasons I'm so curious about her. My family acts really mysterious about the night she left, but I get the feeling they don't have the whole story either." I told him about my conversation with Aunt Sidney and how she let it spill that she'd given Nan money to run away.

When we reached her house, Josh asked if he could come in with me. "I got to know Sidney when I delivered papers here a few years back. I used to mow her lawn and she'd make me lemonade and we'd talk afterward."

"I don't know if she'll remember you," I said. "She gets confused about things. Remember, she thinks I'm my aunt Nan."

"Well, that's understandable if you look that much like her."

Aunt Sidney didn't recognize Josh, but she seemed pleased to have a male visitor. "Are you an artist, young man?" she asked when she noticed his sketch pad.

"He is and he's good!" I said.

Josh flipped open his pad and moved his hand expertly over the page. With a few swift lines, Aunt Sidney's likeness emerged from his pencil.

"That's beautiful!" I said. He had captured the sparkle in her eyes and softened the harsh lines of time in her face.

She beamed when he held it up for her approval.

Josh tore the drawing from his book and we tacked it on the wall beside her bed.

"You made her happy," I whispered to him.

"Your room is ready for you, Nan," said Aunt Sidney. "Maybe you'd like to stay tonight." She turned to Josh.

"My niece and I are quite close," she said. "She even has her own room upstairs. She likes to stay there when things get too heated at home."

We visited for a while and then I gently squeezed her hand and said, "We have to go now, Aunt Sidney. I'll come to see you again soon."

As Josh and I slipped out into the hallway, he said, "You're planning something, aren't you?"

"How did you guess what I was thinking?"

"I haven't known you very long, but I feel like I know you really well. And I saw your face when your aunt mentioned the upstairs room where Nan used to stay. You're going to explore it, aren't you?"

I smiled and led the way to the steep, narrow staircase at the end of the hall. We tiptoed up the stairs so as not to disturb Aunt Sidney. I hated sneaking around her house without permission, but there was something very strange going on in Oxford and I needed answers. I had a weird feeling a piece of the puzzle might be here in this house.

Nan's old room was at the top of the stairs. The moment my hand curled around the ornate glass doorknob, I knew the room inside was long and narrow with shuttered windows on each end and that rose-patterned wallpaper covered the steeply sloping walls. I knew a kerosene lamp sat on the round nightstand beside the small bed and that a braided throw rug lay on the wooden floor.

The door creaked open into darkness and while Josh fumbled along the wall for the light switch, I instinctively reached to the opposite wall and turned the ancient porcelain knob that controlled the ceiling light.

The shadows leapt away. I was not particularly surprised to see the room I had imagined. By now I was getting used to seeing my hunches proved right.

I moved to the little walnut desk under the west-facing

window and lightly ran my fingers over the keys of the old-fashioned manual typewriter.

"This thing doesn't even plug in," Josh commented.

"I can't imagine trying to write a paper without a spell check," I said. "And worse than that, I've heard it was really messy changing the ink ribbons on these old typewriters."

We continued to poke around the room, opening drawers, leafing through the books that lined the little shelf over the window, and studying the paintings on the wall. There was a beautiful one of a young Nan, her face radiant as her golden hair spilled around her shoulders.

"My grandfather painted this!" I gasped as I read the signature.

The gentle strokes of his brush had captured a sweetness in Nan not apparent in the old photographs of her.

He must have loved her, I realized.

"Hey, Alex, look what I found!" Josh's muffled voice called. His legs were sticking from the cubbyhole beside the bed, and a moment later he crawled out, holding a black carrying case. "It's a pool cue," he said, grinning broadly as he snapped open the case.

"What else is there?" I asked.

Josh didn't answer me. He was engrossed in the pool cue, shooting an invisible ball on an invisible pool table.

I peered into the cubbyhole. The light had burned out, so I reached into the shadows. The tight space closed around me and I shuddered. I hate small spaces and have always been claustrophobic.

"Watch out for spiders," Josh said. He laughed when I jerked my hand away.

"There's something else in there," I said as my eyes began to adjust. "It's a backpack!"

I pulled it out and unzipped the pouch on the front of the

pack. "Look! An envelope! And there's money inside—a lot of money!"

Josh set down the pool stick and watched wide-eyed as I counted out six hundred dollars.

"There's a note, too," I said.

"What does it say?"

Dear Nan,

   Please accept this as a gift from me. You and Scott deserve the chance at happiness I never got. Your father will destroy your relationship with Scott. I know this firsthand. Though he is my younger brother, he was always overprotective of me. He did not approve of my one and only love, Howard. Howard was a good man and he loved me. But his family was poor and uneducated.

   My brother threatened him, so Howard went to war, hoping this would give Eric time to cool off. Howard was killed in the war. There was never anyone else for me and I know I will die an old maid.

   I cannot bear to see my favorite niece suffer the same heartbreak. So take the money, Nan. Take the money and run!

Love,

Aunt Sidney

"She left without her money," I said. "That's strange."

"Yeah. What else is in there?"

We dumped the contents of the backpack onto the bed and rifled through my aunt's things. A pair of jeans, a couple of sweaters, and several changes of underwear. A toothbrush and makeup. Nan's driver's license.

"She left her *driver's license*!" I cried. "And here's her

library card and student I.D. Josh, why would she leave all this stuff behind?"

"It is kind of weird." He picked up the pool cue and took another shot at an imaginary ball.

He did not seem to appreciate the significance of what I had found. "Don't you see what this means?" I asked.

"Your aunt left behind her things."

"Nan wouldn't have left her driver's license and all this money. What would they live on? *Air*?"

"Maybe Scott had money."

"Maybe. But six hundred dollars would have gone a long way—especially back then."

"So, what do you think it means?"

"I hate to say this. But I think Nan never left."

14

Tuesday was a cool morning, veiled in a soft, thick fog that turned the houses across the road to fuzzy shadows and muffled the voices of the children running for the bus.

Late for school again, I hoisted Nan's pack onto my shoulders and decided to cut through the park.

What was she thinking the last time she wore this pack? I wondered. I'd read that psychics could discern things about people simply from handling their possessions.

I was beginning to believe *I* was psychic. That had to be the only explanation for how I knew so much about Oxford. If I *was* psychic, then maybe I could figure out what happened to my aunt by wearing her pack.

Where are you, Nan? Are you somewhere far away, happy and painting? Perhaps with a family of your own?

I wished I could believe that. But I suspected something

horrible had happened to my aunt. I suspected she was dead.

Josh thought I was wrong.

"So what if she left behind a few belongings," he'd said as we examined the pile of things I'd dumped from the pack. Her possessions made a sad little pile in the middle of the attic room. "It doesn't mean she's dead," he'd insisted. "She could replace everything she left behind—even her identification. She might have changed her identity for all we know."

"That sounds good," I agreed. "But when I look at her stuff and the money Aunt Sidney gave her, I get a *chill,* Josh! I think something awful happened to my aunt Nan!"

"Hey," he said gently when he saw the tears in my eyes. He slipped his arm around me. "It's okay. She's probably living in France drawing caricatures of tourists or something."

"Maybe. But I have to let somebody know about what we found. I was thinking about asking Mr. Wingate to help, but he probably hates me now because of Kelly's poster."

"What could he do to help?"

"Remember when I told you about the body I found when I was a baby? Mr. Wingate was the reporter who covered the story. My grandparents said he used to be their neighbor, and he always knew about everything that happened around here, even before the police did."

"Well, we've got to talk to him anyway, we might as well ask him what he thinks about your aunt leaving her things behind."

And so we had decided that I would take the pack to school the next day and show it to Mr. Wingate. If he thought it was suspicious, then I would go to the police. But there was no sense in alarming my family without good reason. *Especially* with my frightening theory. . . .

If my aunt *was* dead, I did not think it was an accident. I feared someone had killed her.

My mind floated to Judy Fitzwater.

Two girls. One dead. One missing. Was there a connection? If Judy and Nan were murdered, was it possible to know the truth after so many years?

I'd added my own books to Nan's backpack, making it so heavy that the straps bit into my shoulders as I headed toward Pioneer Park.

Quiet and still in the morning's mist, the park looked like a faded photograph—its colors muted and dulled by the white fog.

I imagined for a moment that the scene before me *was* nothing more than an old photo, taken almost sixteen years before at a sunny picnic and developed by a careless photographer who pulled the print from the fixer before the chemicals could do their job so that now the picture was fading prematurely. I was stepping into another day. A deadly day.

In the back of my thoughts, I knew all along why I'd chosen to come to the park that morning. I wanted to see the pond where Judy died.

I wanted to remember.

All my memories of the Judy tragedy were twisted inside out. Through regression, I had reexperienced her death as if I had been her. Now I wanted to remember through *my* eyes. I wanted to recall the killer's face.

The grass was crusted in frozen dew and the sharp sound of it crunching beneath my feet surprised me.

Pioneer Park was a sprawling square, zigzagging with bike paths and sidewalks. I had not seen the pond before—at least not that I could consciously remember—yet I sensed its location. I headed away from the manicured daffodil and rose gardens and neatly trimmed grass toward the center of the park where the laurel hedges grew wild and tall. The sidewalk here was nearly hidden by weeds, and I followed it as it curved through a grove of cottonwood trees.

There was the pond.

Dank and green and eerily calm.

I sat down on a big rock near the edge of the water and slipped off Nan's pack.

The circular pond was about the size of the school swimming pool. Made from concrete, its sides sloped sharply toward the water. Thick, slick algae grew greenly along the edges. It looked slippery. I could easily imagine someone losing their footing. Was that what had happened to Judy? Did she fall and hit her head as everyone said?

I shut my eyes and tried again to recall that day. *Somewhere* locked in a closet of my mind the memory was there.

The quiet closed around me and I drew a deep breath. The scent of stagnating pool water filled my lungs. It smelled of dark secrets and slimy ripe things. It made me shudder but still I did not remember. Maybe I should try a different angle, I thought and got up and walked around the pool.

Perhaps if I discovered the exact location where I found the body, it would stir a memory.

I moved slowly, my eyes wandering over the lily pads that knitted thickly together along the edge of the water. In my mind's eye, I pictured Judy floating lifelessly. I saw my chubby baby hand reaching out to her, slapping the water. I could almost hear the gentle splashing as I futilely patted her. My hand hitting the water probably sounded like the pond did now, rhythmically lapping at my feet in urgent, slurping waves.

Splash. Splash. Splash.

The sound drew me into a place of clammy, dark things. Cold seeped through my clothes and coaxed goose bumps to rise on my flesh, but I stood calmly, refusing to so much as shiver.

Remember! I silently urged myself. *You can do it!*

I stared into the water, willing the memory to surface. As I did so, something white caught my eye. It was tangled in the lily pads, just at the edge of my vision. At first, I thought I was simply remembering—that the glassy eyes staring up at me through the murky water weren't really there. I blinked, hoping to shake free of the ghastly image.

But the picture would not go away.

I had found another body.

15

For a moment, all I could do was stare at the waxy face. Her long hair lay on the surface of the water, writhing with the slow ripples of the pond.

Something told me this girl had not drowned. Somebody had killed her, and that somebody could be nearby.

I turned and fled.

The path was slippery. I tumbled and fell, scraping the palms of my hand on a rock. I scrambled to my feet, blindly clawing my way through the laurel hedge. As I burst through the bushes, frantic to escape the grisly scene behind me, strong arms wrapped around me. I opened my mouth to scream.

"Alex?" a familiar voice said.

I looked up into Josh's concerned blue eyes. "Hey, what's going on?" he asked.

I buried my face in his chest, trembling as he held me gently. "Oh, Josh!" I cried. "It was so awful!"

"Take a deep breath," he urged. "Just tell me what happened."

"The pond—" I stammered. "There was a girl—she's *dead*!"

He stepped forward. "I better go look."

I grabbed his arm. "No!" I cried. "We have to call the police. We can use Aunt Sidney's phone."

We were breathless when we reached her door.

"My God! What happened to you?" Sequoia said when she saw our faces. Her hair was knotted into a bun, and she reached up with a clay-coated hand to brush away the stray wisp hanging in her eyes. She left a round smudge of clay in the middle of her forehead.

"I need to use the phone." Josh pushed past her. "There's been an accident."

We followed him into the kitchen and I numbly listened as he tried to describe to the police what I had seen. "She said she saw a girl floating in the pond at Pioneer Park and she thinks she's dead," he said.

"She *is* dead!" I said. "Tell them to hurry!"

"A dead body?" Sequoia's face was suddenly powdery white. She seemed to forget the clay on her hands as she nervously fidgeted with her silver bracelets and soon they were spotted with gray. "This can't be happening!"

The police arrived within minutes. Two squad cars pulled in front of the house, and the pair of officers from one car headed straight for the park, while the lone officer from the other car came up to the house. He looked young with his curly red hair and sprinkle of freckles across his pug nose.

"Hi, Fred," Josh greeted him. "This is Alex and Sequoia. Alex is the one who found the body."

Sequoia watched from the doorway, her eyes huge and frightened as Josh and I climbed into the patrol car.

The Oxford police station was a plain, one-story brick building. The policeman ushered us into a corner office and introduced us to Sergeant Bryer, a short stocky man with balding gray hair. I described in detail what I'd seen and he carefully wrote it all down.

Neither Josh or I wanted to go to school afterward. How could I sit in classrooms all day with that grisly picture floating behind my eyes?

Grandma came to pick me up. When she walked into the station, her eyes slid from me to Josh. "You two were together?"

"No," I said. "I was alone when I found the body. I was on my way to school. I ran into Josh right afterward."

Grandma said she would take the morning off to stay with me. "Grandpa's at the dentist, and your mom drove to Seattle to buy extra big cake pans," she said. "You shouldn't be home alone after your horrible experience."

"I'll be fine," I insisted. She made me nervous, the way she hovered around, constantly chattering. I thought I would be more relaxed without her there. But the instant she drove off, I began to feel jumpy.

With my family gone, the house came alive with a voice of its own—sounds I could not hear when Grandpa's radio blared and my siblings bickered. The refrigerator hummed and buzzed and clicked. As a breeze flowed through the garden, the shrubbery scraped eerily against the window. Edward woke from his nap and his toenails clacked across the kitchen floor. The kitchen clock ticked so sharply, I was painfully aware of how time dragged.

It was only noon. I could not bear the idea of being alone for three more hours.

I grabbed my coat and went outside. Sunshine had melted the morning frost. The day had grown surprisingly warm. I began walking. I wasn't sure where to go, but I wanted to avoid the park, so I strolled in the opposite direction. When I realized I was a block away from the police station, something occurred to me.

In the horror and confusion of finding the body, I failed to mention my suspicion about my aunt's disappearance. I had, of course, told the police about finding Judy, because the coincidence of finding two bodies in the same pond was so astounding.

I entered the police station and approached the receptionist.

"Sergeant Bryer is out," she said. "Would you like to talk with someone else?"

"No, thank you. Please tell him Alexis Baxter stopped by. There's something I forgot to tell him." I turned to go, and as I did so, I overheard an officer calling out to another.

"I can't help you out with that, Hugh," he said. "I'm working on the Ferrel case."

"That poor girl. Only sixteen!"

I froze as the words seeped in. *Ferrel.*

Tawny Ferrel.

The girl in the pond was unfamiliar to me.

Tawny was a *live* girl. A giggling girl with animated eyes and smirking, twitching lips—a girl who was constantly flipping her long hair over her shoulder. I had not connected her with the stiff, waxy thing in the pond.

It had not occurred to me the girl I found was someone I knew.

I reeled in shock.

I wanted to stay busy, to be around people. So I walked to the Big Top, planning to work on my mural. When I tried to paint, my hand trembled so badly I could not steady it. After an hour, I gave up and put away the brushes and sank into one of the vinyl booths, my mind on Tawny.

I glanced at the counter where she had stood only a few

days before, just as alive as the group of loud cheerleaders giggling and gossiping in the booths across from me.

I could close my eyes and still see her sulking as she rolled her big blue eyes at her awful uniform.

Our conversations had been short and, for the most part, antagonistic. But I remembered every word, the inflection of *every syllable* she'd spoken to me. Her voice seemed to echo in my ears.

You're the one who tried to run us off the bridge. And, *My mom gets tickets for driving too slow. Girls notice Josh everyplace we go.*

I felt sick to my stomach.

How could someone be so alive one moment and dead the next? I hadn't liked Tawny very much. But her death still shocked me.

"Hey, what's wrong with you? You look like your dog died or something." It was Kelly, who had snuck up behind me. She snapped her gum and grinned as she slid into the seat across from me, and I stared at her, stunned. She was giggling and chattering as if her cousin's death didn't faze her at all. Then I realized she didn't know yet—that very few people in Oxford were aware Tawny Ferrel was dead.

Apparently the police hadn't yet notified her family, and it was not, of course, my place to tell them.

"There was some big excitement in Pioneer Park today," she said. "Did you hear? They found a body in that old scummy pond. I hear it was an old man. I guess he got shot or something."

It's funny how rumors get started. Somebody hears something and they don't have all the details so they embellish, and by the time the story has circled around through dozens of people it barely resembles the truth.

"I could hardly believe it!" Kelly said. "That's the second body found in the pond."

"That's too bad," I mumbled.

"But you know about the *first* one, don't you?" Her eyes were knowing, her lips bent into a strange smirk. She'd obviously heard I'd found Judy Fitzwater's body.

I hadn't told anyone but Josh about finding Judy. Had he told Kelly? It was a painful, personal thing and I felt the sting of betrayal. "Did Josh tell you about that?" I asked. "Did he tell you I found Judy?"

"Nope. My mom did. She remembers when it happened. She was at the picnic that day. But speaking of Josh, have you seen him today? He wasn't at scuba club after school."

I gave a noncommittal shrug.

"Maybe Tawny came back for him," she said. "Maybe they're going to run off together. But knowing her, she's probably stretched out on a California beach right now in that little polka-dot bikini she bought at the mall last week, soaking up the rays."

I nodded weakly, unsure of how to respond.

"Oh, that reminds me," she said. "I have something for you." She stood up and wriggled her fingers into the pocket of her snug jeans, pulled out a folded note, and handed it to me.

Who in the world would send me a note? I wondered as I unfolded it. I didn't know many people in Oxford, and for a moment I stared blankly at the page of neat, round writing. My eyes were drawn to the bottom of the paper as I searched for a signature. When I saw the name scrawled there, I felt like I'd been socked in the stomach.

How could this be possible? I wondered in shock. The note was from a dead girl.

16

"*Tawny gave that to me a few days ago,*" *Kelly explained.* "I kept forgetting to give it to you and it almost went through the wash."

As she smiled at me with unsuspecting eyes, suddenly I could no longer hide my emotions. Perhaps it was wrong for me to be the one to tell her the terrible news. But in that moment, I felt I had no choice. Tears spilled down my face as I reached across the tabletop and grabbed her hand. It felt limp and cold in mine. "Oh, Kelly!" I cried. "Tawny didn't run away."

Her eyes grew serious. "What are you trying to say?" The scent of her bubble gum was suddenly sickeningly sweet and it overpowered the space between us.

I wanted to leap up and bolt out the door. But Kelly was staring at me, waiting for me to finish.

I drew a deep breath. "Something awful has happened to your cousin."

"What happened?"

"She's dead. That wasn't an old man in the park. It was Tawny."

"Tawny? Dead?" Disbelief flooded her face. "No." She shook her head.

"I'm sorry," I offered gently.

"It can't be true!" She jerked her hand from mine. "How do *you* know it was her?"

"I'm the one who found her."

"*You? You* found her?" Kelly's eyes bulged. "She was right about you!"

"What do you mean?"

"Tawny said there was something weird about you." She spoke in a daze, her words pouring out slow and thick like maple syrup from a nearly empty bottle. "Tawny knew it the first time she saw you. Then my mom told us about how you found that Judy girl in the pond when you were a baby. Weird. That's so weird."

"That wasn't my fault. I didn't hurt Judy and I didn't hurt Tawny. I was at the wrong place at the wrong time."

"*Twice!* Oh, my God! I'm going to throw up!" She leapt up and dashed toward the bathroom.

I watched her shaky frame disappear into the ladies' room and wondered if I should follow her. She'd said some awful things to me, but she had just found out her cousin was dead and was probably in shock.

I wiped my eyes and read Tawny's note.

Alex,

   I don't know who you think you are. This is your first day of school and already you're trying to make trouble. I got your note in my locker, and it was just

*about the most childish thing I ever read. Even though
you didn't sign your name, I knew right away who
wrote it.*

*Obviously, you've got your eye on Josh and you're
jealous of me. But that's you're problem. Don't send
me any more threatening notes. And if you do, try to
think of something more interesting than "DIE
BITCH." What did you write that with? Nail polish?*

Tawny

All the air seemed to leave my body as I read her words.
Somebody had sent her a threatening note. *Die Bitch*. The
very words written in Judy Fitzwater's *Beowulf* book and
the same terrible words scrawled across my aunt's mural.

Three girls. Two dead, one missing. Each had received
the same ugly message.

In the Big Top kitchen, I leaned against the grease-
stained wall and shakily dialed the police station. I pressed
my ear to the phone's receiver, straining to hear the receptionist's voice over the clatter of pots and pans.

"I need to talk with Sergeant Bryer," I said. "It's really
important."

"He's not in. Can I have him call you?"

I gave her the Big Top phone number. Two hours later,
he returned my call, his gruff voice pouring through the
phone. He sounded bored as I tried to explain about my
aunt, Judy, and Tawny.

He perked up a little when I told him about the note.
"Bring in the note Tawny got," he said. "We'll have the lab
run some tests on it."

"I don't have *that* note," I said. "I got one from her accusing me of sending her a note. That one said, 'Die Bitch,'
and she said it was written in nail polish. Probably red nail
polish."

"Did you send her the note?"

"Of course not!"

"How did you know it was written in red nail polish?"

"I'm just guessing. The writing on my aunt's mural was in red and so was the writing in Judy's book."

I felt panicked. If he thought I'd sent the note, he might also think I had something to do with her death. "I did *not* send Tawny that note," I said quickly. "A killer is out there somewhere. You've got to do something! *Please!*"

I headed for home, my own words ringing in my ears.

A killer is out there!

I walked fast, suddenly aware of every overgrown shrub, shadowy alley, and abandoned shack—all places a killer could hide.

The day had stretched thin, its last rays of light dying before my eyes. My whole body tensed each time a car passed, its headlights sweeping the street in dusky, gold beams.

What kind of car did a killer drive? Something sleek and dark that whispers close to the road? Or something huge and clunky that chugs along obnoxiously? I found myself looking at each passing vehicle with suspicion.

When I finally arrived home my mother and grand-mother practically pounced on me the instant I walked in the door, slathering me with sympathy and affection.

"Oh, honey!" Mom cried. "We were worried sick when we got home and you weren't here. You didn't walk in the dark, did you?"

"I should never have left you alone," Grandma said.

"I'm fine," I said, reassured as my mother's strong arms went around me and hugged me tight.

"What a horrible thing for you to go through," she said.

"It was awful," I agreed. "I can't get the picture of Tawny out of my head."

"You shouldn't have left," Mom gently scolded. "When you have a shock like that, you should try to take it easy."

"I had to get out of the house," I explained. "I wanted to stay busy. I went down to the Big Top to work on my mural, but I was too upset to paint."

For the rest of the evening, my family hovered around. Grandma made a special spaghetti because she knew it was my favorite, but I was too queasy to eat more than a couple of bites.

Afterward, I offered to help clean the kitchen but Mom insisted she could do it, so I sat at the counter on one of Grandma's swirling stools and rotated back and forth in slow half circles as Mom cleared the table and wiped down the counters.

Normally, True was the one whirling around the stools and she always got yelled at, but Mom just smiled and said, "You seem nervous. Do you want to talk about it?"

"Yes," I said. "I've got a question for you."

She wrung out the sponge and settled on the stool next to me.

"Did it ever occur to you that something bad might have happened to Aunt Nan?" I asked.

"What do you mean?" she asked sharply.

"What if someone hurt her so she couldn't come back?"

"No one would want to hurt Nan. She didn't have an enemy in the world."

"Maybe a stranger hurt her. Anyway, she *did* have enemies. Grandpa hates her—"

"Alex!" she gasped. "What are you *saying*?"

"I didn't mean that Grandpa did anything to her. I was just pointing out that not everyone loved Nan. We're not even allowed to mention her *name*!"

"My father loves Nan. He's just hurt and angry."

"What about that girl who used to be her friend? Nan took her boyfriend away. She hated her, didn't she?"

"Patsy was hurt," said Mom. "She was crazy about Scott, and when Nan took him away, she got married right out of high school, to Gregory Sims, a boy she took up with on the rebound. The marriage didn't work out. I think Patsy pined for Scott a long time. Nan and Scott's relationship hurt a lot of people."

"They loved each other. Aunt Sidney said it was true love. Why didn't everyone just leave them alone?"

She shook her head. "Alex, you don't know anything about it. Nan left before you were even born. Can you please let it go?"

"Not after what happened. I found *two* bodies in the Pioneer Park pond! I don't understand why this is happening!"

She put her arm around me. I stiffened and pulled away.

"Oh, Alex," she said quietly. "This terrible thing that happened to the girl you found has nothing to do with Nan."

"I hope not. But how do you know that? Nobody's heard from her for so long."

She sighed. "Sometimes I worry," she admitted. "But I prefer to imagine her happy and healthy somewhere, leading a productive life."

"But what if something *did* happen to her—"

"Alex, *please*!" she cut me off. "I know you're upset about finding Tawny. And I guess it's natural you'd be a little paranoid. But Nan is my sister. I miss her and I'm concerned about her, yet I know she's always been stubborn. Dad was really hard on her. He told her to never come back."

"What about the rest of you? Why doesn't she contact you or Grandma?"

Her lips tightened and her face drained of color. "There was a big scene the night Nan left. She and Scott did something bad. She's probably afraid if she comes back they'll get in trouble."

"You mean with the *police*?" I gasped. "What did they do?"

"It was before you were born and doesn't concern you, and it's really painful for me to think about it."

"But she's my *aunt*. I have a right to know what happened. Everyone says I'm so much like she was and I feel a bond with her. I don't understand how she could just go away like that without saying good-bye or anything."

"She sent us a postcard. I've told you that."

A postcard.

That postcard contradicted my theory that she never left Oxford. How could she, after all, send a postcard if she were dead?

Suddenly I needed to see it. While Mom was reading True a bedtime story, I lugged out the boxes of mementos again. Grandma saved all letters, so I knew it would be there.

It was at the top of a box of bundles of letters. The postcard depicted a glossy scene of palm trees by a sandy beach. The message on the back was short and unrevealing.

Dear Family,

Hawaii is great. I'm painting the ocean and learning to surf. Don't worry about me if I don't write for a while. I've got lots to sort out. You may never forgive me for what I've done to Daddy, but that is your choice.

Love,
Nan

I read her words over and over. And each time I did, they made less sense.

Something was not right. Yet I could not put my finger on it.

I'm painting the ocean . . .

There it was. The *ocean*? Nan was painting the *ocean*?

How very strange, for she was a cartoonist who favored cluttered pictures with funny people and simple backgrounds. Why had she suddenly taken up seascapes?

The answer was, she had not. I began to tingle from my fingertips to my toes, and I knew with sudden certainty the postcard was not from Nan.

I searched through the boxes for something in her handwriting, and when I found one of her old English Composition papers, at first the writing seemed to match. But then I noticed that the *e*'s and *i*'s just weren't right. Nan's *i*'s always looked like *e*'s, looped and open with just the hint of a dot over them. But the *i*'s on the postcard were all perfectly straight, closed and clearly dotted. It was as if someone had forged her handwriting.

What did it mean?

If only I had the missing pieces of this puzzle.

I saw the secrets in my mother's eyes. Why was she so reluctant to share them with me? What had Nan done that was so horrible she was afraid to come home?

Whenever I questioned my mother about this, she closed up tight. I would just have to find the answers on my own.

Nan was like a ghost. There was nothing much of her here any longer—just a flicker in my mother's eyes, or a painting on the wall. And, of course, there was my resemblance to her. Sometimes it seemed like my face was a monument to her, proof she'd lived before me. The only tangible shreds of evidence on what her last days here really meant were in the fading memory of an aging relative and the long forgotten backpack.

I had tried to explain about the pack to the gruff policeman over the phone. He hadn't seemed too interested. It was almost as if he thought I was making things up. I wondered what he'd say when I actually brought the pack in and presented him with proof there was something strange about my aunt's disappearance.

I reached under my bed, but my hand touched only the dusty floor.

The pack was gone.

Oh, my God! I thought. *I left it at the pond!*

17

It is so dark. And cold. Why am I so cold?

"Come here, darling," a raspy voice croons. *"You know I would never hurt you."*

"No!"

"Don't be that way. I want to see your smile. Where is that pretty smile I love so much!"

"I hate you!" I scream. *"Get away from me!"*

"Alex! Wake up!"

I blinked and looked up into True's scared little face. "You were having another bad dream," she said. "You were talking in your sleep and you kicked your blankets off."

Shivering, I pulled the blankets up around me. My fingers felt like ice.

"Were you dreaming about a monster?" she asked.

"Yes."

"Did he have a round purple head and big, mean teeth?"

"I didn't see his face," I said.

"We'll leave the light on so he won't come back." True climbed back into her bed.

I lay awake trembling for a long time, wondering about this "monster" I had dreamed of. I had a sense of evil. Pure teeth-chattering evil.

It was more than a nightmare.

It was a memory.

As I tried to pick at it, it fell apart, disintegrating like an old letter left out in the weather. I held only bits and pieces of words and thoughts and those soon ran together, smearing into indistinguishable inky blotches.

The details of the dream were gone and I was left with only the feeling of evil along with a fear I'd be too frightened to ever sleep again. Then, thankfully, a soft wave of slumber slid over me and I was out, this time drifting into a warm, cradling world without dreams.

"Dreams always seem intense when you first wake up from them," Josh said when I told him about my nightmare.

"This was more than a dream," I said. We were walking toward our lockers, hand in hand as students stampeded around us. A horrible excitement tinged the morning air as word spread that Tawny Ferrel was dead.

Some of the girls huddled in pale clusters, eyes tiny and pink from crying. A couple of boys were involved in a loud, raucous conversation, shouting details at each other from opposite ends of the hall. "I heard she hung herself!" one yelled as he slammed his locker shut.

"My neighbor said she jumped off a building," the other replied.

"They think she killed herself," I whispered to Josh.

"I know. All kinds of rumors are flying around. When I was sitting outside the school waiting for you a while ago, I heard a bunch of weird stories."

"Is anybody saying she was murdered?"

"Just you." His eyes narrowed in concern. "Alex, I know it's awful what happened to Tawny. And I hate that you had to find her, but you have to get hold of yourself."

I wrenched my hand from his. "What do you mean?"

He sighed and ran his fingers through his curls. "First you think somebody killed your aunt, and now you think somebody murdered Tawny. It's like you're hysterical."

"I'm not hysterical! I'm talking calmly, aren't I? I'm not running around screaming!" I realized, too late, that my voice had risen sharply. I *was* beginning to sound hysterical.

"Hey, it's okay." He pulled me into a hug. "All I'm saying is that we don't need to jump to conclusions about what happened. That's all."

"Everyone thinks my aunt ran away. But they don't realize she left her backpack with her money and identification."

"Bring the pack in to show Mr. Wingate. He can look at the situation objectively."

"The pack's gone," I said. "I took it off yesterday morning at the pond. After what happened, it didn't even occur to me to realize it was missing until last night when I went to reach for it."

"What about the money?"

"It was in the pack," I said with a groan. "I lost six hundred dollars—and my textbooks, too!"

"The police must have picked up the pack," said Josh. "It's part of the crime scene now."

"I called and asked them about it. They said they'd combed the area and no one found a pack."

"Wow. That's a lot of money to lose."

"Yeah. And it wasn't even *mine*." I reached into my purse and pulled out the postcard. "Look at this. This is the postcard that Nan supposedly sent right after she left, but if you compare the writing to one of her papers it doesn't match." I shakily held out the evidence while he scrutinized it skeptically.

"It looks pretty close to me," he said.

"Look at the *e*'s and the *i*'s. The ones on the postcard look funny."

"Yeah. I guess they are kind of different." He didn't sound convinced.

"*Two* teenage girls died and another just disappeared! Somebody has to *do* something."

"The police will take care of it. If there is a murderer out there, they'll find him."

"If there is a murderer out there, he's been running loose for almost twenty years. What makes you think the police will do something now?"

He just looked at me sadly, and I realized for the first time he had lost a friend.

"Oh, Josh," I said. "I'm sorry. I know this is hard on you, too. Tawny was your friend."

"We went to school together since the seventh grade. I can't believe she's dead. I never knew anybody our age who died before."

"It's a shock," I said. "Maybe I am jumping to conclusions about what happened to the girls. But what if somebody *did* kill them?"

Josh didn't have an answer for me, but I vowed to find someone who would listen to me—someone who could convince the police to do something about the horrible string of tragedies. "I'm going to see Mr. Wingate," I told him. "Maybe he'll remember something about the day Judy Fitzwater drowned."

Bruce Wingate was a husky man with a friendly round face and bright red hair. His desk was piled with papers and black-and-white photographs, which he was busily shuffling through when I peered in the doorway.

"Excuse me," I ventured. "I need to talk to you."

"I know who you are."

I lifted my hands imploringly and said, "Mr. Wingate, I'm really sorry. I could hardly sleep last night thinking about it. I know I've caused both you and Anita a lot of pain, but I swear I didn't mean for it to happen."

He stared at me sternly as I squirmed uncomfortably. Then, suddenly, a smile replaced his frown. "Come on in and sit down. I was young once, too, I know how things can get out of hand. You come from a good family. I know your mother and grandmother very well. Why don't we put this incident behind us? What I really need right now is a cartoonist for the school paper. I heard you are good."

"I'll bring something in to show you," I said, excited in spite of myself. I'd always wanted to see my work in print. "There's something else I wanted to talk to you about, Mr. Wingate."

"What's on your mind?"

"Do you remember when Judy Fitzwater drowned in the pond at Pioneer Park?"

"Terrible tragedy. I was a reporter for the *Oxford Journal* and I covered that story."

"I know. I read your article."

"I wasn't sure if your family had told you what happened."

"They didn't. I didn't see the article until we moved here. I found it in one of my grandmother's scrapbooks. It's creepy to think I found a body when I was a baby."

"You were so little, you probably don't remember." A question rolled through the statement.

I shook my head. "You're right. I don't remember. But I wish I did. If I saw something more—if I saw it *happen,* then maybe I could remember something about Judy's killer. Do you have any idea why they never caught him?"

"Killer? There's no killer. The coroner ruled it a drowning. She slipped and hit her head. Plain and simple."

"In your article you wrote that Judy was murdered."

He grimaced and tapped his pencil on the edge of the desk. "I was an eager young reporter. In fact, that was my first story. I thought it would be my ticket to becoming an investigative reporter. If I cracked a big case, I was sure I'd have an open door to the big city newspapers."

"You mean you made stuff up?"

"I reported what my eyes and ears told me. I never lied, but I sometimes slanted articles to make them more exciting." He smiled apologetically. "I'm sorry the article upset you."

"But you must have thought something was suspicious," I persisted. "Or you wouldn't have suggested Judy was murdered."

He opened his mouth as if to say something, then quickly clamped it shut again. "Some things are better left in the past," he said.

"I wish I could remember what happened."

"You were just a baby. You couldn't possibly remember that far back. Besides, there's no reason to. You've got to put this behind you and move on."

"I can't now. It's happening all over again."

"What do you mean?"

"You heard about Tawny Ferrel?"

He nodded.

"Do you know how she died?"

"I've heard the rumors."

"I found her body in the pond at Pioneer Park."

"My God!" His eyes reflected shock as he stared at me.

"It's really strange, isn't it? First I find a body when I'm a baby, then I come back to town fifteen years later and find another body in the same spot!"

"It is an eerie coincidence."

"I wish it were a coincidence. But this is *too* weird. It's like I have some connection with these girls drowning. I just don't know what it is."

"What do the police say?"

"They're not telling me anything. And they don't seem too interested in my opinion."

"If I were still a reporter, I'd do a story on this. It's definitely an odd angle."

"There's more. I think something happened to my aunt, too. She disappeared a couple of years before Judy died. The family thinks she ran away, but I found something she left behind—something that makes me think something bad happened to her, too."

As I told him about finding the backpack, he listened intently. But when I came to the part about losing the pack, he shook his head. "I know from experience that the police in this town need to see concrete evidence before they'll investigate something like this. If you can find the pack, it would be helpful to your cause. Do you have anything else that indicates something happened to your aunt?"

The only thing my family had left of Nan were old photographs, some of her paintings, and the lone postcard she had supposedly sent from Hawaii.

When I got home that day, I went through the box of mementos again, not sure what I was looking for. But I knew it when I saw it.

It was a small square color photograph. There was Nan, happy and smiling in a bathing suit, holding hands with a handsome bushy-haired boy. Next to them stood a chubby woman with a little brown wiener dog tucked under her arm like a football.

One glance, and I was certain the woman was Scott's mother. They did not look like mother and son. Yet I knew they were. Just as I knew so many of the odd facts about Oxford.

What about Scott's family? I wondered. Did they know what became of him?

There was no listing for Dewitts in the phone book. And I could not come right out and ask my mother or grandparents how to find Scott's mother. But Oxford is such a small town, all I had to do was wander down to the grocery store and strike up a conversation with the cashier.

"Scott Dewitt's mom?" said the bubbly, gray-haired checker. "After her husband died several years ago, she moved to the Turtle Trailer Park in Kettleburg, just a couple miles from Oxford."

I walked to the nearby bus stop. Fifteen minutes later, I was on the bus headed north toward Kettleburg. If Dottie Dewitt could tell me something about what happened to my aunt, the sooner I talked to her the better.

It was a short ride and the old diesel engine rumbled noisily as I was jostled around in my seat. I peered out the dirty window at the acres of strawberry fields and thought about what I would say to Dottie.

Kettleburg was even smaller than Oxford. The main street consisted of a small grocery, a drugstore, and a gas station. On the corner sat a little pink building, topped with an oversized sign that read, EMMA'S BAKERY. Sweet smells wafted from the open window, and I stood for a moment inhaling the intoxicating scent of baking bread.

The trailer park was not hard to find. I spotted the entrance as I passed the bakery. A green sign, shaped like a turtle, swayed from two rusty chains on a curved pole. Beside it a straight asphalt road led to the trailers. Stretched out in neat rows along the riverside, the dwellings had a permanent feel. Almost all had little wooden porches built around the front doors. Many had small grassy lawns, and some of the shrubbery towered over the trailers as if they'd had many years to grow and engulf the compact metal homes.

I stopped the first person I saw, a frazzled woman with a

pair of twin toddlers in tow. "Do you know where Mrs. De-witt's trailer is?" I asked.

"Dottie Dewitt is the manager," she told me, as the little blond boys tugged at her legs. "Her trailer is right over there."

I followed her gaze to a long silver trailer wrapped in a cedar deck. Birdbaths and statues of deer filled the small square of her yard.

My rap at the door was answered by a muffled chorus of angry dog barks.

"Shut up!" someone shouted. "Scout, no! Oscar, stop that!"

The trailer rocked with the commotion, and I waited patiently for her to get things under control so she could open the door. But the barking never ceased and a moment later she cracked the door and a river of wiener dogs spilled out and circled around the porch, yipping at my feet.

"Petey, no!" Mrs. Dewitt screamed as she threw the door wide open. She was a large woman with a round pink face. "Oscar, stop it! Petunia!"

"How many do you have?" I gasped, as wobbly, brown dogs swarmed around me.

"Enough," she said. "If you're from the high school selling candy, I already bought some."

"I'm not selling anything. I just wanted to talk with you for a few minutes."

"Mitzi, no! *Oscar!* Petey! Jojo, don't you bite that nice girl!" She reached down with a rolled up newspaper and swatted one of the brown dogs who was snarling at my ankle. "Watch out for Jojo," she warned. "The others are friendly but he'll take a big chunk out of your leg."

The dogs were galloping around me in circles and I'd already lost track of Jojo. To me, the wiener dogs looked exactly alike and the fact that one of them wanted my leg for lunch made me uneasy.

"Come on in," she said. "Have a seat."

I sat in a squat orange chair while she fumbled around in the kitchen. I quickly took in the cramped surroundings—the owl-shaped candles lined up in a row atop the small television, the worn yellow carpet that gave way to daisy-patterned linoleum when it reached the narrow kitchen, the corner shelf of shiny trophies of swimmers frozen in action, and the long thin couch beneath the dusty window. None of it was familiar.

A framed photograph of Scott hung over the television. He was a handsome boy, with smiling green eyes, feathered blond hair, and a square masculine chin.

Nan's true love.

"I was going to make us some tea, but I can't find my glasses."

"There they are." I pointed to a pair of square brown glasses on the coffee table.

When she slipped them on, her smile froze. "Nan?" Bewilderment crept into her voice.

"I'm Nan's niece, Alex."

She forgot the tea and sank down onto the couch opposite me. "You gave me a start. I couldn't see you clearly until I put my glasses on. You look so much like Nan. She was my Scottie's girlfriend."

"I know. That's why I'm here."

"Have you heard something?" Bright, red blotches of excitement appeared on her cheeks. "Have you heard from Nan? Do you know where Scott is?"

"No. Nobody in my family has heard anything from Nan for years."

Her voice shriveled, becoming sad and limp. "I should know better than to get my hopes up like that. I know the truth, just like I'm sure your grandparents know the truth."

"The truth?"

"About the kids. Scottie and Nanette. They're both dead."

18

"*Scott doesn't even call on Christmas or Mother's Day.*" Dottie's voice cracked. "He was such a thoughtful boy. He wouldn't hurt me like this if he could help it. That's why I know he's dead. I know it deep in my bones, but every once in a while I think I'm wrong—that the phone will ring and I'll hear Scott's voice. Or maybe there will be a knock on the door and I'll see him there, tall and smiling with a good story about why he went away."

"Maybe he will come back," I said, trying to comfort her.

"It would be easier if I knew the truth. The wondering and waiting are the hardest. If he's dead, I wish I had proof. Then I could at least know he's not suffering." She forced a tight little smile. "But your family knows all about this, too. It must be just as rough on your grandparents as it is on me. I feel for them—even though your grandpa doesn't think too kindly of me."

"Why?" I asked.

"We had words when the kids disappeared. Your grandpa blamed Scott for his accident—and I tell you it *was* an accident. It wasn't Scott's fault."

"Do you mean when he lost his hand?"

Her voice trembled. "I'd give *both* my hands for one year with my son."

It was one of those things people say as if they believe a supreme power will descend and bargain with them—as if limbs or years of life can actually be traded away.

The sudden white anger on Dottie's face as she clenched her fists made me think she blamed Grandpa. "He's so sorry about his hand," she said. "But he didn't do anything to find Scott and Nan. His own daughter!"

A moment later she composed herself. She pulled one of the wiener dogs into her lap and ran her thick hand over the length of his body. "Of course, you can't really know what goes on inside of people. I'm sure it's tough on him and your grandma, not knowing what became of their daughter, not knowing how she died."

"They think Nan is alive. They got a postcard signed with her name shortly after she left."

"But the writing doesn't match Nan's, does it?"

"How did you know?"

"I got a postcard from Scott." She stood up and squeezed down the narrow hallway to a closet where she pulled out a shoe box. "Here," she said, handing me a postcard, identical to the one I had found at home.

I turned it over.

Dear Mom,

   I am fine, so don't worry about me if you don't hear from me in a while. Hawaii is great. Nan and I are both busy surfing and stuff.

   Scott

"It's like somebody forged his writing," Dottie said. "I tried to get the police to investigate, but they didn't take this seriously. They insisted he'd run away. If he hadn't sold his car right before he left, maybe they would have believed me. The police thought he sold it so he could buy a plane ticket. You know, sometimes I still see his old car driving around here because a fellow in the area bought it. Every time I spot that old blue clunker, my heart catches. I half expect to see Scott behind the wheel."

"I think Scott and Nan's disappearance has something to do with what happened to the other girls."

"What other girls?"

I told her about Judy and Tawny.

"I don't know nothing about Tawny," she said. "But I remember when Judy died. She was the police chief's daughter, you know. I heard she died of a drug overdose, and her daddy didn't want her name dragged through the mud."

So that was why Bruce Wingate had changed the slant of his articles!

I gasped as I examined the postcard. "Look at the *i*'s," I said excitedly. "And *e*'s! They look like the ones on the postcard from Nan!"

Dottie looked at me sharply, her pupils boring into me like pinpoints. "What do you mean?"

"If the postcards *were* forged, they were both forged by the same person!"

Three minutes later, I was sitting beside Dottie in her old dusty station wagon, roaring toward Oxford. There had been no time to consider the consequences of bringing her home—to imagine what Grandpa would do if he walked in and found her there. She had insisted on seeing the postcard right away. "If somebody hurt Scott, that somebody must be the person who forged the kids' names," she said. "Too many years have gone by with nobody doing nothing about the missing kids. I know I won't be able to sleep tonight until I see that postcard."

So we had piled into the car, Dottie and I and the dozen wiener dogs.

I breathed a sigh of relief when we pulled up and saw no cars in our driveway. My mom and grandparents were out. The members of Grandpa's rose garden club took turns tending the roses in Pioneer Park, and this morning I'd heard him tell Grandma that today was his turn. It was quarter after four now. He wasn't due back until five.

Don't be early, Grandpa, I silently begged. Since no one was allowed to so much as breathe the name of Nan, I wasn't sure how he would react if he came home to find her boyfriend's mother in his home.

When Dottie opened the car door, half the wiener dogs escaped. Edward, who had been snoozing on the front porch, awakened and pranced across the yard with ferocious yips.

"Edward, no!" I cried.

"Mitzi, down!" Stop, Petey! *Boris!*"

We danced around in the flurry of frenzied pint-sized dogs, making awkward attempts to break up the commotion.

Edward was outnumbered, and I hated to imagine how Grandma would feel if he got hurt. I finally managed to scoop him up, just as Dottie remembered she had doggie treats in her glove compartment and lured her dogs back into the station wagon.

I quickly ushered her into the house, anxious to show her the postcard before Grandpa got home.

"The place looks the same." She paused in the doorway. She'd been so eager to see the postcard, but now she dawdled, roaming into the living room and scrutinizing the family photos. She snorted and tossed her head in disgust.

"What's the matter?" I asked.

"There's no pictures of Nan. And where are her trophies?"

"Trophies?"

"She was a swimmer like my Scott." Her eyes glowed with pride. "That boy swam like a fish!" She continued to scrutinize the row of family photos lined up on the mantle. "I thought this one was Nan at first, but that's you, ain't it?"

"That's my eighth grade picture," I said. "Grandpa doesn't like to be reminded of Nan."

"His *own* daughter!" she exclaimed. "Course, I never got along great with that girl." She quickly glanced at me, as if worried she'd said too much. Then she shrugged and said, "We were like oil and water. We just couldn't mix."

"That's too bad."

"Nan wasn't good for Scott. But I never tried to break them up like your granddaddy did."

I left her in the living room and went to find the postcard.

"It's the same all right!" she gasped as I handed it to her. "Those *e*'s and *i*'s sure look the same." She held the two postcards up, side by side, pinching them at the corners with her chubby fingers. "Maybe I can finally get the police to pay attention."

She sank onto our living room couch, shaking her head as she continued to examine the postcards. I glanced at the clock. "Maybe we should get going—"

The front door squeaked open, and I heard the loud clomp of Grandpa's gardening boots on the tile floor in the front hallway. "Who's here?" he called out good-naturedly. "There's a car full of weird little dogs in our driveway."

He charged around the corner, the smile leaking from his face when he saw Dottie.

"They happen to be *purebreds*!" she snapped.

"What are you doing here?" he demanded.

"Grandpa, *please*. I invited her."

Dottie marched over to him and waved the postcards under his nose. Her voice was an odd mixture of grief and triumph as she said, "*See!*"

"What's this?"

"It's the postcards someone forged Scottie's and Nanette's names on. *Now* do you believe me? *Now* will you try to do something about it?"

"You're not making any sense," Grandpa said.

"Don't try to make me look like a crazy woman. That's what you done before. This time your own granddaughter brought me the proof. Somebody killed the kids. That's the *only* reason my Scottie wouldn't come home to me. Somebody killed them, and I want that person brought to justice!"

"Nan is not dead. And Scott wasn't the angel you thought he was." He stepped close to Dottie, anger glaring in his eyes as he waved his prosthetic hand in her face.

"Scott didn't do that to you!" She sounded suddenly frightened.

"I was there!" Grandpa roared.

When he blurted out what Scott had done to him, she covered her ears. "No!" she shrieked. "Scott would not do that!"

"But he *did*," he said. "And my daughter was in on it. I saw her there. I saw her eyes. And I saw that she wanted me to die. They left me alone to die."

19

His arms are around me and it is nice. So, so nice. "I love you," he whispers.

"Me, too," I murmur. "Forever and always. I don't want to ever go home, Trout."

"Your father won't like that."

"I don't care! I don't care about anyone but us."

"Alex, you're making noise in your sleep again."

"Sorry, True." I rolled over, burying my head under the pillow. I drifted away, trying to find my way into the sweet dream again.

"There you are, darling. Come to me, my love."

"No!"

"I'll take care of you," he says in his raspy voice.

"No! Where is Trout?"

He laughs so coldly it feels as if his teeth are gnawing on my bones.

"What did you do to him?" my voice rises hysterically. *"What did you do with Trout?"*

"Trout went swimming. Appropriate, isn't it?"

My glance flies to the lake. The water is black under a stingy portion of moon. A tiny white sliver like a snipped off fingernail. "Trout!" *I shriek.* "Are you out there, Trout?"

"He can't hear you now, my dear."

"Trout!" I awoke, my eyes bulging, my throat hoarse as the scream ripped from my throat.

"Alexis, are you okay?" My mother was shaking my shoulder. She and True stood over my bed, blurry-eyed and yawning, hair poking out in all directions. "We couldn't get you to wake up."

"Where is he? What has he done to him?" I cried, hot tears wiggling down my cheeks.

"Who?" Mom asked, putting an arm around me.

But already the dream had vanished, like mist in the wind. "I don't remember," I said. "A fish person. Or something. I loved him."

"It was a nightmare," she said gently. "It's understandable you're upset. Especially after that scene with Grandpa tonight."

"I wish you would have told me the truth about what happened," I said. "I never would have brought Dottie to the house if I'd known." I shivered, remembering the ugly wave of wrath that tore from my grandfather.

"Scott pushed me into the machinery!" he'd yelled. "That's why he doesn't come home. He's afraid he'll go to prison for what he's done to me!"

"They're dead!" Dottie had screamed back. "Our children are *dead*!"

"Get out of my house!" said Grandpa. "Get out! Now!"

Dottie crumbled into tears, turned, and dashed clumsily down the walk. I'd stood and watched, dismayed as the station wagon chugged toward the corner, wiener dogs circling madly inside.

The horror of what my aunt Nan had done made me cold and weak. That evening my mother and grandmother had scurried about, whispering huskily to each other as Grandpa stewed in his chair in the living room.

As I listened to them, I finally managed to piece together the story. My grandfather did not approve of Scott and had forbidden Nan to date him. But she rebelled and threatened to run away with Scott. A terrible scene erupted, and Grandpa told his daughter if she left the house, she was never to return. Then she and Scott showed up at the factory where Grandpa did repair work on equipment at night. The three of them argued some more and finally Scott and Nan left. But a little later, as the machinery thundered and roared, Grandpa spotted a shadow on the wall and knew someone was creeping up behind him. He glanced up and saw Nan in the doorway, staring at him. He felt Scott grab him from behind and shove him. He fell into the machine. When Grandpa awoke, he was in the hospital, his hand and daughter both lost forever.

"Try to get some sleep," my mother said now. "It's been an awful couple of days."

It certainly had. The worst of my life, almost as bad as the horrible nightmares. I did not want to slip into the dark dream again.

I ached for the light, fuzzy dream where I felt loved. *Trout.* That was what I had called the boy in my dream. What did it mean?

I felt for him the way I felt for Josh. Perhaps that sounds strange. Josh was a real live boy and Trout was a dream boy. A shadowy figure that moved through my subconscious. But Trout appeared often in my dreams in the following days, and whenever he embraced me, I felt that same loving warmth I felt from Josh.

*"Are you Josh or are you Trout?" I asked him once. "I
love you both, you see, but it is so hard to tell you apart."*

*He smiled, a glowing dream smile. "We are the same
person, Josh and I."*

It did not make sense.

"We are the same person."

How could Josh and Trout be the same person?

I puzzled over it, dismissing it as another jumbled, silly
dream. Yet Trout seemed so *real*.

My dream life became just one more confusing element
in the strange enigma my life had become—until the night
an unlikely person gave me the answer.

The week leading up to that night was an intense time. I
attended the funeral for poor Tawny and cried when they
lowered her casket into the ground. The paper reported her
death as an accidental drowning, but I suspected the police
were still investigating.

Meanwhile, Josh and I were growing closer daily. We
saw very little of each other outside of school, as my
mother still forbade me to date him. But how could she forbid me from talking to somebody at school?

Josh and I ate lunch together every day, taking our trays
outside to sit at the picnic table as the sweet smelling leaves
drifted down around us. We held hands under the table, and
I was so aware of the sparkling sensation of his fingers
curled around mine that I barely tasted my lunch. Most
days, I returned my tray to the cafeteria still laden with
food.

Of course we always sat together in psychology class.
And in art class we huddled close, advising each other on
our drawings. Though Josh's style was realistic and I was a
cartoonist, we still appreciated each other's work.

He shared my excitement when Mr. Wingate made me
the *Weekly Scoop* cartoonist. My first assignment was for
Environment Week at the school. I was to draw a cartoon

of a cheerleader, leaping in the air. "Make her cartoon balloon say, 'Oxford High wipes out litter!' Mr. Wingate had instructed me when he dropped by art class. "And draw lots of litter overflowing from the trash can."

"I know Alex will do a great job," Anita said sweetly. I was relieved that she seemed to have forgiven me for my part in the poster prank.

She looked a little embarrassed when a couple of boys snickered as Mr. Wingate affectionately patted her shoulder before he left. "I'll give you extra credit for drawing the newspaper cartoon," Anita told me. "But with your talent, you'll get an A without the extra points."

I was glad she was no longer upset with me.

Those lighthearted moments of lunch in the sunshine and drawing cartoons were like little islands of safety in a sea of horror—happy times when I could forget for a while the unexplained events in Oxford that still haunted me.

Dark questions nagged at me, sometimes waking me from a sound sleep.

What drove my aunt to hurt her own father? Why did she disappear so completely? And why did I find two dead girls in the same pond, sixteen years apart?

It was Tuesday when a key piece to the mystery slid into place. My view of the world was about to turn upside down and inside out. But I didn't know that as Josh and I sat on the weathered, gray dock and watched Forgotten Lake ripple around us.

"If you confront your fear of water, it will help you get over it," he said. "It will make you strong."

He was scheduled to help Tom with scuba lessons. I had told my mother I was interested in learning to scuba dive and that I wanted to watch the lessons. It was true. I *was* interested in scuba diving—if I could first get over my fear of water. In fact, I had attended the scuba classes each day after school for the last week. So far it was all classroom work and I had done well on the written tests.

Roger had advanced me part of my pay for the mural work, and I had purchased a mask and snorkel. Josh loaned me some fins, and the rest of the equipment I had borrowed from the school. Now all I had to do was get up my courage to go in the water. I had not really lied to my mother. I *had* developed a sudden interest in scuba diving. I simply neglected to mention the fact that Josh was one of the instructors.

"Do you think you'll get your nerve up for the first scuba lesson, today?" he asked. We sat side by side, arms around each other, enjoying the golden afternoon as he waited for Tom and the students of the scuba class to show up. The sun shone brightly through the brilliant orange of the maple tree leaves, and a soft, sweet breeze ruffled the tall grass that grew at the water's edge.

"I don't know if I'm ready to scuba dive," I said. "Tom says I can try it today if I like, because I did okay on the classroom tests."

"What do you mean, *okay*? You aced those tests!"

The classes had been under way for six weeks when I started sitting in on them a few days earlier. Impressed with how quickly I'd caught up, Tom pronounced me ready for my first underwater lesson.

"It's one thing to pass a test," I told Josh. "But it's a whole different thing to try the real thing."

"You don't need to be scared," he said. "I'll be there with you."

"I don't want to be afraid. But I *am*." I gazed out over the lake. It was bright with sunshine—*too* bright, and I shielded my eyes against the glare. Sizzling with sunlight, the water looked as if it would be hot to the touch. But I knew it was cold. A cold, dark place.

"They never should have flooded it," I said. "This place

wasn't mean to be underwater." Nan's mural depicted Old Oxford as a cozy town with quaint houses and happy people. A place where sunshine kissed the ground and flowers burst from the earth—not a dark, watery grave for trees. "Just think of all the trees that died," I said, shuddering as I pictured the slimy black stumps beneath the water.

"The lake is beautiful, Alex," Josh said. "You could learn to appreciate it. Once you get used to it, you might even like swimming."

"I'm not even sure I could do it again. What if I jumped in right now and sank?"

"You know you can do it, Alex! You didn't drown that day you got caught under the boat. You *swam*."

I gave into the smile tugging my lips. "You're right. I still don't understand it. It was like I knew instinctively what to do."

He squeezed my hand. "I don't want to push you on this. But it would be great to have you along when I scuba dive."

"I'd like that, too," I said. "Since I'm wearing shorts, maybe I'll wade out into the lake later and try to get used to the water."

"It's pretty cold," he said.

"I discovered that the other day. But it's not the cold that bothers me."

It was so nice to confide in someone. I was no longer embarrassed to discuss my water phobia with Josh. It seemed I could tell him anything. And as we sat on the dock, waiting for Tom, I found myself talking about my aunt. "It's upsetting to know she did something so awful," I told him. "I can't believe she stood by and watched someone push her own father into that machine!"

"I know. If the night watchman hadn't wandered in and found him, he would have bled to death."

"Grandpa said she *wanted* him to die!"

"No wonder he's so bitter."

"How could she have done that, Josh? How could she have stood by and watched someone hurt him like that?"

"You never know about people," he said quietly. "Maybe she was a sociopath. In psych class last year, Tom said you can't spot sociopaths by looking at them."

"You think my aunt was *crazy*?" I asked.

"Sociopaths aren't crazy. They just don't care about anyone's feelings but their own."

"But my aunt wasn't like that, Josh. She just *couldn't* have been!"

"Because she looked like you?"

"She looked like I do. She painted like I do. I feel like I know her."

"You're trembling." He cupped his hands around mine. He drew them to his lips and gently kissed my fingers.

"Hi, gang!" It was Tom, striding toward us, in full wet suit gear. I almost didn't recognize him. "So, Alex," he said, "are you going to try snorkeling today?"

"I don't think so. I don't feel too good."

"What's the matter?"

I glanced at Josh. He nodded at me. "You should ask Tom about what we were talking about," he said.

"Tom, you knew my aunt," I said shakily. "Was there something wrong with her?"

He sighed and sat on the edge of the dock, his flippers dipping in the water. "She had some problems," he said.

I described what I had learned about the night she left. He did not look surprised. I guess when you live in a small town, secrets get out. "I heard how your grandfather lost his hand," he said. "It was a shock for everyone who knew your family."

"How could she have done such an awful thing?" I asked. "How could she have done that to her own father?"

"I never understood it," he said quietly.

"Josh says she could have been a sociopath."

"That's possible."

"But you were her friend! Don't you know?"

"Sociopaths wear a mask, so to speak. They let the world see what they want it to see. They might look and act normal, but inside they are different from the rest of us. Actually, one percent of all females and three percent of males are sociopaths."

"You mean there are killers all around us?"

"Not all sociopaths are killers. Basically, a sociopath will do whatever is necessary to get what he or she wants. They have no empathy for others' feelings. They simply don't care about anyone else's pain. But that does not mean all sociopaths are killers."

"But some of them *do* kill!"

"Yes. Some kill for money. Some kill for what they perceive is love. And some kill just for pleasure."

"Not my aunt!" I said. "Anita says she was so nice to her. Nan taught her how to draw and inspired her to love art—"

"Anita was just a little girl," Tom interrupted. "She didn't see the signs of trouble in Nan like some of us did."

"So you *did* notice there was something wrong with Nan?" I said.

He tightened his lips and shook his head. "I was just a teenager myself back then. I certainly wasn't qualified to evaluate her."

"But you *remember* her, don't you?"

"Why is this so important to you, Alex?"

"I've always felt a bond with my aunt."

"But you've never met her."

"Everyone says we're so much alike."

"Ah," he said. "I see. You're afraid you might be a sociopath, too."

Was that it? Was I afraid that if Nan was bad, then I was, too?

Josh squeezed my hand. "Alex isn't a sociopath," he said reassuringly.

I smiled at him and said to Tom, "I'm just so confused about things."

Josh said, "Alex thinks her aunt is dead."

Tom looked at me sharply. "Has something happened to Nan?" His voice was filled with shock.

I found myself telling him about finding Nan's pack and my fear she never came home because she couldn't. "I talked to Scott's mother," I said. "She says he didn't run away. She thinks he was murdered."

"I talked to Scott the day he left," said Tom. "In fact, he sold me his Fairlane."

"The Fairlane was *Scott's* car?" asked Josh.

"That's right," said Tom. "He apparently sold me the Fairlane so he and Nan would have money to live on. I knew he was going to take off because he dropped several hints about it. They were obviously planning something."

"Dottie mentioned that Scott sold his car," I said. "But she still thinks he and Nan were killed."

"If *you* had done something as awful as Nan, would you come home?" Tom asked.

"I can't imagine doing something like that," I said.

"But if you *had,* you could be in big trouble. Nan left her things behind because there wasn't time to get them. She probably thought they'd killed the old man and had to get out of town fast."

It made sense. If Nan was so evil she'd hurt her own father, then who knew what else she was capable of?

I had been imagining her as a girl like me, and had based my feelings about her circumstances on my own life. I would not have run away without money or my personal possessions, but I also would not have stood by quietly while someone hurt my father.

I tried not to think of Nan as I sat on the dock that afternoon, watching Tom and Josh give scuba lessons. The class consisted of seven students—eight counting me. I didn't know any of the kids very well, except for Kelly. I was getting to know her a lot better than I wanted to. It seemed that whenever I was with Josh, she'd pop up.

Why can't I get over my fear? I wondered as I watched the class pull on their scuba gear and wade out into the lake. Feeling left out, I opened my sketch pad which contained my cartoon for the school paper.

It was good and I felt a rush of pride. I had begun by penciling the drawing in, and now I was adding the finishing touches with a felt-tipped pen. I'd drawn the cartoon big, so when it was reduced for printing the flaws would be less noticeable. I'd taken great care with every line. The cheerleader was so animated, she looked as if she'd leap off the page.

Josh had said my cartoon was great. I was glad we had our art in common. I wished I could share his love for the water, as I watched him bob beneath the surface, demonstrating a procedure to Kelly. When she slipped off her mask and glanced at me, an undeniable smirk played on her lips.

She knows I'm scared! I realized. I forced myself down to the water's edge where I tentatively stepped into the shallow water. The hairs on the back of my neck pricked to attention as I gazed out over Forgotten Lake.

Why was I so afraid?

In a flash, I remembered the words of Dr. Trollen: *The symbol of the unconscious is water.*

Was it the water I was scared of? Or my own unconscious?

Maybe I was afraid of remembering something bad—

afraid to dip into my memory and see the dark thoughts swimming there. I thought of Judy's tragedy. Was that memory lurking just below the surface?

The gritty sand squished between my toes and small sharp rocks bit into the soft soles of my feet as the cold lake sloshed around my ankles. Drawing a deep breath, I waded up to my knees. Each step sent another wave of apprehension through me, and I shivered so hard my teeth chattered.

"Watch out for the drop-off," Tom called out to me. "If you walk a few more feet to the left, you'll find yourself in deep water."

That was enough to make me freeze. I stopped and trailed my fingers in the water, deliberately splashing my legs. I was determined to get used to it.

"I'm bored," Kelly complained. "When are we going to do something exciting like explore a shipwreck or something?"

"Maybe next week we can all dive down and explore the old theater," said Josh.

"Negative," Tom said. "That building is a death trap. Not even experienced divers should go near that place."

"Adults are always spoiling our fun!" said Kelly.

I wished I had her bravado. I wished I could be out there with them, standing between Kelly and Josh. Each time she reached up and grabbed Josh's arm or stood too close to him, I felt a flash of jealousy.

I knew he was not interested in Kelly, yet it still bothered me to see another girl clinging to him. In fact, it angered me so much I summoned a surge of courage. I gulped in a big breath of air and before allowing myself to be afraid, I closed my eyes and ducked my head underwater.

I surfaced and my arms reached out instinctively. I began paddling. I swam in slow lazy circles, my gaze trained on the creamy white clouds floating in the sky. I was swimming! It was not because I *had* to, but because I *chose* to. I felt a wonderful rush of power.

"Good job, Alex!" Josh called out.

"What's the big deal?" Kelly asked snootily.

Ignoring her, I swam to shore and shook myself like a wet dog, spraying drops in all directions. The class got out shortly and most of them left quickly. But Kelly stayed and she, Tom, Josh, and I sat on the dock and ate the cookies she'd made. "You like them, Josh?" she asked.

"Chocolate chip is my favorite," he said.

"That's why I made them," she said coyly.

I was relieved when her mother finally drove up in a squat yellow car and honked her horn.

"There's my mom," said Kelly. "I've got to go."

"I haven't seen Patsy in ages," said Tom. "We went to school together." He waved his arm and called out, "Hey, Patsy! How are you doing?"

She got out of the car, her short red hair glinting in the slanting afternoon light, and headed toward us. As she drew near, her resemblance to her daughter was clear. Kelly had her slight frame, full chipmunky cheeks, and suspicious darting eyes.

"Hi, Mrs. Sims," said Josh.

"Hello, Josh," she said, but her eyes were on my face. I squirmed uncomfortably as they flicked over me, moving from the top of my head down to my feet and then sweeping upward again as she openly appraised me. She tossed her head, as if what she saw displeased her.

"She's Nan all over again, isn't she?" said Tom.

"There certainly is a family resemblance," Mrs. Sims said crisply.

"I hear you're going to be volunteering at the school newspaper," said Tom.

"Yes. Bruce asked me to oversee the pasteup and layout of the paper. I have a degree in graphic arts, you know."

"That's right," said Tom. "I remember when you were up against Anita for the art teacher's job. Where did you end up working?"

"I'm waitressing at Drake's Fish House."

"Working at the newspaper will be a nice change of pace," said Tom.

Kelly snorted. "Too bad they're not going to pay her," she said, and her mother shot her an annoyed glance.

"Volunteer work can be really rewarding," Tom said quickly. "You'll be seeing more of Alex. She's the new school cartoonist and she's just as good as Nan was."

"That's nice," Patsy snapped and turned to Kelly. "Ready?" she asked. "I've got a roast in the oven and it's going to dry out if we don't get home fast."

Her reaction to me was unsettling. Why had she looked at me like she hated me?

Patsy.

Was this the same Patsy who used to be Nan's friend? The Patsy who had dated Scott before Nan took him away?

"Was Patsy friends with my aunt?" I asked Tom.

He laughed. "At one time. Remember when I told you that sociopaths don't care about other people's feelings?"

"Yes."

"The way Nan treated Patsy is a perfect example. Patsy was dating a boy named Scott. Nan took up with him and didn't care who it hurt."

"Are you saying my aunt *was* a sociopath?" I asked, confused. "A little while ago you said you couldn't evaluate her."

"I can't," Tom said. "I'm just trying to answer your questions." He sounded concerned. "I can see this really troubles you, Alex. I'm here if you need to talk."

"Thanks," I said.

"How could Patsy hold a grudge against my aunt after all

this time?" I asked Josh. "She acted as if *I* was the one who stole her boyfriend!"

"You girls can be pretty vicious," he said with a laugh. "I heard Kelly doing an impersonation of you today and it wasn't very flattering."

"What do you mean?" I asked. "What did she do?"

"Oh, nothing," he said, realizing he had said too much.

"*Josh!* Tell me!"

He shrugged. "You know Kelly. She's just weird, so don't take it personally. But she was doing an imitation of you being afraid of the water."

I felt a flash of red-hot anger and along with it a wave of determination. I looked Josh in the eye and said, "Okay, that does it. Next time I'm going in."

20

"*Anita used to show up to meet Tom after the scuba lessons,*" said Josh, as we drove toward my house. "I wonder why she wasn't there this afternoon."

"Maybe she's with Bruce today," I said.

"Could be," he said. "But let's not worry about them. What about *us*? What will your folks say when they find out I gave you a ride home?"

"I don't care. I'm tired of them telling me who I can be friends with. But I don't think it's going to be a problem today because it looks like no one's home," I said as I noticed that my mother's and grandparents' cars were gone.

As Josh and I got out of the car, Gertie Olson, our round, gray-haired neighbor, beckoned to us from the other side of her picket fence. "Your old aunt has taken a turn for the worse." She peeled off her gardening gloves. "I was watering the roses when your family came running out and jumped into their cars. Your mom asked me to tell you they're all over at the house. She wants you to head over there to pay your last respects."

Aunt Sidney was dying!

I had not known the old lady long, but I felt as if the long fingers of grief were twisting my heart into knots as I climbed back into the car beside Josh and we headed toward her home. "I'm sorry," he said softly.

"I just hope she isn't suffering," I said.

My family had gathered in Aunt Sidney's kitchen, where Mom was helping a red-eyed Sequoia make tea. Grandpa was staring out the window, his mouth set in a grim line, and the kids were sitting at the table.

"What is Josh doing here?" Mom demanded when we walked in.

"He gave me a ride home from scuba lessons," I said.

Mom's eyes narrowed and she opened her mouth as if she was about to launch into a lecture.

"I'm a friend of Sidney's," Josh said quickly. "I used to mow her lawn."

Mom's face softened as she said, "The doctor says she could go at any time. We're taking turns sitting with her. We thought it would be too overwhelming for her to have all of us up there at once. Grandma's upstairs now. Why don't you go on up there, Alex, and hold Aunt Sidney's hand for a while."

"Can Josh come up with me?" I asked. "Aunt Sidney likes him."

"I suppose it would be all right," she said.

"I never knew a dead person before," said Toby as he dumped sugar directly from the bowl into his tea.

"Are the angels going to come and get Aunt Sidney?" asked True. Her face was pinched and scared.

"Of course they are." Mom patted True's shoulder. "Aunt Sidney is going to heaven."

Grandma met us at the top of the stairs. She looked a little startled to see Josh, but she gave me a hug and said, "You might be shocked when you see Aunt Sidney. She's not functioning very well. She can barely talk, and when she does she's pretty incoherent. Hold her hand and talk softly to her. She'll probably know you're there even if she can't show it."

I was glad Josh was with me as we entered the dimly lit room. The ever-present television was silent and the lights were off. The fat red candle burned on the nightstand. The flame quivered oddly, splashing the wall with jerking distorted shadows. Aunt Sidney was a pale crumpled figure, squirming restlessly beneath layers of quilts.

I shut my eyes and saw her for a moment as she'd looked in the family album—proud and straight in her Sunday best as she gazed steadily at the camera. She'd worn a bright pink dress that matched her rosy cheeks, and her silver hair had been combed up into a bun. It was my favorite picture of her.

"I'm here, Aunt Sidney." I touched her hand. It was limp and cold. Josh walked softly around the bed and gently took her other hand. We stood like that for a while, speaking quietly to her and each other.

Our presence seemed to calm her. She lay still. The blankets rose and fell slightly with her breaths. "I'm glad she's resting," I whispered to Josh.

Suddenly her eyes flew open. She looked about the room. "Oh, Virgil! You've finally come for me. Edith, you look as fat as ever!" she added, laughing.

"Who is she talking to?" Josh asked.

"Virgil was her younger brother and Edith was her cousin," I said. "I've heard Grandpa talk about them. They died years ago."

"Well, I'm ready to go!" She spoke animatedly, her voice strong and clear. "I see you've brought Elmer along.

And there's baby Tess and Nickie. Mama is here, too. Hello, Mama."

I followed her gaze, but saw only our shadows melting on the wall.

"Nan." She looked directly at me. "It is so nice you've come back. But you must stay this time." Her head twisted on the pillow as she looked for Josh. "Scott, be good to her. You've both got another chance now."

"Aunt Sidney, try to rest," I said.

She smiled, her eyes aglow. "Nan, listen. I know what I'm saying. You *are* Nan, just as that young man across from you, who you call Josh, is Scott. You kids are back and you've got to stay for a while. Don't let the bad one stop you this time."

Josh came around the bed and put his arm around me. "Maybe we should get your grandpa."

"Say good-bye to him for me," she said brightly. Her features slumped. Her eyes flickered shut as her hands lay quiet at her sides.

A warm breeze filled the room, swirling around us. Josh's arm tightened around me. The breeze seemed to move through me, and I felt the hairs on the back of my neck prickle.

"Where is that breeze coming from?" he asked. It ruffled his hair, lifting the curls off his face. The candle flame flickered wildly. As the wind whooshed past, the light blew out. We were in the dark.

Josh gasped. "*What* was that?"

"I think," I said, my voice shaking, "I think that was Aunt Sidney's soul leaving her body!"

21

"*You cannot make sense of the last words of someone so sick,*" my mother said. "Aunt Sidney was incoherent all night long."

We'd just arrived home from the memorial service. Mom and I were on the porch swing. The chains stretched and squeaked with our weight as we swayed gently in the late morning sunshine and sipped ice tea.

I was desperately trying to make her understand what had happened the night Aunt Sidney died. I closed my eyes, remembering how Josh and I had stood in the dark room, motionless for a long moment after the candle blew out. "She's dead, Josh," I'd said and then we had rushed downstairs to get the family. Of course I'd immediately told them about her last words. They had seen no special significance in them. When we described the forceful wind that flew through the room, my mother and grandparents dismissed it as a draft from the cracks around the windows.

"I felt it, too," Josh had whispered to me. "There was an energy in that room. It was as if she moved through us on her way out."

He did not, however, seem to understand the meaning in Aunt Sidney's last statement.

Only I—and perhaps Sequoia—seemed to realize what she was trying to tell me. Now, when I tried to explain this to my mother, she shook her head and said, "That's crazy, Alex."

She would not even consider the possibility I had once been her sister.

"What about all the things I knew about Oxford?" I asked.

"You've heard me talking about them, of course. And you've seen plenty of photographs."

That night in Aunt Sidney's kitchen, when I relayed the old woman's last remarks, Sequoia had slipped me one of the books from her Eastern Philosophy class. It included cases of reincarnation, and as I read these, I learned that many people who claim to remember other lifetimes don't look anything like their previous forms. A lovely African-American girl believed she'd been an old Irish man with deformed ears, and a squat, plain woman remembered life as a graceful, long-limbed dancer. But some cases reported uncanny physical resemblances between two lifetimes. I seized on this now and demanded, "Why do I look so much like Nan? And why do I draw just like she did?"

"Genes, Alex," Mom said flatly. "It's not uncommon for someone to inherit features and talents from a close relative. True looks a little like your dad did with her curly red hair and blue eyes. She also has his musical ability. Toby inherited Grandma's pug nose and fair skin. And *you* happen to look like Nan."

"*Exactly* like she did! So much like Nan that people who knew her practically faint when they see me!"

"It *is* unusual for a child to look so much like her aunt, but not unheard of," she said. "Genes are like the roll of the dice. You never know what characteristics a child may inherit."

This logical perspective made sense. My artistic ability and resemblance to Nan could simply be the luck of the draw. My feelings of déjà vu could be explained away by the fact I'd visited Oxford as a baby.

For a moment, we sat quietly as I digested Mom's side of the argument.

It is crazy! I chided myself.

I'm me.

Nan was Nan.

Yet I was not convinced. Aunt Sidney's voice had rung with such calm certainty as she'd spoken her last words.

And then there was Josh. The moment I first saw him, it had been as if we'd always loved each other. Who could explain his drawings of his "mystery girl"—the distinct heart-shaped face, slanted green eyes, and lopsided dimples captured by his pencils? I shared those features with Nan. He had been drawing her a whole year before he met me.

Aunt Sidney had come right out and said that I was Nan and Josh was Scott. If this was true, did it mean that Josh held a memory of me from our other lifetime?

Was it all just gibberish? Or had my old aunt somehow fixed on the truth in her last moments?

"What if it *is* true, Mom? Aunt Sidney was lucid right before she died. She wasn't just rambling incoherently. And it's so spooky the way I know so many things about Oxford—things that I don't remember you telling me. What *if*? What if I *am* the reincarnation of Nan? Who's to say it's not possible?"

"I don't believe in reincarnation." She set her iced tea

down on the porch railing. "And if I *did,* this still wouldn't make sense because Nan's not dead."

"Mom—"

"And another thing you're overlooking. Nan is an excellent swimmer and you've always had that fear of water."

"I'm starting to overcome it."

"Yes, and that's good. But Nan started swimming at three, and you're just now learning. It was hard for you at first, right?"

"Yes," I admitted with some relief. For I did not *want* to be Nan. I did not want to be the girl who stood gleefully by and watched her own father injured.

If I *was* Nan, did that mean I carried the evil of her deed?

A breeze blew across my shoulders and I shivered.

If I am Nan . . .

If I am Nan, how can I ever again look at my grandfather's plastic hand without a crush of guilt?

Or did Nan get paid back when *she* was murdered? Did that absolve me of all guilt?

If I *was* the reincarnation of my aunt, had I already paid for my mistake? Was that why Nan was killed? Was this my karma? Or did I still carry a debt? Was I about to be punished some more?

My mind whirled in confusion. There were so many things to consider.

If I am Nan . . .

If I am Nan, why am I back? Is it to make things up to my family? Or was I destined to be a famous artist, and since I had not fulfilled my fate the first time around, had I returned as me?

The wind plucked up, rattling the low branch of the maple beside the porch so it released a sprinkling of leaves. I watched the sparkle and flutter of orange and gold as the leaves drifted lazily toward the lawn.

By next spring those leaves would disintegrate, becoming

part of the earth. Perhaps someday a new maple would spring from the same ground the dead leaves had nourished.

Life would go on, in one form or another.

"Will you please let this go now?" Mom asked.

I stared at her, my lips pressed tightly together. I could make no such promise.

"Alex, *please*."

"Mom, it was like she was trying to warn me about something."

The meaning in Aunt Sidney's words was obvious to me. Why didn't everyone else see it?

"Somebody could have murdered me," I said. "Maybe they killed Scott, too, and now he has come back as Josh."

She regarded me through worried eyes. "I know it was a shock finding Tawny Ferrel in the pond. Watching Aunt Sidney die was hard on you, too. But you have to get a hold of yourself, Alexis."

"I'm not saying I believe this. I just think we should consider it."

"I think you should see a counselor, honey," she said quietly.

"But I could be in danger! Aunt Sidney practically spelled the whole thing out for us. Right before she died she said, 'Don't let the bad one stop you this time.' "

"What is that supposed to mean?"

"That's what I'm trying to tell you!" I cried, my voice rising in frustration. "Don't you see? The 'bad one' stopped us last time. That could mean somebody killed me. What if they try to kill me again?"

If I put myself in my mother's shoes, I could see why it was so hard for her to understand my perspective. She did not, after all, know what it was like to meet someone for the first time and recognize them, as I had recognized Josh.

And how could I explain that overpowering rush of déjà vu that met me each time I turned a corner in Oxford?

"I just don't know what to think about all this," Mom said. Shaking her head, she went into the house to help Grandma make lunch. I curled up on the porch swing, leafing through the book Sequoia had loaned me. As I read, a passage caught my eye: *"Many patients have come to see me with unexplainable fears and obsessions,"* said Dr. Herrod. *"Over the years, I've discovered a startling trend while regressing patients through hypnoses. Once I was working with a patient who was so terrified of heights she'd have anxiety attacks when she sat in the balcony in the theater. I hypnotized her and asked her to go back to the source of her fear. She told me it was the year 1824 and that she was standing on the edge of a cliff. The ground beneath her crumbled and she fell to her death.*

"I've discovered many similar cases since. The phobias we experience in this life are often directly linked to trauma in a past life—in many cases, the last incarnation's death."

I sat upright and read the passage again. *Trauma in a past life!*

Could that be the reason for my fear of water? Was I simply remembering something that had happened to me in another lifetime?

I'd thought I had it all figured out when I learned I'd been here as a baby.

When I'd been inadvertently regressed in class, I'd concluded I was simply remembering that day as a toddler when I'd wandered away from the picnic and saw a girl die. My natural assumption was I had vicariously experienced *Judy's* death in the pond.

Now I knew differently.

Now I knew I was remembering my *own* death!

I closed my eyes, recalling the terrifying vision. I could still feel the murderous grip around my ankle as I was yanked beneath the water.

Nan, my mother had said, was an excellent swimmer.

An excellent swimmer.

If an excellent swimmer drowns, everything changes. If she is born again, she could carry the terror with her into her new life.

I closed the book. With shaking hands, I set it on the seat beside me. A cold tremor rolled through me. My teeth began to chatter. A killer was prowling around Oxford, perhaps planning his strategy at this very moment. He killed Judy. He killed Tawny. He killed Nan. Would he try to kill me again?

It had been quiet in Oxford all the years I was away. *Why?* Not one girl was murdered in that time. Could I somehow be the key to his rage? If that was the case, then what was it about me that triggered his anger?

"Would you like a cupcake?" Mom asked, popping her head out the door. "I'm practicing a new kind of flower design." She held up a yellow cupcake topped with an orange swirling blossom.

Numbly, I accepted the cupcake and set it on the railing. "I want to read something to you," I said and read aloud the passage about phobias carried into new lifetimes.

"You can't believe everything you read," she said. "That book has you all worked up. Remember when you were little and you'd beg me to let you watch scary movies on TV? Afterward you'd be afraid to sleep with the lights off. This is the same kind of thing."

"It's not the same."

"Honestly, Alexis, you really do let your imagination run away with you." The words were barely out of her mouth when the phone rang. I rushed inside to the kitchen to answer it.

"Mind your own business," a raspy voice warned. "Or you'll end up like the others."

A shiver shot through me and my knees buckled. I sank into the chair against the wall. "Who is this?" I asked.

Click. He hung up.

"It was a prank phone call," Mom concluded when I told her what had happened. "Probably kids playing a joke."

Had it been a kid? Perhaps someone from school? The voice was indistinguishable, as if it was disguised. I had the impression of lips hidden behind a handkerchief as he talked. It could have been a man. It could have been a woman.

Or it could have been a child playing a joke. Yet, I knew it was *not*.

It was the bad one.

I recognized the raspy voice from my dreams.

Come to me, my darling. I will not hurt you.

I had known him when I was Nan and I had tried to run from him then. I had not run fast enough and he had caught me. I shuddered, remembering the cruel grip on my ankle as I was pulled into the dark depths.

"Alex, you've got to calm down," Mom said. "I talked with Tom at the service this morning, and he's agreed to counsel you after hours at the school."

So *that's* what she had been discussing with him as they huddled together at the car after we'd sprinkled pink rose-buds on Aunt Sidney's grave.

Half the town had been there, on the grassy hill behind the old church. We'd all joined hands and sung one of Aunt Sidney's favorite hymns. It was beautiful. As our voices rose into the trees, the sun splashed a dappled pattern of gold flecks on her tall marble gravestone. I was no longer sad for her. I had, after all, felt her leave her body. I was sure she was in a better place.

But I was frightened for myself and Josh.

"I don't need a counselor, Mom," I said.

"You're confused and you need someone to help you get straightened out." The tremor in her voice told me she thought I was cracking.

She was not the only one to think I was crazy.

22

In the following days, I tried to make them all understand.

"You're nuts," Toby scoffed. "Dead is dead. People don't come back to life. Worms eat them and they turn into dirt."

"You've been under a lot of stress," my grandmother told me.

Even True watched me through big, scared eyes.

Then one afternoon Grandpa surprised me by showing up at the Big Top as I worked on the mural. He lumbered over to the booth beside me and plopped down. "Can you take an ice cream break?"

"That sounds nice," I said. "But I have to clean up my paints so I can drop my cartoon off at the school paper. They're going to press tonight, and Mr. Wingate asked me to turn it in before six so Patsy Sims can finish the pasteup."

He looked at his watch. "It's four-thirty now. I can drop your cartoon off on my way home. You can stay and work on your mural a little longer if you like."

He bought us each a banana split and we settled in a corner booth. "Don't tell your grandmother we spoiled our dinner," he said conspiratorially. He dipped into the ice cream, a fond smile crossing his lips. "Nan always loved banana splits."

It was the first time I'd seen him sentimental about his daughter. I stared at him, stunned.

"We were close at one time," he said.

Why was he suddenly discussing the one person we were never supposed to mention?

He set down his spoon. "I'm worried about you, Alexis."

That, of course, was the answer. Like everyone else, my grandfather was worried about me.

"Your mother told me you think Nan is dead and that you are her reincarnation."

"I know it sounds insane," I said.

"But do you *believe* it?"

"I'm pretty sure I do. Right before she died, Aunt Sidney told me I was Nan."

He nodded and his lips turned inward. "Yes, I know."

"It is strange she never came home, don't you think?"

"Nan did something very bad. Did you know that?"

"I heard Mom and Grandma talking about it. Nan and Scott hurt you. Why would they want to do that?"

"It's a long story—something I don't like to talk about. I tried to put it behind me, but since you've been here it's gotten all stirred up again. You're stubborn like Nan, Alexis. And I suspect you won't let this go until I tell you everything."

I sensed my ice cream melting, but I set down my spoon and kept my eyes on my grandfather's tired face. The long kept secrets were finally leaking out and I did not want to risk breaking the spell.

"Nan was my special girl," he said. "She was the happiest, bubbliest baby on earth. Don't get me wrong—I've always loved your mother, but Suzie and Grandma were sort of a team. Suzie was our firstborn and your grandmother doted on her. They enjoyed doing the same things—cooking and sewing and entertaining company. Nanny was an artist like I was."

His steel eyes melted into liquid gray and he actually laughed as he said, "When she was two years old she crawled up into my lap when I was drawing. I let her have one of my pencils and she worked on my picture with me. Of course she just scribbled, but the joy in her eyes told me she was going to be an artist. That made me so proud."

"You taught her to draw," I said. It was a statement, not a question.

"Yes. I built her her own little easel and we'd spend hours drawing together. She always liked cartooning, and I used to do a little of that myself. Nanny was good. When she was a teenager, we liked to talk about how someday we'd do a comic strip together. The first father-daughter cartoonist team."

His whole face seemed to sag. "Then she met Scott. She was never the same after that. I knew he was trouble from the start."

"Why?"

"His father, Bob Dewitt, was a bad man and the apple doesn't fall far from the tree. Bob was my supervisor at the jam factory."

"I thought you were an artist."

"The cannery was my second job. I was a freelance graphic artist and made a pretty good living at it. But we hoped to send the girls to college and your grandmother and I were trying to build our nest egg so we could afford to do some traveling. So I picked up a few shifts at the cannery doing maintenance on the machinery at night. I'd worked there when I was putting myself through art school so I knew the ropes. But Bob made trouble for me from the beginning. He was always blaming the equipment failure on me. I knew he was spending the company's money on liquor and women—money that should have been used to purchase new parts for the machinery."

"Why didn't you quit?"

"We needed the money. I wasn't going to let anybody push me out of a job. I wanted to leave on my own terms in my own way. At any rate, I disliked Scott from the moment I met him. He kept Nan out late, and she started breaking all the rules of the household. If I said anything to her about it, she'd fly into a rage and tell me to mind my own business. Your grandma said it was just normal teenage rebellion, but what she did to me was *not* normal."

My gaze was drawn to Grandpa's plastic hand, lifeless on the table beside his banana split. I could not imagine losing my hand—to never feel a paintbrush dancing between my fingers again! What did he feel when he looked at a blank easel?

A ripple of guilt moved through me. "I'm sorry." I spoke so hoarsely, it came out in a whisper.

"*You* did not do this to me, Alexis. Let's get that straight. You and Nan are two entirely different people."

"I'm just like she was."

"You've inherited some of her characteristics, but you're a good girl. My daughter had some problems, but I loved her so much I was blind to them."

"What kind of problems?"

"She was obviously disturbed. A normal girl would not have done what she did. The police wanted to find Scott and Nan and arrest them for assault. Maybe I should have let them. At least then Nan would have come home and we could have gotten her some help. But I refused to press charges. She is, after all, my daughter. At the time, I thought I was doing the right thing."

"I thought you told her to never come home."

"I may have said that in anger. But I did not mean it." He picked up his spoon and made a halfhearted stab at his ice cream. "I think the more time goes by, the harder it is for her to come home."

Maybe she is home!

I glanced at my hands. Long, slender with graceful fingers. Artist's fingers. They felt so natural, splashing new color into Nan's mural. The faces of her cartoon people gazed down at us from the wall, jolly and animated.

"Nan was confused," Grandpa said. "That doesn't mean you have to repeat her mistakes."

"What about your mistakes?" The words flew from my lips before I could stop them.

His mouth dropped open in surprise. Then he smiled and said lightly, "Are you saying I wasn't the perfect father?"

"Well, you didn't give Scott much of a chance. You hated him from the beginning just because he was Bob's son. That's not fair."

As he contemplated his ice cream, I wondered what memories drove the flicker through his eyes. "It's funny you should say that," he finally said, his voice oddly low. "Nan once said the exact same thing."

23

Monday afternoon, after school let out, I met Tom in the school counseling office for a session Mom had set up for me.

"What's going on in your life, Alexis?" he asked. "What would you like to talk about?"

I settled into the cushy vinyl chair next to his desk and smiled self-consciously. "Where should I start?"

"Your mother filled me in on some things, but I'd like to hear your version."

"What did she say to you?" I demanded. "Did she tell you I was crazy and that I was running around with a criminal?"

"Those are pretty strong words," he said slowly. "She did mention Josh. I understand you are not supposed to be seeing him."

"Mom doesn't want me to *date* him. But how can she tell

me not to talk to him at school? What am I supposed to do at scuba lessons? *Ignore* him?"

"Your friendship with Josh appears to be far from casual."

"You can't stop feelings," I said.

He nodded. "I was a teenager once, too. I know what it's like to have raging hormones."

"I'm not talking about *that*! I mean I have serious feelings for Josh."

"But you're attracted to him?"

"Of course! But it's more than that. I *love* him!"

"It's normal for a sixteen-year-old girl to have a crush on a boy like Josh. He's a jock and pretty girls are always falling for jocks."

"Nobody understands," I said. "I wouldn't care if he was a computer geek. I love him for what's inside. I feel like I've known him forever."

He tapped his pen on the corner of his desk as he appeared to be thinking this over. Finally he said, "When your mother told me you've been disturbed lately, I was not surprised. I sensed something was wrong that day at the lake when you asked me all those questions about Nan. You seem to relate very strongly to your aunt."

"You don't know the half of it!" I said, and found myself launching into my reincarnation theory.

Tom leaned back in his chair, crossed his legs, and folded his hands over his knee. His eyebrows arched quizzically as he waited for me to finish.

I forged ahead, despite the disbelief in his narrowed brown eyes.

"I know it sounds crazy," I said, "but this town was familiar to me from the moment I arrived." I paused, hoping to see a glimmer of understanding, but his skeptical frown made me forget what I was going to say next and suddenly I was stammering like an idiot.

The story came tumbling out as I tried to explain about Nan, her drowning, and my belief I was her all over again—back in Oxford to solve my own murder.

When I was done, a small tight smile crossed Tom's mouth. "Just how much of this other life do you claim to remember?"

"Only bits and pieces. It's like I have only a few pieces of a puzzle."

He shook his head, and his voice held a note of pity as he said, "We all like attention, Alex. And I realize you don't get much of that at home."

"You think I'm saying all this for *attention*?" I cried indignantly.

"Your mother has two other children to take care of and she's busy trying to start her own business. It's understandable you might feel she's ignoring you at times."

Frustrated, I searched for the right words to express how wrong he was. But his unwavering gaze had rattled me into silence.

"Being sixteen isn't easy," he said. "Remember, I was there, too, once. I had a rough home life and I went through a really awkward stage when I was a bit of a nerd—"

"Tom, *look*!" I pointed at the closed office door, where a shadow moved across the opaque, glass window. "I think someone's listening to us," I whispered.

Tom sprung from his chair and as quietly as a cat stalking a mouse, he crept across the floor. His pudgy fingers grasped the doorknob and he yanked it open.

There stood Deke, a look of surprise sweeping his dense, crooked features. "I didn't know anyone was in here," he said sheepishly. "I, um, was cleaning the window."

"Where's your squeegee?" Tom asked crisply. "Last time I washed a window I at least needed some water."

"I was just going to get it," said Deke. He poked his head

through the door. "Don't worry, little lady. I didn't hear any of your secrets." The smirk on his face said otherwise.

The men stared at each other for a curiously long time. Unspoken words of animosity sparked between them.

Tom finally spoke. His voice was low and cool. "These sessions are private."

Deke snorted. "I know enough about the people in this town to stir up trouble if I wanted to. But I don't want to."

Tom shut the door. "It's okay," he said to me. "I don't think he heard anything."

"I think he *did*! I noticed a shadow out there for a few minutes, but I didn't realize it was a person until he moved. Deke's always slinking around, eavesdropping."

"You've got to stop overreacting to things, Alex. You sound paranoid."

I took a deep breath. "Okay. I'll try. But it's hard to relax knowing there might be a killer running around Oxford."

"That's the kind of thing I'm referring to. If you go on and on about murders and reincarnation, nobody will believe anything you say. People really will believe you're crazy."

Perhaps they will, I thought. Yet how could I keep such thoughts locked inside me?

I needed those close to me to understand. Most of all, I needed Josh to understand.

We were in this together, whether he believed it or not.

"Deke was eavesdropping on my counseling session," I told him.

We had met at Forgotten Lake after my session with Tom and were unloading our scuba equipment from the trunk of his car. "Why was Deke so interested in what you were talking about?" Josh asked.

"That's what I'd like to know. What if he has something to do with all the weird stuff that happened in Oxford? Maybe he was listening in to find out what I know."

"He's been around here for a long time. Do you think he knew your aunt Nan?"

"He knew her," I said. "He made some remark to me once about how she didn't care about anyone else's feelings. He scares me, Josh."

His eyes sparked with concern. "Just make sure you're never alone with him. I couldn't stand it if anything happened to you."

"Hopefully I'll be around for a while—that is if I don't drown." I looked down at the clutter of scuba gear I'd borrowed from the school.

"You'll be fine. The school equipment is old, but it's safe. Besides, *I'll* be with you."

It took us ten minutes to wiggle and writhe our way into the wet suits. My suit fit snugly, like a second skin, but it was uncomfortably warm.

"You'll feel better when you get in the lake," Josh said.

At the water's edge, I looked down at the tangled pile of scuba equipment. "How am I ever going to sort this all out?"

"It just looks confusing. I'll be back in a few minutes to help you put on your gear. I left my underwater watch up at the car." As he headed up the hill, I reached down and grasped the heavy tank's harness. With a slow, easy motion I swung it gracefully up onto my back.

I felt like a sea monster with strange appendages as I glanced down at the riddle of straps and hoses hanging off me. I should have been stumped. Yet I was not. Instinctively, I began to snap buckles and straps together. Without even thinking about it, I slung my mouthpiece over my right shoulder and my gages over my left.

Josh returned, amazement in his eyes. "How did you get the tank on your back by yourself?"

I shrugged. "I just used a little leverage."

"What about the straps and harness?"

I smiled. "Nan helped me."

"This is spooky, Alex," he said as he checked my equipment and gages.

It *was* spooky. Yet I felt a sense of eerie calm. "She scuba dived, you know."

He shook his head. "Stop it, Alex. It's really not funny anymore."

"I'm not trying to be funny. Didn't you hear what Aunt Sidney said to us? I am Nan and you are Scott."

"That doesn't mean anything. Sidney was out of it half the time. You know you couldn't make sense out of the things she said." His eyes were a troubled blue as he stared out over the lake. "Ready to get in the water?" he asked abruptly.

"Yeah. This stuff is heavy and I'm getting really warm." My legs trembled with the weight of my gear as I backed toward the lake.

"No wonder," said Josh as he slung his own tank over his shoulder. "You've got a hundred pounds of gear on your back."

I glanced at the still water behind me and a shiver of apprehension snaked through me. I was about to submerge myself in a place that frightened me so much I could barely stand to look at it. I took a deep breath and walked into the lake.

Long strings of icy water seeped into my wet suit. With each step, I seemed lighter. By the time I had waded to my chest, I felt weightless.

Josh smiled at me as he waded in beside me. "Okay, let's go through our final checklist," he said. "Check your gage. Your tank is full of air. Always look at your watch when you enter the water and note the time. This is important because you want to surface before you run out of air. And *whatever* you do, always remember to surface slowly or you'll get the bends. If you come up too fast, the air in your lungs could expand and burst like balloons. It could kill you."

We bit down on our mouthpieces and drew several breaths. Our regulators were working. "Spit in your mask and then slosh it around in the water," he instructed. "That will keep it from fogging up."

We faced each other. Josh pointed at the water. *This was it!*

We slowly stooped down. The water crept up my neck. The sharp coldness sloshed against my chin. I wanted to cry out, but was afraid to breathe. As we sank to our knees, the water rose, level with our eyes. My stomach clenched in panic.

The bulk of my gear was suffocating. The straps and belts seemed to tighten around me. I wanted to tear from the water and rip everything off. I started to rise. Josh's hands gently touched my shoulders.

I looked into his eyes. They were huge, magnified by the mask and the water—giant, reassuring eyes that seemed to fill up the space between us.

We knelt on the rocky bottom of the lake, and Josh nodded as I prepared to take my first underwater breath.

Fear lapped at the corners of my mind. All my instincts shouted, No! You cannot do this! You cannot breath underwater. It is unnatural!

But I *could*. I sucked on my mouthpiece and my lungs filled with air. It was incredible. I was defying the laws of nature. I felt a wonderful rush of exhilaration and power.

Alexis Arlene Baxter is underwater! The realization sent a renewed surge of courage through me.

I drew slow, deep breaths and after a moment, began to relax. I was submerged in a watery realm, yet I felt insulated. My wet suit had warmed and my breath was guaranteed.

The boy I loved was beside me and we moved gracefully

beneath the lake—slow and easy—as if we were walking on the moon. Gravity as I knew it no longer existed.

The roar of my own breath drowned out all other sound, and I stared in wonder at the glistening white bubbles rising above me.

The underwater world was a soft contrast to land. Everything appeared bigger and more rounded. When a fish drifted lazily by, I reached up my hand in slow motion and touched it. It skittered away in a flash of silver.

We practiced clearing our masks, buddy breathing by sharing one hose, and removing our tanks to prepare for a free ascent.

The time passed quickly and I felt a sense of disappointment when we surfaced.

On the shore, I chattered excitedly about how natural it had felt for me.

Josh was strangely quiet as he peeled off his wet suit. Finally he asked, "Are you sure you haven't done this before?"

"No," I said. "I am not sure. That's what I've been trying to tell you, Josh. I did this when I was Nan."

"This whole thing is too weird. What happened to the good old days when the hardest thing I had to deal with was whether or not to order curly fries with my burger?" he asked and laughed a little too loudly.

An odd half smile stiffened his lips. He looked away from me, but not before I saw the dark flicker cross his eyes.

"You're scared," I said, as realization swept over me.

"Hey, I'm not scared. But I'm no fool either. Something really strange is going on, but we should stop jumping to conclusions until we get the facts. You're letting yourself get carried away with this reincarnation stuff."

"Why won't you even consider the possibility we may have been here before?"

"Look, I don't want us to be Scott and Nan. They were messed up people. It's creepy to think I could have the soul of a killer."

"Scott and Nan didn't kill anyone."

"They pushed your grandfather—"

"He didn't die!" I interrupted. "Scott and Nan made some mistakes, but that's what reincarnation is supposed to be about—learning and growing. If we were them, then we've evolved in this lifetime."

"How do you know?"

"Because we're good people, Josh."

"What about this karma stuff you're always talking about? If we were Nan and Scott, then how do you know we're not going to be punished for what we did? It doesn't matter that your grandfather lived. They intended to kill him. They cold-bloodedly pushed a human being into a machine that ripped off his hand. He would have bled to death if the night watchman hadn't found him."

I opened my mouth to protest, but no words came out. For I could not argue with Josh. Everything he said was true.

24

For days, I had been struggling with the same fear Josh had expressed.

How could I blame him for his feelings?

Scott and Nan had done an evil thing.

Was there anything more evil than a child trying to kill their own parent?

"I can think of only one thing," said Sequoia. "And that's when a parent hurts their child."

It was Tuesday morning and I had stopped to see Sequoia before school. Her roommate, Cassie, had opted to move away after Aunt Sidney died. My grandparents were letting Sequoia stay in the house until it was sold. It felt strange knowing my old aunt was no longer there, yet her presence seemed to linger.

"Sidney was a cool old broad," said Sequoia. "I'm going to miss her."

"She knew Nan and she loved her," I said. "She didn't seem to see any evil in her."

Sequoia shrugged. "I think Sidney was an evolved soul. She was a forgiving person. Maybe she understood why Nan had problems."

"Nan didn't just have problems," I said. "If she could do that to her own father, then she had a serious black spot on her soul."

Her soul.

My soul.

I shuddered.

"Every time I look at Grandpa's plastic hand, I get sick to my stomach," I said. "If *I* did that to him, how can I ever make it up to him?"

"You probably can't."

"So what do I do? Carry the guilt with me *forever*?"

She grinned. "I'd think a severed hand should be worth at least a couple of lifetimes of suffering."

I didn't laugh. "I'm not joking, Sequoia. How do we ever make up for the times we hurt people? I still feel awful about the poster Kelly made of Anita and Mr. Wingate. I wish I hadn't let her use my camera."

"Everybody does things they feel bad about," she said. "Maybe it's all part of the reason we're here. Maybe when we're sorry enough, we've learned a lesson and we can move on."

"Does that mean that something has to happen to me to make me more sorry?"

"You mean like a punishment?"

"Karma."

"You could have been born with one hand missing," she said. "That would have been appropriate karma."

I wiggled my fingers in front of her. "But I wasn't. Maybe I'll have an accident."

"I wouldn't worry about it."

"But I *do*! I think my boyfriend and I are the reincarnations of a couple of kids who did something horrible. We were *bad* people! But there's an even *worse* person running around Oxford who probably killed us eighteen years ago. I keep having nightmares about him."

Sequoia patted my shoulder. "Why don't you go to see Dr. Trollen? She could help you get this whole thing in perspective. I take her class on Wednesday nights. Why don't you come with me and we can talk to her after class?"

"That's a good idea." I glanced at my watch. "Uh-oh. I better get going. I'll be late for school."

I was eager to get there to see my cartoon in the school paper.

I spotted a stack of newspapers outside the office. I grabbed one. It was still warm—"hot off the press," as they say. The sharp scent of ink filled my nostrils as I flipped it open. It was the typical high school paper, just four pages long, and I spotted my drawing immediately, centered at the top of the second page, right above the article on Environment Week.

I smiled. In the reduction process, the lines of my drawing had become crisp and clean. With a rush of pride, I realized it was as good as those in the big city newspapers.

When I walked into psychology class later that morning, I saw that several students had picked up the newspaper and were browsing through them.

"This is the cartoon you were drawing at the lake," Kelly commented.

"Yeah. I worked really hard on it."

Courtney, who was sitting beside Kelly, leaned over and grabbed the paper away from her. "You're a good artist," she said.

"Let me see," said Kelly, snatching the paper back. "*Wow!* I can't believe Mr. Wingate let you get away with this!"

"With what?" I asked, puzzled, I stared down at my drawing, wondering what in the world she was talking about.

Then I saw it. Two small words written on a piece of garbage—a piece of garbage I had drawn. Two words. They were ugly and familiar. They were written in my handwriting, yet I had not written them.

Die Bitch!

"I didn't write *that*!" I cried. "Somebody altered my drawing."

"Who would do that?" Kelly asked.

"That's what I'd like to know!" I said. "How come your mom didn't catch it when she was doing the pasteup?"

"The writing's so small," Kelly said. "She probably didn't notice."

Word of my hidden cartoon message spread quickly and I was summoned to the principal's office where I was faced with the disapproval of my grandmother, Mr. Wingate, and Mr. Cline.

As I followed Mr. Wingate into Mr. Cline's office, Grandma leaned over her desk and said, "She wasn't raised to behave like this, Bruce. Alexis has been under a lot of stress."

"That may be so," he said, turning to me. "But how can I trust her to draw another cartoon for us?"

I felt horrible.

Somebody was threatening me: *Die Bitch*. The proof was there, in black and white in a published cartoon. It was obvious the message was for me. Nan had gotten her threat through her mural, Judy in her book, and Tawny received hers in her locker. Now I had received mine. But instead of running to my rescue, everyone was accusing *me* of defacing my own drawing.

"Somebody tampered with my cartoon," I told them all. "My life is in danger!"

Tom made time for me at lunch and I met with him in his office. "It is in your handwriting, Alex," he pointed out.

"Why would I spoil my own cartoon like that?" I asked.

"I don't know, Alex. You tell me."

"I *didn't* do it!" I cried. "Somebody is threatening me. It's the same threat the other girls got. I think the police should know about it."

He pushed the phone across the desk toward me. "It's probably a high school prank. The police are busy solving *real* crimes, but if it will make you feel better, call them."

As he watched, I dialed the police and asked for Sergeant Bryer. "I've been threatened," I said and relayed all that had happened. A moment later, I hung up, deflated. "He didn't take it seriously," I said. "He thinks I'm nuts."

Tom smiled sympathetically. "I'll keep my eyes and ears open. As guidance counselor, I learn an awful lot about what happens around this school. Whoever wrecked your drawing will probably tell somebody and I'll eventually hear about it."

"Thank you," I said, but I was not reassured.

Surprisingly, it was Grandpa who came to my defense that night at the dinner table. The story of my cartoon scandal had spread to the grade school, and Toby laughed as he passed me the mashed potatoes. "Everyone thought it was really cool it was *my* sister's cartoon."

True was eating dinner at a friend's house, and Mom was delivering her first cake for her new business. Grandma fluttered around, setting out extra rolls and refilling milk glasses, while Grandpa listened intently as Toby described the hidden message in my cartoon.

"I know a lot better swear words than bitch," said Toby. "I can help you with your cartoon next time, Alex."

"I didn't write those words in my cartoon," I said. Then I added sadly, "I don't think there is going to be a next time. Mr. Wingate wants me off the paper."

"He was understanding about the poster prank," Grandma admonished. "But everyone has their limits."

"I *didn't* do it!" I cried. "Why would I ruin my own cartoon?"

"Who knows why teenagers do anything?" she asked.

Grandpa was watching me, his gray eyes glowing. "I know you were proud of your drawing," he said. "I believe you, Alexis."

I was startled. "You *do*?"

"I'm an artist, too," he said simply.

"I called the police and told them about what happened to my cartoon, but they don't take it seriously."

"What do you think they should do?" he asked.

Obviously someone was threatening me. But I sensed my family would not believe me. They already thought I was losing my mind. I was not about to add to their doubts about my sanity, so I just shrugged and said, "Tom and the police think it was a practical joke. But I still wish they'd do something about it."

"It's an ugly prank," said Grandpa, "and I'm sorry it's got you so upset. But you should listen to Tom. High school kids are always pulling things like this."

It would have been nice to agree with Tom and Grandpa—to dismiss the sabotaging of my cartoon as a silly gag. And perhaps I would have, if it had ended there.

25

"Are you ready to go?" Trout asks.

I smile at him. I love him so much I think I will burst. "Yes. All my stuff is stashed at Aunt Sidney's. I'm all ready except for one thing. I want to say good-bye to Daddy. I can't leave on such bad terms."

"You'll never talk sense into him."

Trout goes along with me and we park in the far corner of the lot, beside the grove of alderwood trees.

It is late. The sky is black and the air is crisp. The factory is dark. Hand in hand, we walk across the parking lot, the sharp crunch of gravel beneath our feet as we head toward the maze of low, rectangular buildings.

I cannot see and I stumble. Trout catches me.

"We should have brought a flashlight," I say. "You'd think there'd be more lights on."

"You know my old man. He's such a cheapskate," he

says. "He doesn't want to pay the electric bill to keep the factory lit at night."

"Daddy's like that, too," I say. "He's always yelling at us to turn off the lights. You'd think our fathers would get along. They have so much in common."

Daddy's building is the only one lit. Harsh white light radiates from the small square window where he is working. A machine whines and hums and drones, and we recognize his bulk bending over it.

He has left the door open and we walk in and surprise him.

His face is swept red, his large bulbous nose so bright it looks like he will explode in anger. "How dare you bring him here!" he sputters.

"I love him," I say. "I'm sorry that you can't accept that, but I'm seventeen years old."

"You are still a child in the eyes of the law!" Daddy roars. "Until you are eighteen you must do what I say. And I forbid you to see him!"

"I will be eighteen in three months," I say. "I will make my own decisions then. Do you think I will stop loving him in three months, Daddy? I will love him forever!"

Trout squeezes my hand. "And I love your daughter," he says. "If you love her you wouldn't hurt her like this. Can't you see how this is tearing her up?"

"Don't you advise me on my relationship with my child!" Daddy shouts. He lunges toward me and grabs my arm, yanking me from Trout.

"Daddy, no!" I shriek.

Trout leaps in between us and shoves my father hard in the chest. "We tried!" Trout yells. "You'll be sorry for what you've done to us!"

"Don't you threaten me!" Daddy cries.

Tears stream down my face as we run out. My father's

angry voice follows us, his words raining on us like harsh pelts of hail.

I've calmed down some by the time we reach the car. "We used to be so close," I say. "I can't leave like this."

"You tried," Trout says bitterly. "If he won't listen to reason, what else can you do?"

"I shouldn't have brought you with me. I should have known that would just make him mad. I want to go back in. I want to talk to my father on my own."

He revs up the engine and drives the car around the factory, closer to Daddy's building so I won't have far to go in the dark. "I should walk you to the door," Trout says. "You shouldn't be out by yourself."

"It's not far," I say. "It will just make him mad again if he sees you. Don't worry. I'll be fine."

But I feel scared the moment I turn the corner and the car is out of sight. I move quickly through the shadows as icy fingers of apprehension squeeze my stomach. I see through the window that Daddy has gone back to work. His face is still red. He is still angry.

When I step into the hallway, I pause by the pop machine and peer in at my father. His back is to me now. His shoulders are strong and square, and I remember all the piggyback rides he gave me when I was little. Something twists in my chest. What will I say to him? What can I possibly say to make him understand?

I am so angry at my father, yet I still love him. Frustrated tears burn my eyes. "Daddy?" I say, trying to make my voice heard over the machine. But it drowns me out.

As I hesitate in the doorway, a shadow moves out from behind the pop machine. I am staring straight into the barrel of a gun.

• • •

"What are you doing here in the middle of the night?" Josh blinked and yawned. "When I heard you rapping on my window I thought you were a burglar."

"Burglars don't knock," I said through chattering teeth. "I had another dream. It was so awful." I looked up at his surprised face, framed in the window of the old farmhouse.

"Alexis, you're crazy."

"I-I need to talk to you. It can't wait until morning." I stood in the tall, dewy grass, shivering in the light sweater I'd grabbed when I dashed from the house. I hadn't taken the time to find my coat for fear I'd wake my family.

"Hold on a minute," he said. "I'll be right out."

A moment later he joined me on his front lawn, his eyes small and sleepy and his voice a husky whisper as he said, "Let's take a drive. My mom's out of town, but I don't want to wake my sister. Here, you wear my helmet."

I slipped the shiny black dome over my head, and he helped me adjust the straps under my chin. Then he pushed his motorcycle to the end of the street and when we were out of earshot of the house, we hopped on and roared into the night.

Josh drove us to the pier on the lake. I huddled in his arms and told him about the dream. "I was remembering," I said. "I saw all kinds of details. You had a nickname. I called you Trout!"

"That's strange."

"I remembered what happened to us! We didn't hurt my grandfather. Somebody else was there. Somebody evil."

"The bad one," he said quietly.

"Yes! The one Aunt Sidney warned us about. But I woke up before I could tell who it was!"

"It could have been just a nightmare."

"That was not a regular dream. It was like the others I've been having. I'm remembering when I was Nan. Oh, Josh! Please say you believe me!"

He tilted my chin so I looked up into his eyes. They were warm and brimming with love as he softly said, "I believe you, Alexis." He kissed me—a sweet, gentle kiss that tasted slightly of sleep and warmed me all the way to my toes.

"You're the only one in the whole world who believes me," I said. "You're the only one who understands."

We held each other under the moonless sky. A breeze tripped over the black lake, coaxing ripples into waves that slapped the shore.

The water was a shadow.

Dark.

Inky.

Invisible in the night.

It churned restlessly, like an animal who had slept too long. Its green, musty odor thickened the air. I could taste it—sour and frightening on my tongue.

"I should get home," I said. "Before somebody notices I'm gone."

I held tight to Josh as the motorcycle sputtered and whined to life. The surrounding forest was a dusky blur and soon we were on Swing-Low Street with the sharp black night racing past us. It seemed that every cell in my being vibrated with the thrumming of the engine. My mind tilted dizzily as we leaned into each corner.

Someone believes me!

The realization was exhilarating.

I had lived before. I was not crazy. Josh believed me. That was all I needed to know for now.

The narrow beam of the cycle's headlight cast a long white finger onto the dark road ahead. A small animal—a raccoon or a rabbit—skittered across our path and vanished into the velvety woods.

As I pressed against Josh and peered over his shoulder, two dots of light appeared in his rearview mirror. Someone was behind us. The car weaved, its headlights zigzagging in and out of the oval of the mirror. It was quickly upon us, snaring us in the intense glare of its halogen headlights.

Josh glanced down at the mirror. I sensed him tense. With the twist of the throttle, he gave the cycle some gas. We shot forward, leaving the car behind.

A moment later, its headlights loomed large in the mirror. They seemed to swallow us whole, and I knew the car was about to hit us.

The impact was an odd sensation. The world slowed until I felt caught in a single frozen frame of time.

This is it!

That thought was like a caption, written in sharp black letters under the crystallized moment.

And then the picture changed. *I am going to die.*

We were lifted into the air, but I felt no terror as the road beneath us vanished. A surprising sense of euphoria filled me. It was as if a warm, gentle hand was lifting us effortlessly toward the sky, and for a brief moment I felt incredible freedom.

Next thing I remember, I opened my eyes to see two tiny red taillights disappear in the distance. An eerie quiet hovered over us, interrupted only by the steady click, click, click of the motorcycle wheel turning brokenly.

"Josh!" I shrieked.

His limp figure lay in the ditch, illuminated by the beam of the motorcycle headlight.

26

The morning clouds were tinged with pink, and the first golden rays of the day swept across my front yard as I headed up the walk. The newspaper was gone from the front stoop, so I knew the family was up. I opened the front door and the rich, earthy aroma of brewing coffee rolled out to greet me.

My mother and grandparents were at the kitchen table and three pairs of sleepy eyes widened in surprise when they saw me. "Alex!" Mom cried. "I thought you were upstairs in bed!"

At the sound of the deep throaty rumbling of an engine, Grandma pulled back the curtain just as the sleek, black automobile chugged around the corner. "That looks like Tom's car!" she said.

"It is. He gave me a ride home."

"Where have you been?" Mom's voice sparked with irritation.

I gazed steadily into her eyes. "I was at the hospital. Josh and I were in an accident last night. Somebody ran into us! I think they did it on purpose, but the police think it was a drunk driver."

An instant of shocked silence followed. Then I was bombarded with the tornado of angry words I knew would ensue.

"Were you on that motorcycle?"

"Were you wearing a helmet?"

"How could you disobey us like that?"

"I hope you learned something from this!"

"You're grounded, young lady!"

"How dare you sneak out of the house!"

I folded my arms across my chest. "Don't any of you care what happened to Josh?"

"How is the boy?" Grandma squeaked.

"He has a severe concussion," I said, a catch in my voice. "*I* was wearing his helmet! The doctors don't know how bad his injuries are. He might never be okay again!"

"How awful!" cried Grandma.

Grandpa stared solemnly at the table, and Mom jumped up and ran to me. "Thank God you're okay!" she cried.

I stiffened in her arms and she released her hold on me. "Is that all you can say?" I said, as the tears I'd been fighting rushed down my face. "Don't you care anything about Josh? You're probably hoping he won't get well so I can't see him anymore."

"Alexis! That's a terrible thing to say. I wouldn't wish something like that on anyone."

"Josh *is* going to get better." I grabbed a napkin and blew my nose. "I'm going to help him. You can ground me until I'm fifty, but I'm going back to the hospital and I'll stay there until the nurses kick me out!"

I'm not sure how I let Tom talk me into going home in the first place. I must have been in shock and unable to think clearly, for I could not imagine sleeping. The boy I loved could die because *I* was wearing his helmet. If he had not insisted I wear it, it would have been me lying in that hospital bed. My whole body ached from the impact of the crash. The doctors had checked me over. Other than a few bruises, I was fine.

I stomped up the stairs to get my coat and money for the bus. When I came back down, my grandfather was standing in the doorway with the car keys jingling in his hand. "Forget the bus," he said. "I'll drive you."

I settled into the cushy black seat next to him in his big, sleek car. I drew a deep breath, trying to relax. His car always smelled of licorice, and I found this somehow comforting.

He drove in silence until we were out of Oxford, headed along the freeway toward the hospital. "You are stubborn just like Nan," he said. The statement rang with unexpected tenderness.

"She didn't hurt you on purpose," I said. "Grandpa, I had a dream. There was somebody else at the cannery that night. He had a gun."

He trained his eyes on the road, but I knew he was listening because a little muscle on the side of his brawny neck twitched convulsively.

"I don't know who it was," I continued. "But he jumped out from behind the pop machine."

Grandpa looked at me sharply. "How did you know about the pop machine?"

"I was there! I saw everything. I saw you in your blue coveralls bending over a big black machine. I heard everything you said!"

I repeated as much of the dream dialogue as I could remember. When I was finished he said, "You know things you have no way of knowing. That does not mean you are Nan's reincarnation. There is another explanation. Psychic ability runs in our family. My sister, Sidney, was psychic and so was my mother. Maybe you've been having visions about things that happened in the past."

"Maybe."

"Sometimes psychic people embellish when they remember their visions. They add a little something extra in the retelling to make it more interesting."

"I don't lie!"

"I'm not accusing you of anything. It's just that you have a very vivid imagination. And remember, we're talking about a *dream* here. That's a very different thing than reality."

"Nan and you were always so close. Why would she—"

"It's painful for me to hash over that night."

"She didn't mean to hurt you! Someone else did. The bad one!"

"Nobody else was at the cannery. *I* was there."

How could I argue with him? All I had was a dream—wispy images that were already beginning to evaporate from my consciousness.

When we reached the entrance of the hospital, Grandpa offered to come in with me. "You must be exhausted after sitting in the hospital all night," he said. "Did you sleep at all?"

"No. And I'm really not tired. You don't need to come in with me, Grandpa. Tom promised he'd wait there until Josh's mom showed up. I won't be alone."

All night long, I had stayed in the waiting room. When no one could reach Josh's mother, I had called Tom, who rushed right down. We'd sat together in the stiff vinyl chairs, drinking bitter, watery coffee from the machine and taking turns asking the nurses for news on Josh.

"He's still the same," they had told us. "No one but family is allowed in to see him."

Tom had assumed I'd already called my mother and I did

not correct him. At dawn, he'd insisted on driving me home, saying, "You need your rest. I'll stay at the hospital until Josh's mom shows up, and if there's any news I'll call you."

I saw now, as I walked into the waiting room, he had kept his promise. He was lying down on a narrow couch, snoring softly. I touched his shoulder. His small eyes flew open in alarm. "You're back already?" He sat up. "I finally got a hold of Josh's mom. She's on her way."

I knew her immediately as she rushed in with her black raincoat flapping behind her. Her tiny upturned nose and mane of fine blond hair were her own, but the full mouth and high forehead were Josh's. Her eyes were small and red and frightened. The nurse at the front desk ushered her in to see Josh. When she emerged, Tom tried to calm her. "We're all pulling for him," he said gently.

"I knew that motorcycle was dangerous," she said. "I wish he'd been driving his car."

"I'm surprised he wasn't," said Tom. "He finally paid it off a few days ago."

"Who would run him off the road like that?" she cried.

"Probably a drunk," said Tom. "The police were here last night. Alex told them everything she could remember. They think it was an accident."

"No!" I said. "It wasn't an accident. Somebody deliberately tried to hurt us. I told the cops that. They're so stubborn they won't believe somebody's trying to kill—"

Tom caught my eye and nodded at Mrs. Shelldrick, who seemed to have no color left in her face. I clamped my mouth shut. What was the point in frightening Josh's mom?

"The guy who hit the kids probably panicked," said Tom. "He took off before the police could get there."

"Would you like to see Josh, Alex?" Mrs. Shelldrick asked.

I went in alone to see him. When I stepped into the dimly

lit room, I was struck by the strong, sterile scent of hospital disinfectant.

It was eerily still. A curtain was drawn around the bed next to Josh's, and from within came the hoarse, rhythmic breaths of a respirator.

Josh lay motionless in his bed, his dark curls a stark contrast to the wide, white bandage around his head. I gasped at the deep, purplish black eyes swollen in his pale face. His big hands were folded limply across his stomach.

Beside his bed, the steady beep, beep, beep of a cardiac monitor played counterpoint to the sound of the other patient's respirator.

"Oh, Josh!" I whispered. Gingerly, I perched on the edge of his bed and touched his hand.

I could barely breathe at the thought of him so motionless. Josh, the athlete. The boy who was always fidgeting. How could this be the same person?

I shuddered, contemplating the thin veil that separates us from death.

Josh stirred. Weakly, yet purposefully, he squeezed my hand.

27

Sequoia and I waited in Dr. Trollen's small, cluttered office. "She's traveled all over the world," Sequoia said as we looked at the jumble of small statues and wooden figures adorning the walls and shelves.

"I hope she has some answers for me," I said. The bookcases were jammed with books. In fact, they occupied every corner of the room. They were stacked on the desk, the floor, and even on the shabby green couch. Surely one of those books held a pertinent explanation for the enigma my life had become. If Dr. Trollen had read them all, she would know how to advise me.

She arrived late for our appointment, her short gray hair windblown, her cheeks flushed. Her eyes were bright and encouraging as she listened to my strange tale. She nodded often as if my story made sense. "How terrible." She clucked her tongue in sympathy as I told her about the motorcycle accident. "It is possible you two are soul mates, destined to stay together for many lifetimes. How is he?"

"The accident was last night. He's in bad shape," I said. "I was with him at the hospital all day. He's still not talking."

She tilted her head and smiled kindly. "Everything is going to work out. Things happen for a reason. Your story is a very interesting one. I have documented cases like yours. It is not uncommon for a soul to return to the same family to clean up unfinished business. You may very well be the reincarnation of your aunt, but who is to say for sure?"

"I look almost identical to her!"

She nodded her head knowingly. "Yes, yes. I've heard of such things, also. Tell me, Alexis. Have you ever had a spontaneous regression?"

"What's that?"

"Some people may be going about their day-to-day business—washing windows or feeding the cat or what have you—and then, suddenly, something triggers a past-life memory. One woman I know of was putting a bandage on her little daughter's scraped knee when she suddenly recalled being a nurse in World War I. She saw her hands wrapping a thick, white bandage around the bleeding leg of a soldier and heard the thunder of artillery in the background.

"Thousands of cases of spontaneous recall have been documented in India, Africa, the Far East, the United States—and, well, you get the picture. It is far from uncommon."

"Alexis is always having feelings of déjà vu," Sequoia said. "She'll see something for the first time and feel like she's seen it before."

"Spontaneous recalls are much more than a sense of déjà

vu," said Dr. Trollen. "The person experiencing one actually has the sensation of being somewhere else."

"I experienced that when you regressed me in class," I said. "I've had it happen in dreams, too. But never out of the blue when I was awake. Do you think I could have a spontaneous recall if I keep my mind open?"

"Perhaps, or you may never have another experience."

"What is it I'm supposed to do?" I asked. "Why have I come back?"

"If you are the reincarnation of your aunt—and remember we have not established that as fact—if you *are*, then you know better than anyone. Your soul carries knowledge with it. You have things to accomplish here. If you don't accomplish these things, then perhaps you will the next time around."

"I could come back here *again*?"

She shrugged. "Possibly. Or maybe you've already learned whatever lesson you are to learn. Or you may have taught something to someone else. Perhaps that was your purpose here. The web of life is so fantastically complex, no one can say for sure what another's destiny is."

She must have noticed my frustration for she said, "I'm sorry. I have no clear-cut answers for you. Just follow your conscience and you will do the right thing."

Though my visit to Dr. Trollen was interesting, it did not solve my problem.

I still did not know the name of the "bad one." I still did not know who had hurt Scott and Nan.

A killer was loose in Oxford, and I had no idea who it was.

Unsure where else to turn, I dove back into Grandma's disorganized boxes of mementos. Perhaps they held the answer to the mystery.

Everybody in Oxford is connected to everybody else.

I remembered Grandma's words as once again I reached

into her musty closet and lugged out the boxes of scrap-books. I pulled down several boxes and peeked inside, wondering where I should start. A box on the top shelf caught my eye. It was labeled "Nan" in fading black felt pen.

Excited, I pulled it down. The first thing I saw was a but-ton eye, peering up at me out of the tangle of possessions from the past. I reached into the box and my fingers brushed something soft and fuzzy. I pulled it out.

The teddy bear was obviously well loved. He was miss-ing an eye. His painted-on paws were worn and faded as if he'd been played with often.

Why don't I remember? I wondered, as I propped him up on the floor. If this were Nan's special bear, why didn't I feel the twinge of déjà vu I so often experienced?

Turning him over, I realized why I did not remember him. He had not been my bear. He was Tom's. For pinned to his back was a note.

Dear Nan,

I hope Oscar Bear gets along with you as well as he did me.

All my love,
Tom

I read the date on the note and did some quick calculat-ing. Tom had been in the seventh grade when he gave his bear to Nan. I was touched. Apparently, he'd once had a crush on her.

Did Tom remember the good in Nan? Or had his happy memories of her been erased when he'd heard she had tried to murder her own father?

Sociopaths don't care about anyone's feelings but their own.

That is what Tom thought of Nan. He thought she was a sociopath. And sometimes, I had the feeling, he thought I was one, too.

A sudden rush of determination surged through me. I wanted to prove to everyone that Nan had been a good person—that *I* was a good person. If only I could solve the mystery of her disappearance! If only I could find the proof she had been murdered—that someone else had pushed Grandpa into the machine!

I rummaged through the boxes with a renewed ferocity. Apparently, Nan had saved every greeting card given to her, because the box was stuffed with them. I paused to examine one from Patsy. It depicted a fluffy orange kitten, eating a piece of birthday cake. Inside, in neat, rounded letters it said, *To my dearest friend on her fifteenth birthday, your pal, Patsy.*

Apparently, the card had been sent before Nan battled with her for Scott.

A folded note was tucked inside. The date at the top indicated it had been written nearly a year later. *Nan, you bitch. I know the only reason you wanted to be my friend was so you could get to Scott. Well, you've got him. But you'll never be my friend again. Patsy.*

I reeled at the word "bitch."

Death threats flashed through my mind—all those creepy notes in blood red!

Die Bitch.

Patsy, of course, had not come right out and said, "Die bitch." But the note dripped with venom.

Could it be . . . ?

Could Patsy be responsible for the murders?

I quickly dismissed the idea as I visualized her slight frame. She certainly did not look like a killer.

When I found the picture of the Oxy Roxy, a strange prickling spidered over me. I stared at the eight-by-ten photograph, struck by the sight of the gray, concrete building with the light bulb-laced marquee which announced, *Saturday Night Fever*.

I recognized the Oxy Roxy. I knew the cold, smoke-colored walls and the velvet curtained ticket booth in the corner of the picture.

But most of all I remembered the people.

They stood in a group, as if in a class picture. Familiar faces from the past peered out at me from beneath strange hairstyles. Most of the group was dressed alike in brown blazers over white shirts. Apparently, they were in uniform.

Nan stood in the front with Tom and Scott on either side.

She worked in the theater! I could almost feel the sticky carpet beneath her feet as she directed people to their seats. And I could almost smell the buttery popcorn as she scooped it into red and white striped cardboard buckets.

I closed my eyes, hoping another past-life regression would overtake me.

Nothing happened.

Sighing in frustration, I studied the faces in the picture. Did I recognize them because I knew them now? Because I'd seen other photos of them? Or was I remembering them from my life as Nan?

That is the hard part—knowing if I'm actually recollecting something or simply piecing things together from what I know now.

A blond girl about seven or eight stood in front of Nan, who placed her hands protectively on the younger girl's shoulders.

Scott was handsome, with his dazzling grin of even white teeth and flash of blond hair. But I barely recognized Tom. He looked scrawny and gawky. His Adam's apple dominated his skinny neck. Big ears jutted out from beneath a closely cropped haircut. Patsy stood beside him, grinning in the same chipmunky manner I associated with Kelly.

As my eyes roamed over the faces, my heart sped at the sight of the stubble-faced man in the corner. He wore a white T-shirt and jeans and stood apart from the others, shoulders slouched, hands dipped deep in his pockets. It looked like Deke!

I flipped the photograph over. Nan had written the names of the people on the back. She'd identified Deke as the projectionist. The little girl with her was Anita.

I arrived at school early the next day, with the photo tucked in my math book.

I hoped when I showed Anita the picture, she would remember something that could help me.

"Anita?" I stepped into her classroom. I gasped in horror at the sight before me. All of the tables were overturned, the students' paintings had been ripped from the wall, and foam from the fire extinguisher covered Anita's desk.

I stood frozen a moment as I took in the damage. Anita's ceramic cup was broken, its pieces scattered across the piles of shredded colored paper. Her sweater lay in a puddle of red paint beside her desk.

Who would do something like this? Who would do such a sick thing?

Then I saw it. A twisted message written in the red paint. He had used her sweater to scrawl the threat across the floor in letters two feet tall. Those now familiar words grabbed me by the stomach and squeezed. Two small words with terrifying power. *Die Bitch.*

28

"*What happened?*" *a deep voice boomed.*

I whirled to see Mr. Wingate and Patsy Sims in the doorway. "Where's Anita?" asked Mr. Wingate.

"I don't know," I said. "I just got here and found this mess."

He shook his head slowly, his eyes full of something that resembled pity. "You have problems."

"You think *I* did this?" I asked.

"What is it, Bruce?" Anita appeared in the doorway next to him. "Oh, no!" she cried as her wide eyes swept over her classroom. "What happened?"

"We just arrived," said Patsy. "We were looking for you so you could show me the pasteup program on the computer."

"Look what it says there!" I said, pointing to the puddle

of red paint. "That's a threat, Anita! Somebody wants to hurt you!"

"Oh, Alex," she said limply. "I've tried to be your friend."

"I didn't do this!" My voice was high and defensive as frustration bubbled up inside of me. "I was looking for you and found it like this."

Nothing I could say would convince them. I had a reputation as a troubled girl—a girl who conspired to take candid, embarrassing photos of teachers. A girl who told lies. A girl who wanted attention so badly she would plant ugly messages in her own cartoon.

A few minutes later, I was in Tom's office as he leaned back in his creaky wooden chair and regarded me with concern. "I thought we were making progress," he said.

"I *didn't* vandalize Anita's room!" I said. "I wouldn't do something like that."

"I want to give you the benefit of the doubt, Alex."

"But you don't believe me?"

"I didn't say that," he said quietly. "Let's not worry about what *I* believe, let's concentrate on what *you're* thinking. What's going on inside of you right now?"

"I just wish everyone would believe me!" Frustrated tears stung my eyes. I blinked them away.

"You are obviously distraught. I know the last couple of days have been hard on you. You're worried about Josh, aren't you?"

"Of course! I don't know why I came to school today. I should be at the hospital with him."

"His mother is with him today. I called a few minutes ago to check on him."

"How is he?"

"Doing a little better. He's not out of the woods yet."

"I was there last night. He still wasn't talking. I'm going to see him after school."

"Do you need a ride?"

"Thank you," I said. "But Josh's mom loaned me his Fairlane. She said she knew how much I mean to Josh and that if he could talk, he'd tell her to let me drive it so I could come see him." My voice broke. "I feel like the accident was my fault. If I hadn't gone over there in the middle of the night, it never would have happened."

"So *that's* what's really bothering you."

"That and the fact somebody wants to kill me! A maniac is running loose. He killed Tawny and Nan and now he wants to kill me and Josh and Anita!"

"That's quite a statement."

The phone rang and Tom picked it up. "It's for you," he said with surprise as he handed it to me.

"Hello! This is Alex." I nearly dropped the phone when a raspy voice croaked, "Watch yourself or else."

I covered the mouthpiece. "It's him!" I hissed.

"Who?"

"The bad one! The one who's been hurting people!" I handed the phone to Tom, who listened a moment and said, "No one is there. He hung up."

"But you heard him! You heard him when he asked for me!"

"Yes. Did you ask a friend to call you here, Alex?"

"You think I had someone call me here just so you'd believe me?"

"I'm not accusing you of anything. I'm simply asking questions. How am I supposed to know what's going on with you unless I ask?"

"Please believe me, Tom!"

"Whether or not I believe someone is stalking you is not important. In spite of everything that's happened, I still believe *in* you. You're a good person. I'm on your side."

"Am I going to get in trouble for something I didn't do?"

"No," he said. "Mr. Cline doesn't have proof that you are

the vandal. And he knows it would violate your rights to punish you without evidence. We'll let this go until we investigate further."

As I drove to the hospital that afternoon, my mind whirled with all that had transpired. My dreams seemed to hold a key. I vowed to begin writing them down.

Suddenly one of the details of my dream popped out at me. Trout. That had been my dream boy's nickname. Was this the proof I needed to show I *had* lived before as Nan?

I had just passed Kettleburg. I turned the car around.

"Sure Scott had a nickname," Dottie said. Her face was pink from surprise. I'd apparently interrupted a meal. She wore a napkin tucked in her blouse and both were splattered with orange food.

"What was it?" I asked. "What was his nickname?"

"Petey! Stop that! Mitzi!" She booted the snarling brown dogs out of the doorway with her slippered foot and plodded out onto the porch, shutting the door behind her.

"Well, my boy swam like a fish," she said. A proud smile inched across her wide face. "Some of his friends called him Trout."

"I knew it!" I cried.

Her eyes popped open as I launched into my strange tale. "I saw something about reincarnation on one of my talk shows," she said. "I always knew my Scott would come back to me if he could. Does he remember me?"

"Josh doesn't remember anything specific," I said. "Certain things are familiar to him—like the Fairlane. And he was drawing pictures of *me* a year before I moved here, so I guess he was remembering me when I was Nan."

"If he remembers his girlfriend, then he's sure going to remember his own mother!" she snapped.

"I don't know what he remembers now," I said sadly. "He's in the hospital."

Dottie insisted on going with me to see him. "You're driving Scott's car!" she exclaimed when she saw the rounded form of the Fairlane nudged against the curb.

"It's Josh's car now. He bought it from Tom," I explained.

"It's so unfair." She crawled into the car. "My Scottie's sweet soul is back and now he might leave me again."

"Josh is going to be all right!" I said. "He *has* to be!"

All the way to the hospital she talked about Scott. "I wonder what he'll do when he sees me," she said.

"Don't expect too much," I warned. "Josh isn't even sure if he believes in reincarnation. I don't want to upset him, especially when he's so sick. He's not talking yet and we shouldn't stay for more than a couple of minutes."

When we walked into his hospital room, she gasped at the sight of his bruised and ashen form. I went to him and lightly kissed his forehead. "I've brought someone to see you," I whispered. His closed eyelids were a pale, fragile blue.

"Scott?" Dottie inquired. "Scott, it's Mama!"

She sat on the edge of the bed and the mattress shifted dramatically with her weight, rolling Josh's body slightly. He stirred in his sleep.

"Scottie!" she squeaked.

His eyes flickered open and he stared blankly into her fleshy face.

"Water," he croaked. "Can I have some water?"

He was talking! I dashed out of the room and called out to the nurse. She raced back with me. She leaned over him. 'Squeeze my fingers, Joshua," she said as she held out two fingers.

I held my breath.

"Good boy!" the nurse said, and I sagged with relief.

The nurse brought the doctor in and we waited outside.

He emerged a few minutes later, smiling broadly. Josh was going to be okay!

I'd been nervously pacing as I waited to hear the news. And I had all but forgotten Dottie. She followed me back into the room, and as we stood over his bed I glanced at her, expecting to see my relief mirrored in her face. She stared back at me accusingly.

"What's the matter?" I asked.

"Hrrumph!" she said. "I shouldn't have come here. It was a waste of time. That boy is *not* my son!"

29

"*I shouldn't have let you get my hopes up*," Dottie said as we headed away from the hospital.

"I'm sorry. I didn't expect you to believe me. No one else does."

"I'd think I'd know my own son. I looked into that boy's eyes and I did not know him."

"If Josh is the reincarnation of Scott, he could look different in this life."

"I'd recognize his soul. If my boy's soul was occupying a *monkey's* body, I'd recognize him!"

"I don't think people come back as animals."

"What makes you an expert? I heard that people *do* come back as animals."

"I guess no one really knows for sure," I said.

She shook her head, her gray curls bouncing. "All I know is the dogs probably jumped up on the table and ate my dinner by now. It was my last can of spaghetti. I didn't make it to the market today because my car broke down."

"Are you hungry? We could stop somewhere."

"Burger sounds good. Love those cheeseburgers."

I drove toward the Big Top and Dottie cheered up as she told me how she liked her burgers. "Extra onions and pickles. That's the way they're best."

"Sounds good," I said, because my appetite was coming back, too.

Josh was awake and talking! He had smiled at me before I left. "I'm glad you're okay, Alex," he'd whispered.

"It sure brings back memories, riding in this old car again," Dottie interrupted my thoughts.

"It's familiar to me, too," I said.

"Don't start that reincarnation stuff again. You sure look like Nan. But that doesn't mean you are her."

"I might be."

"If you're Nan, tell me where Scott's hiding place was."

"Hiding place?"

"In this car here. He didn't know I found it. He had a place he stashed stuff. Cigarettes and things. He couldn't keep secrets from me though. I found the hiding place but I never let on. I figured he was going to do what he was going to do. This way I could check up on him."

Forgotten Lake shimmered in the late afternoon sun, and I rolled down the window as we passed it. A rush of cool, moist air flowed through the car, and goose bumps prickled my skin. "I don't remember a hiding place," I said.

Dottie grinned triumphantly.

"That doesn't mean I'm *not* Nan. I don't remember much about my other life. Certain things are familiar to me and others have no meaning. I don't know why."

"Oh, well. It used to be right up here." She reached up and pulled down a corner of the headliner, the thick sheet of fabric covering the car's ceiling. A puff of dust clouded the air. "Well, I'll be! There's something up there. It looks like a cassette tape."

"Josh's cassette player is in the backseat."

Dottie leaned over the seat and grabbed it. She jammed the tape in and slipped on the headphones. "You can hardly understand it. It's all scratchy."

"Let me hear." I pulled off to the side of the road and put on the headphones. The garbled voice was indeed scratched. "I can't understand it either. Wait. He's saying something about a fight."

"Probably one of those lovers' quarrels he had with Nan. She was always nagging him, and they'd get to fighting."

"They didn't get along?" I was surprised.

She smiled smugly. "He got along better with his last girlfriend, Patsy. Me and her got along like a house afire. I'm holding on to this tape. It was probably Scott's."

"It might be Tom's," I said. "He had the car a long time."

When we pulled into the Big Top, it was dinnertime and the place was packed.

Most nights, you can find just about every other person in Oxford there and tonight was no exception. Kelly's mother was picking up a to-go order and Dottie threw her thick arms around her. "Patsy!" she exclaimed. "We was just talking about you. I was telling Nan here—I mean *Alex*—that you was always Scott's favorite girl."

Patsy's pink lips curled into a pleased smile. "We had loads of fun, he and I."

"There's Tom," I said to Dottie. "Let's ask him about the tape."

He sat with Anita at a corner booth. Their hands were clasped together under the table. She smiled stiffly when she saw me watching and pulled her hand away from Tom's. Avoiding my eyes, she sipped her pop.

"Say, Tom," Dottie blurted loudly as she hobbled toward them. "Did you know about Scott's hiding place?"

Everybody in the place turned to watch.

"Did you know about the hiding place in the Fairlane?" she asked again.

Tom looked confused.

"Well, *did* you?" she demanded.

He shrugged.

Dottie's eyes flashed as she looked at me. "Told you. He don't know about it. That tape I found was *Scott's*!"

"We found a tape tucked up in the ceiling of the car," I explained. "We think it's got Scott's voice on it."

I forgot all about the tape after I dropped Dottie off at her trailer. Half an hour later she called.

"I've got something you won't believe!" she squealed.

"What is it?"

"I need a ride to the police station. I left a message for Sergeant Bryer to call me, but I don't want to wait for him. I need to go right down to the station and give them the tape. I asked my neighbor to drive me, but her baby's sick."

"I'll drive you!" I said. "But tell me what's going on."

"I played the end of the tape and I've got it all figured out! I know who done it! I know who killed my Scott!"

"Who?"

"Oh, blast it! Shut up, dogs. Someone's at the door. Just get over here fast, okay?"

30

I *was unable to pull into Dottie's driveway because an ambu-*lance was backing out. I recognized Sergeant Bryer's thick frame as he bent over a clipboard on the hood of his police car. I parked behind him. "What happened?" I asked. "Is Dottie okay?"

"She had a stroke," he said. "She's on her way to the hospital."

"Oh, no!"

"The doctors at Burgess General Hospital are good," he said kindly. "My grandmother went there when she had a stroke and she's doing fine now. She's eighty-two and walks a mile every morning."

I sank onto the curb, my knees trembling. "This is so strange," I said slowly. "Do you think someone did something to cause her to have a stroke?"

"Why would somebody do that?"

"She called me about an hour ago. She asked me to take her to the police station because she'd found proof somebody killed her son and my aunt!"

"I got a message from her, but all it said was she wanted me to call her." Sergeant Bryer's eyes narrowed skeptically. "She never could get over the fact that boy ran away. You two have been egging each other on with your theories."

"This isn't just a theory. We found a tape in Scott's old car. When we first played it, the voices sounded garbled. But when Dottie played the other side, she heard something."

"What?"

"I don't know," I said, frustration welling up inside of me. "Somebody came to her door so she had to hang up. Do you think that person could have—"

He lifted his hands as if he were stopping traffic. "Hold on. We don't know anything about what she found."

While I waited on the stoop, he went into Dottie's trailer only to emerge a few minutes later, empty-handed. "No tape." He shrugged. "Her tape recorder is empty."

That night I slept fitfully. When I awoke the next morning, I called the hospital and learned Dottie was in intensive care. It was too early to tell the extent of her injuries.

Once again, my stomach churned guiltily. Had I gotten her so riled up with my reincarnation theory that it gave her a stroke?

Another possibility snaked through the back of my mind. What if someone had deliberately hurt her? Her "stroke" was suspicious. The tape, after all, was missing.

I felt more compelled than ever to speak to Anita. *I had to warn her again!*

I drove Grandma to work, arriving half an hour before school started. I hoped to find Anita alone in her classroom. As I approached the art room, I spotted Deke ambling toward me. My insides seemed to freeze as my gaze fell on the object in his hand. It was a pack. An army green pack with a silver buckle. Nan's pack!

Deke's had it the whole time, I realized. I had dropped the pack by the pond, the morning I found Tawny. Did that mean he had been there, too?

Why was it so important for him to conceal Nan's pack?

I had to tell someone! *Tom!* Would he be in his office? By the time I reached him, I was out of breath.

"Slow down!" Tom interrupted me as I stammered about what I'd seen. "I can hardly understand you."

"I've had this weird feeling about Deke for a long time," I said. "Remember that pack I told you about? The one I found at my aunt Sidney's?"

"Nan's pack."

"Yes! I left it by the pond the morning I found Tawny's body. Deke has it! I just saw him with it."

"Okay, let's go have a look," Tom said. His presence was reassuring as we descended the stairs.

"The basement gives me the creeps," I said.

"Basements are like that. Especially big dark ones like this."

"Thanks for coming with me. I know I seem hysterical sometimes, but there's so much going on."

"That's okay, Nan."

"Nan!" I paused as we reached the landing. "Tom, you called me Nan."

"Freudian slip. You *do* look like she did. You even act like she did."

"I *am* Nan."

"Alexis." His tone was flat. I couldn't see his eyes in the shadows, but I sensed the disapproval flickering through them.

"I know you two were good friends," I said as I deliberately slipped back into referring to Nan in the third person.

"I found a note you wrote her when you were in the seventh grade. It, um, sounded like you *really* cared about her."

His laugh rattled with embarrassment. "I had a huge crush on her in junior high when I was in an awkward stage, but when we got older she started chasing *me*."

We reached Deke's room. The door was ajar, and Tom nudged it. It creaked open.

"There it is!" I pointed to the shelf.

Tom reached for it.

"What are you doing?" It was Deke! He sauntered cockily into the room, with Burrel shuffling behind him.

"Alex thinks this is her pack." Tom's voice was frostily calm.

Deke snatched the pack from him, turned it upside down, and, with a vigorous shake, spilled the contents onto his desk.

I blinked at the pile of scrunched pop cans and flattened paper cups.

"Garbage?" Tom asked.

"One man's trash is another man's treasure," Deke said. "You've heard that before, haven't you, Tom Turkey?"

"Don't play games, Deke." Tom said. "And don't call me that."

"He hated that when he was in high school!" Deke's laugh was low and nasty. "Tom Turkey had a turkey neck. Gobble, gobble, gobble." Deke smirked at me. "You know Tom and I used to work together at the old movie theater? Tommy and I go way back!"

"What's with the garbage?" Tom interrupted.

"I don't collect it. *Burrel* does! He brings it to me and it's not polite to refuse a gift." With a wave of his hand, he indicated the long shelf of strange clutter. "Burrel gave me all of this. Didn't you?"

"What happened to the things that were in the pack?" I asked.

"Burrel, buddy?" said Deke. "You heard the little lady. What did you do with her stuff?"

Burrel hung his head and spoke so quietly we had to strain to hear him. "I threw it away in the back of the garbage truck. I love watching that great big hydraulic arm smashing things."

"So I never had this lady's things, did I?" Deke prompted him.

He shook his head. "No, I bring you the pack, Deke. I threw all the other stuff away. You never saw it."

Was he telling the truth? I wondered. Or was Burrel lying to protect his friend?

31

My first class was about to start by the time we emerged from the basement. There was no time to talk with Anita. I decided it would just have to wait until lunch.

At noon, I headed for her classroom, only to find the door locked.

I poked my head in the school office. "Grandma, have you seen Anita?" I asked.

At her desk, Grandma unwrapped a thick, sloppy sandwich from a square of tinfoil. It dripped shreds of lettuce and mayonnaise and smelled sharply of tuna fish. "She always rides her bike home for lunch," she said. "If you hurry you might be able to catch her. But that Anita moves real fast on her bike—drives like a crazy woman."

The bike rack was behind the school, right beside Deke's garden. A row of bicycles were shackled to posts, and I scanned them quickly for Anita's blue bike. It was gone. I looked up, just in time to see the flash of gold of her hair as she pedaled around the corner.

I headed for the cafeteria where I bought an egg salad sandwich. I found a corner table and sat beside a pair of girls I did not know. They flipped their shiny hair and whispered and giggled to each other about a hunky boy at the next table. When they glanced at me, I smiled self-consciously and picked up my sandwich. It was lonely with Josh gone. I bit off a corner of my sandwich. It tasted bland and dry.

How could I eat knowing Anita could be in danger?

I knew I could not wait to talk to her.

Follow your conscience and you will do the right thing.

Dr. Trollen's advice rang in my ears. *Follow your conscience . . .*

I *had* to warn Anita. Even if she did not believe me, I had to warn her again. What if something happened to her and I had done nothing to try to prevent it?

Five minutes later, I was back in the Fairlane, headed down the steep hill, wondering what she would think when I appeared at her door. How could I convince her I wasn't a crazy student trying to harass her? If I remained calm and matter-of-fact, perhaps I could persuade her to listen to me.

I was planning my strategy as I rounded the corner and neared the bottom of the hill. For the second time that day, I was met with the sight of an ambulance. It was parked in the middle of the street, red light spinning as an attendant shut the back door. It pulled away and its siren started howling as I approached.

Then I saw it. A twisted tangle of blue metal and tire at the side of the road.

A bicycle. A *blue* bicycle.

I rolled down my window. "What happened?" I yelled to the policeman who was directing traffic.

"Accident. Move along now."

"That looks like my teacher's bike," I said.

"It was Anita Barnes from the high school," he acknowledged. "Bad accident. Wheel came off her bike."

I found Tom in the teachers' lounge. "I've got bad news," I said. "Something has happened to Anita."

He jumped up, spilling his coffee as he cried, "What is it? What's happened?"

"She was in an accident on her bike. Only I don't think it was *really* an accident. The policeman said her wheel came off. Somebody must have tampered with it."

He turned white and dashed out into the hall, with me at his heels. He glanced over his shoulder and shouted at me, "Where did they take her?"

"I'm not sure."

Tom phoned the police and learned Anita was on her way to Burgess Hospital. I followed him out to his car. "I tried to warn her," I said. "But I didn't get there in time."

"What do you mean?"

"I had a bad feeling ever since she got that threat when her room was vandalized." I told him about Dottie's accident and the missing tape. "Half the town was at the Big Top last night when she was talking about the tape. Did you notice if Deke was there? Could he have overheard Dottie?"

Tom fumbled in his pocket for his keys. His hand was shaking so badly he had trouble putting the key in the door. "Deke was there playing video games last night," he said. "But I don't remember if he was there at the same time as you."

"He doesn't like Anita," I said. "He's always making rude comments about her. The bike rack is right near the boiler room. What if he tampered with her bike?"

"Deke's got a smart mouth and he's usually busy offending somebody. But I can't imagine him deliberately hurting someone. And I can't imagine *anyone* wanting to hurt Anita."

As I watched Tom speed out of the parking lot, I wanted to kick myself. Why hadn't I tried harder to warn Anita?

I now knew three people in the hospital. It was no coincidence! Somebody had deliberately hurt them all.

The next morning I learned Anita had broken her wrist, had a mild concussion and numerous deep scratches over her body. But she was going to be okay.

Mr. Wingate said it was better if I didn't visit her. "She's very upset. I think it's best if she only sees those she knows and trusts right now."

I felt a pang. Anita didn't trust me. But something in Mr. Wingate's voice told me he did not think this was an accident. "What do you mean by those she trusts?" I asked. "Does Anita think someone sabotaged her bike?"

"Let's just say she's been a little uneasy ever since her room was vandalized." His words were as cool as crisp blocks of ice.

Did she think *I* had caused her accident?

Tom checked on Dottie and reported that she, too, was recovering but had no memory of the last weeks.

The good news was Josh was feeling better.

"He's getting out of the hospital on Wednesday," I told Mom. "His mother has to work that day, so I'm going to pick him up."

We were in the kitchen where she was squeezing a squiggly yellow border of frosting on a large round cake. "When's he going back to school?" she asked.

"His doctor wants him to take it easy for another week."

"That's probably a good idea. Do you think I should add pink or yellow roses to the cake?" Hands on her hips, she stepped back and regarded her creation with a frown.

"Yellow." I wondered, *Is that all she's going to say*?

I had been expecting a lecture about Josh. I stared at her,

waiting. When she continued to fuss over her cake, I came right out and asked, "So you're not going to tell me to stay away from Josh?"

"Nope."

"Good. But what's Grandpa going to say?"

"He's the one who told me I should let you date Josh. He said that forbidding Nan to see Scott was the biggest mistake of his life. It drove her away from our family." Her large gray eyes were as soft as velvet as a faint smile curved her lips. "We don't want to lose you, too, Alex."

I threw my arms around her.

She hugged me awkwardly.

On Wednesday I drove the Fairlane to the hospital to pick Josh up.

"It's *my* car," he said, as he hobbled toward the Fairlane on his crutches. His skin was a washed-out white, and bruises still stained the hollows of his eyes. "I want to drive."

"Not yet," I said. "You look awful."

"Thanks a lot!" he said, but he got into the passenger side. When he didn't argue, I knew he was still weak from the accident. I hated to burden him with my fears, but he needed to know.

"It's got to be Deke," he said when I finished filling him in on the details. "I've always thought he was strange."

"I think so, too. How do we convince the police to investigate him?"

"That's going to be tough. Especially since they don't think a crime's been committed. I just found out they think Tawny's death was an accident."

32

Crunch, crunch, crunch. The gravel crackles and crunches beneath my feet.

If only I can make Daddy understand, I think as I approach his building. He is inside, and I stand in the doorway watching him a moment before he sees me. His back is to me. His shoulders are square and strong. My heart twists as I remember the piggyback rides he used to give me when I was little.

"Daddy?" He cannot hear me because the machine is thundering. A shadow moves from behind the pop machine. I stare into the barrel of a gun.

I fix on it a moment, then my eyes shift upward. The menacing figure before me is wearing a ski mask and the hollows of his eyes are pools of darkness in the dim light.

The bad one.

I know he is evil, yet I do not recognize him.

I look to my father for help, and the bad one follows my gaze. Daddy is still hovering over the machine. The bad one edges toward him as Daddy begins to turn toward me. He looks right into my eyes. I open my mouth, trying to shout a warning, but the bad one is too fast. He raises his gun and brings it down hard on the back of Daddy's head. I rush forward as my father slumps into the machinery.

"You're coming with me!" the raspy voice says as he twists my arm up behind my back. I feel the cold, hard gun pressed against my ribs.

Thursday morning, when I woke up from the dream, it remained vivid in my mind. The sharp pelts of water from the shower did not wash it away. It was still there—clear and real—as I brushed my teeth with minty, green paste and dressed in my jeans and sweater. It was still there as I sat at the breakfast table, amidst the commotion of my family.

I watched True eat her cereal with big, sloppy, sleepy bites so that she spilled most of it down the front of her pink dress. Toby read the sports page aloud in a grating tone, and my mother and grandfather did their best to ignore him.

I could not wait to tell Grandpa about my dream.

I tried to warn you!

I wanted to yell it at him. I wanted to grab him by his shoulders and shake him. *Don't you understand, Grandpa? I tried to warn you. I tried to warn you, Daddy!*

Daddy.

I watched him from across the table. Lined, angular face. Serious gray eyes. Silver hair, too long in the bangs, so that when he bent forward to read the newspaper they covered his eyes. His features had become dear to me.

I had known him before. He gave me piggyback rides

and taught me to draw. And then the bad one ripped us apart.

"Grandpa, I need to talk to you," I said. "It's important."

"I'm giving your grandmother a ride to work," he said. "She's got to be at the school early this morning. From there, I'm heading over to the nursery to pick up mulch for the plants. If you'd like a ride to school, we can talk after I drop Grandma off."

It was frosty morning and the heater in Grandpa's car was not working, so we sat shivering as we watched Grandma scurry up the steps and into the school.

"What was it you wanted to talk to me about?" Grandpa asked.

"I had another dream."

"Alexis." His voice was softly skeptical.

"I tried to warn you! He had a gun and he hit you on the back of the head. You looked at me right before he attacked you. I tried to warn you, Daddy!"

"I'm your *grandfather,*" he said flatly. "I love you dearly, but you are not my daughter, Alexis Arlene. You are my *granddaughter.*"

"Now I am. But it wasn't always so. You used to give me piggyback rides."

"Your mother must have told you about the piggyback rides I gave to her and her sister."

"No. I *remembered!*"

His shoulders quaked as he began to silently cry. Big, sloppy tears crawled down the lines in his face and dripped from his chin.

Watching him, I felt like I'd been socked in the belly.

"Grandpa?"

"It breaks my heart," he whispered. "It breaks my heart that Nan went crazy and now you—now you—"

"I'm not going crazy."

My words could not convince him.

As I watched my grandfather drive away, the crisp morning air seemed to seep right through my skin. I couldn't stop shivering.

School would not start for another hour, but I had nothing else to do, so I went into the office and watched my grandmother bustling about. "It should be warming up pretty soon," she said when she noticed my teeth chattering. "Help yourself to some hot chocolate. There's some packages of the instant kind next to the coffeepot."

"My, it really is chilly," she said, clutching her sweater. "I wonder what the problem is this time. Deke or the furnace?"

When she asked me to go find him, I wanted to object but had vowed to remain calm. Everyone thought I was cracking and I was not about to give my family another reason to find me paranoid.

As I headed down the hall, my breath escaped in feathery wisps. I shivered partly from the cold and partly from the prospect of an encounter with Deke. Chances were he was drunk again. Grandma said he was supposed to get here by five a.m. to fire up the furnace. It was almost seven, and the school felt like an icebox.

The moment my foot touched the basement floor, I knew something was wrong. It was usually warm close to the furnace room. Today an icy chill sank to my bones and the air was scented with the acrid scent of natural gas.

It's just my imagination, I told myself, remembering Tom's admonishing words in our last counseling session.

You've got to stop overreacting, he'd said. *It's not healthy.*

I swallowed hard and took a few tentative steps toward the boiler room. What happened next happened so quickly, my brain had no time to tell my feet to run. It began with a terror-stricken cry that sliced right through me. I would have thought it was the sound of an anguished animal, except that this cry was in the form of a spoken word. "Noooooooooooooo!"

A rush of icy air whistled past me as if the basement were drawing a sudden breath. My ears popped as a thundering roar rolled over me. I watched in horror as the door to Deke's room buckled out. Jagged orange tongues of fire encircled the frame. A cloud of dust engulfed me. I scrambled madly for the stairs.

I must have been in shock as I stumbled into the hallway because all I could do was stare dazedly at the teachers and a few early bird students who spilled from the classrooms. People shouted and shrieked, running every which way. Nobody seemed to know what to do.

"Out of the building, *now!*" the principal yelled.

A strong arm slipped around me and guided me toward the exit.

33

The Big Top parking lot was jammed with cars full of teenagers.

Mr. Cline had ordered the school closed for the investigation into the explosion. Most of the Oxford High students had gravitated to the favorite hangout.

A couple of kids from my scuba class had offered me a ride and now I joined the drove of students who were stampeding across the parking lot.

I glanced up at the giant clown face. His grotesque smile seemed more sinister than usual. I thought I saw a flicker in his eye, as if something had moved past the window.

Inside the Big Top, students were crammed into the booths. Some spilled into the aisles, and Roger was running to find extra chairs.

The room hummed and buzzed as the kids excitedly speculated on what had caused the explosion.

"I heard it was a Mafia hit," a stout boy shouted.

"Deke was probably involved in drug trafficking," another retorted.

"One of the cops said he got drunk and left the gas on," a frizzy-haired girl said.

Josh arrived in the midst of the excitement. Kelly had taken her mother's car and picked him up. He was still pale and shaky. The bruises around his eyes had deepened to a black and crimson shade. But he was smiling.

"Josh," I said. "You shouldn't be up and around." I shot Kelly an accusing glance, but she just smiled smugly.

A group of kids got up, vacating a corner booth, and we swiftly took possession. Josh sat beside me and, much to my annoyance, Kelly plopped down on his other side.

Despite the fact Deke had probably been killed, the somber mood was tinged with exhilaration. Though most of the students showed little sign of grief, Courtney Blaine was sobbing intermittently. Kelly reached around Josh and nudged me. "Looks like someone *else* is trying to be the center of attention," she said pointedly.

"If that's not the kettle calling the pot black, I don't know what is," I snapped.

"Is Courtney a relative of Deke's or something?" asked Josh.

"Nah," said Kelly. "She always gets hysterical about everything."

"I need to talk to you privately," Josh whispered in my ear.

As it turned out, we didn't get any time alone together until that evening. By then, the whole town was chattering about the news.

I'd learned about it at the dinner table, when Grandpa got up to answer the phone. He came back to the table, shaking his head. "That was Mr. Cline. They found part of Deke's mandible in the rubble. That's all that was left of him."

"What's a mandible?" asked Toby.

"Jawbone," said Grandpa. He pointed to his chin and wiggled his jaw. "That's the thing that moves when I talk."

Deke was dead.

I would not say I felt joy over the death of another human being, yet I felt relief. For I did not need to be afraid any longer.

"Looks like Deke got his karma," Josh said when I drove over to his house after dinner. "When you hurt people the way he did, it's always going to come back to you."

"Now that he's gone, how will we ever find out what happened to Nan and Scott?"

"That's what I wanted to talk to you about," he said. "You're not the only one who's been having dreams. Last night I had one of the strangest dreams I ever had. I saw something, Alex. It's not really clear, but I know the bodies of Scott and Nan are still here in Oxford."

"*Our* bodies!" I said.

He nodded solemnly. "I'm starting to think you're right. At first I though the reincarnation thing was crazy, but the dream I had was so real. I was Scott in the dream."

It was a wonderfully warm feeling to have someone on my side, especially when that person was Josh. I hugged him. "I'm so glad you believe me," I said.

"I wish none of it was true. The dream was awful. We were dead."

"Where were our bodies?"

He shook his head. "I don't remember. The nightmare started to fade as soon as I woke up."

"If we can find Scott and Nan's bodies, everyone will know they were murdered," I said slowly. "That's the proof we need. Grandpa will finally believe Nan didn't hurt him. If my body is buried in Oxford, I'm going to find it."

34

Deke's garden glowed in the moonlight.

"How are we going to move the statue?" I asked.

"Don't ask me," said Josh. "This was your idea."

The garden had seemed like the logical place to start. It all clicked together when I remembered Grandma mentioning that Deke had started his garden the year Nan disappeared. First he had put in that silly statue of the Labrador. It had sat there, alone in the center of the stretch of dirt for a whole year before he'd planted a row of peonies.

The garden now overflowed with daffodils, pansies, and every imaginable color of carnation. It was bordered with a protective fence of rosebushes.

Why, I wondered, had a man like Deke felt a sudden compulsion to plant a garden?

The answer could be that he was hiding something—something like a body. When I'd broached the subject with

Josh, he'd been skeptical at first. "I don't know," he'd said. "That would be pretty stupid of him to kill someone and then bury the body in his own garden where it could be connected to him if someone found it."

After tossing this around for a while, he had agreed that Deke was not the smartest man in the world.

So here we were, under the full moon, like a couple of ghouls searching for corpses.

Josh grabbed his crutch and hobbled over to the statue. Rocking it gently, he exclaimed, "Wow. This thing weighs a ton."

I joined him and together we tried to drag the statue off the concrete slab. As we attempted to lift it, Josh gasped sharply and his face wrinkled in pain.

"Are you okay?" I asked, concerned.

"No problem," he said, but I knew he was hurting.

"Hold on a second. Let's use our heads and find another way to move this thing."

"Shhh," Josh hissed. "I hear something."

I froze at the distinct crunch of footsteps on gravel. Somebody was coming!

Before we could react, the bushes parted and a familiar pale face peered in at us. "What are you guys up to?" a squeaky voice asked.

"Kelly!" I whispered. "Where did you come from?"

"I couldn't sleep," she replied. "I went out for a bike ride and saw you guys over here."

Why did I get the feeling she was not telling the truth? Had she followed us here, or was it simply a coincidence?

"This is weird," she said. "What are you doing in the middle of the night in Deke's garden?"

"Shut up and give us a hand," Josh said and put her to work beside me. She was stronger than she looked, and we dragged the statue off the corner of the slab where it plopped softly in the dirt.

"What are you looking for?" she asked.

"We think Deke buried something in here." I bent to lift the slab.

"Wait a minute," Josh said. "Let's use some leverage." He wedged the shovel's blade under the slab and easily slid it to the side.

"Buried treasure!" Kelly gushed.

Josh and I exchanged a glance. Ignoring her, I grabbed the shovel and started digging. The dark, loamy earth broke easily. I scooped up several light shovelfuls and tossed them to one side.

I was looking for my own body!

I shuddered and tried to push away the horror of what I was doing. My heart raced. My mouth was dry as paper.

I gripped the shovel handle tightly, plunging the blade into the dirt. It struck something hard. "I found something!" I gasped.

I felt sick to my stomach. I looked at Josh. He took the shovel from my trembling hands and gently scraped away some soil. "This is it," he said somberly.

Kelly and I crowded in to see. There, framed against the black earth, bones gleamed pearly white in the moonlight.

35

We stood for a long moment, staring at each other.

"What is that?" Kelly shrilly demanded.

"A skeleton," said Josh.

Her eyes popped open wide. Josh dropped the shovel and backed away from the grave.

"Oh, my God!" I said. "We did it! Oh, my God!"

It was decided by mutual consent that Kelly would go home and phone the police while Josh and I stood guard.

The police arrived in minutes, though it seemed more like an hour.

Finally! I thought. *Finally I have proof!*

"Okay, where's the body?" Sergeant Bryer asked.

Josh squeezed my hand as he pointed to the hole where the bones lay exposed. The sergeant bent over the grave and a moment later he laughed. "Poor Scruffy," he said and held up the small skull of a dog.

Three days later we had not lived down the humiliation. The whole town was laughing at us. We now had a reputation as "those crazy kids who reported a murdered dog to the police."

As it turned out, the dog had been Deke's. He was a black Labrador who had died of natural causes many years before. Apparently, the garden was a monument to him.

"Hey, Sherlock!" Mark yelled. "Dug up any dogs lately?"

"Nope," Josh retorted. "I haven't dated your sister in a couple of months."

Josh and I were at the Big Top, sharing a vegetarian burger as I put the final touches on the mural.

"You've done a great job!" Roger said as he emerged from the back with two thick chocolate shakes. He set them in front of us. "The shakes are on me. Thanks for working so hard on the mural, Alexis."

"Thank *you*," I said. "The shakes look great."

Rachel poked her head out of the kitchen doorway. "Hey, Dad! Where are the hamburger buns?"

"Should be right there in the cupboard," he said.

"I looked and they're not there!"

Roger shook his head. "It's the darnedest thing," he said to us. "That's the third time this has happened this week. I must have some awfully big rats. Yesterday a block of cheese disappeared. Maybe I should hire you two guys to catch the culprit." He winked at us. "I heard you're quite the detectives."

"We do dogs, not rats," Josh said.

Roger chuckled to himself as he headed back to the kitchen. It seemed there was no escaping the jokes.

"Don't worry," Josh said. "Everybody will pick on us until somebody else makes an ass of themselves. Then they'll forget about us."

I went back to work on the mural, and Josh stretched out

in the booth, slurping the last bit of chocolate from his shake as he watched me. "You sure spend a lot of time on the detail," he commented as I touched up the Oxy Roxy Theater. "You even painted the name of the movie playing on the marquee."

"*Saturday Night Fever* was showing when Nan and Scott worked at the theater," I said. "I saw it in that old photograph and decided to use it on the mural to make it authentic."

He stared a long time at the Oxy Roxy. "That's how we used to get in." His voice was oddly flat.

"What do you mean?"

He pointed at the little door on the side of the Oxy Roxy. "That's the utility access door. I had this image of us, crawling in there after the theater was closed. We'd sneak in with our friends and eat popcorn and show the movies in the middle of the night."

"Wow. Maybe you just had a spontaneous regression!"

"It was just a fleeting thought. But it's got me thinking about the Oxy Roxy. I'm getting a really powerful feeling a clue might be down there. Scott and Nan worked there right before they disappeared. If I can dive down and get inside, then maybe I'll see something that will trigger a memory."

"That place is a death trap! You heard what Tom said. And you're supposed to be taking it easy. It would be stupid to attempt a dive like that even if you were in perfect shape."

"I'm feeling better every day." He was still staring at the mural, his eyes glazed and distant.

"Josh!"

He smiled. "Don't worry so much."

"Just promise me you won't do anything stupid."

"Cross my heart!"

I gathered up my paintbrushes. "I'm going to the washroom. As soon as I get cleaned up, I'll be ready to go."

Fifteen minutes later, my paintbrushes were washed and lined up neatly in their plastic carrying case. I emerged from the rest room to find Josh talking with Sergeant Bryer. "If you hear anything let me know," the sergeant was saying.

"What's going on?" I asked.

"Burrel Osworth's mother reported him missing." Sergeant Bryer slowly eased his bulk from the booth. "She hasn't seen him in a week."

I set my paint box on the table. "Do you think something happened to him?"

He shrugged. "He's disappeared before. He's got the mind of a six-year-old in the body of a fifty-year-old man. He's Irma Osworth's only son and she dotes on him. You know how mothers worry."

"He sleeps in the park sometimes," Josh said. "But I haven't seen him there for a while."

As the door closed behind Sergeant Bryer, something occurred to me. I turned to Josh. "What if—" I said. "What if Burrel died in the school explosion?"

"I don't think so. They found the fragment of only one jawbone."

We both had the thought at the same instant. I saw it sparking in Josh's eyes, but I was the one who spoke it. "Maybe it was *Burrel's* jawbone!"

He nodded as horror dawned in his eyes. "That would mean Deke is still alive!"

"We should tell Sergeant Bryer what we're thinking," I said.

Josh ran his hands through his curls and sighed deeply. "Yeah, *right*. Like he's really going to believe what we have to say."

"I guess we don't have a lot of credibility," I agreed.

He snatched his keys from the table. "Let's talk about it on the way home."

Josh's car was parked in the far end of the parking lot, right next to the phone booth. As we passed it, the phone rang shrilly. We glanced at each other. It rang again. Josh reached in and snatched up the shiny black receiver. "Howdy," he said. "Hello? Guess they hung up."

We were three steps away when the phone began to ring again. "That's strange," I said, as a bristly apprehension slithered through me.

"Don't answer it," said Josh. "Somebody's playing games."

Brrring! It rang with an urgency. I shrugged and stepped into the booth. "Hello!"

"Die bitch," a raspy voice said.

I dropped the phone as if it were a red-hot skillet.

"What is it?" Josh asked.

"It's *him*! He's still alive!"

Josh picked up the phone and listened. "He hung up. How did he know to call here?" He looked around, his eyes sweeping every corner of the parking lot.

"He must be watching us!" Hysterical, I ran into his arms. "Let's call the police."

We drove a couple of blocks away and stopped at another phone booth and called Sergeant Bryer, who took the information with his usual lack of enthusiasm.

The rest of our afternoon was spent at Forgotten Lake, speculating on the odd turn of events. We sat in the car and stared out over the water. "Is it possible?" I asked. "Could Deke really be alive?"

"It sure looks that way."

"I'm scared, Josh."

His arm went around me. I leaned my cheek against his chest and was comforted by the sound of the strong beat of his heart. "I'm not going to let anything happen to you," he whispered.

The determination in his words frightened me. I pulled away and looked into his eyes. *"Josh?"*

"The answer is there." He nodded toward Forgotten Lake, and I could see in his face he was already picturing himself exploring the secrets of the Oxy Roxy.

"No!" I cried. "It's too dangerous. At least wait until you're better. You could ask Tom to go with you."

We headed back to town and when he pulled up in front of my house, Josh sounded distracted as he said, "Try to get some rest."

"Is that what you're going to do?"

"That's right," he said, but I did not believe him.

36

I *knew something was wrong the moment I pulled up in front* of Josh's house. His motorcycle was parked under the covered driveway, but his car was gone.

After he'd dropped me off, I had spent an hour in my room, turning the day's events over in my mind. I could not relax. I kept picturing Josh diving into Forgotten Lake's dark waters. I borrowed Mom's car and drove to his home.

The windows of the square white farmhouse stared at me blankly, as if to say "no one is here."

I knocked on the door anyway, lifting the black metal knocker and rapping sharply. Its hollow echo filled the air. I waited, but the only answer came from a crow high up in the alderwood tree. No one was home.

With creeping dread, I rounded the house. There was my wet suit, dangling from the hook on the back porch, where I had hung it the week before. I was not surprised to find the hook beside it empty.

On the drive over to Josh's, the dull teeth of fear had been there, all along, nibbling on the back of my mind. I knew where Josh was. He was diving in Forgotten Lake, exploring the Oxy Roxy.

It's a death trap.

The memory of Tom's warning splashed across my mind in a prickly wave of foreboding. Hands shaking, I grabbed my wet suit and gear, threw it into the trunk of my car, and sped off.

Tightly knitted clouds of gray cloaked the sky as I drove toward Forgotten Lake. The sun had sunk low in the sky, and the air rushing through the open car windows already smelled of night—sharp and cool and dankly green.

I gripped the steering wheel and pressed the accelerator to the floor. A hard lump of fear burned in the pit of my stomach. Josh was in no shape for a dive, even in the safest conditions. I blinked away an image of him, still and pale, at the bottom of the lake.

I had planned to stop and call for help, but the first couple of phone booths I passed were occupied.

What if Josh is diving right now? I worried. What if he passed out and drowned in the extra couple of minutes it took me to stop and phone for help?

If he is in trouble, I reasoned, then I can get to him as fast as anyone else. So I raced along the narrow, curving road and when I reached the lake, I turned into the parking lot so sharply my tires spun in the loose gravel, showering the side of the road with rocks.

His car was parked beside the pier and I pulled in behind it.

I scanned the beach. *Josh, where are you?*

Forgotten Lake mirrored the steely dome of the sky. I stretched my gaze across the vast wrinkling water. A thin wind coaxed the lake into motion so it seemed to be sucking and slurping on the edges of the shore.

I ventured onto the pier, my feet slapping an urgent rhythm on the worn, gray wood as I hurried to the end. I looked in the direction of the Oxy Roxy, where I knew the old theater was slowly decaying in its underwater world, just thirty feet from the edge of the dock. There were the telltale bubbles of a diver.

I dashed up to the car and began carrying my equipment down to the dock. Ten minutes later, I'd wrestled into my scuba suit at the water's edge.

My knees were rubbery and weak as I struggled under the strain of the heavy equipment and made my way across the dock. I awkwardly lowered myself onto the ladder, my feet dipping into the water. Suddenly, I recognized a ragged figure, rummaging through the garbage can at the foot of the pier.

Burrel!

Burrel is alive.

If Burrel is alive, then Deke must be dead!

I froze. If Deke is dead then who—?

Who?

Who had made the menacing phone call? And what about the threatening notes? According to Josh, Burrel could not read or write.

He's harmless. Everyone believed that. But what if Burrel *wasn't* harmless? What if he just fooled everyone into thinking he couldn't read or write?

He straightened up and though his face was in shadows, I sensed his eyes upon me.

There was no time to worry about him now. Josh needed me. I glanced at the trail of bubbles rolling to the surface. I pushed away from the dock.

A lifetime of phobias came back to haunt me now. Fear

of water. Fear of tight spaces. What if Josh was inside? Could I actually go into that dark, old theater?

Josh! That was all that mattered. The fear melted away as I clenched the mouthpiece tightly between my teeth and descended toward the source of the bubbles. As I did so, a sharp pressure filled my ears. I stopped and tried a trick Josh had showed me. With a yawn, I equalized the pressure in my ears. The pain melted away.

I swam beneath the surface, down into a deep, shadowy place. Faint light filtered from above as the ominous gray mass of the Oxy Roxy loomed before me.

I hovered a moment, searching for a sign of Josh's bubbles. But only *my* bubbles disturbed the quiet stillness of the watery realm.

I've lost his trail, I realized. My eyes swept the cold, concrete structure and I thought of haunted castles.

Death trap.

Was Josh inside?

I hesitated. If he *was* in there, how had he gotten in? The double doors were barred with thick, heavy boards.

Perhaps he was exploring the other side of the submerged theater.

I floated around the building, legs kicking gracefully behind me. As I turned the corner, I swam into a school of fish. Their bright, silver underbellies flashed as they seemed to turn with one mind.

I circled the old theater, and when I reached the far side, I saw it. A small metal door near the floor of the lake. It was the one Josh had pointed out to me in the mural! I dove toward it. Here the water was murky, as if another diver had kicked up the silt moments before. I yanked on the door and to my surprise, it swung open.

I aimed my flashlight into the hole and shuddered at the tight space. I did not want to go inside, but Josh might be in trouble. Time was running out.

I plunged ahead and followed my light's long milky beam down the corridor.

Suddenly the area opened up.

I was inside!

With an arcing sweep of my flashlight, I searched the huge room. The Oxy Roxy was still intact. It was an eerie scene. The ceiling hung high above me and strands of green algae dripped from the balcony. The rows of seats looked as if they were waiting for mermaids to occupy them so the show could begin. The thick velvet curtain that once draped over the screen now floated ominously toward the ceiling.

I felt as if I were flying as I soared through the water above the seats, searching for Josh. He was nowhere in sight.

I swam toward the dark doorway that I knew led to the lobby. The lobby felt close and cramped. My flashlight seemed brighter in the smaller space. I aimed it toward the concession stand and was startled to see a school of fish darting in and out of the big broken popcorn machine.

I glanced down at my air gage. I was nearly to the red zone, my reserve. I had only fifteen minutes of air left!

Had Josh come and gone without my seeing him?

Perhaps he had found another way out. I took one last look around and headed back the way I had come.

I swam through the tunnel-like hallway, hastily grabbing the sides of the wooden walls. My hand closed around a knob and I pulled on it, trying to propel myself faster. To my amazement the door swung open, and with it a rush of thick, dark water. The motion had created a suction and it brought a grisly surprise.

A skeleton lunged out, long golden hair writhing and twisting in all directions.

Inches from mine, its black eye sockets stared vacantly back at me. Its jaw opened and closed as if it were laughing at a macabre joke. I pushed away from the opening, trying to escape the grotesque image. The skeleton came with me—her long hair tangled in my regulator. Together we did a horrifying dance. Her bony arms flailed dizzily at her sides and her head bobbed up and down while I struggled to get free.

I heard the strange gurgle of my own scream, distorted by the water.

Somehow I broke loose. The bony figure was left behind as I burst outside. I forced myself to stop, as I remembered Josh's warning.

Never surface quickly. It could kill you!

I took a deep breath and exhaled, then followed my bubbles slowly upward.

I was several feet from the surface when it happened. A strong grip closed around my ankle.

37

I *struggled wildly. My arms thrashed out in front of me.* My hands reached desperately for something to grab onto. I tried to scream again and kicked ferociously at the thing that had my leg. It loosened its hold and I swam free. I popped to the surface, like a cork flying from a champagne bottle.

A moment later someone bobbed from the water and I found myself looking into a familiar face. His brown eyes were magnified by his thick scuba mask. Tom!

I stared at him in horror. I ripped my mouthpiece out and shrieked, "Stay away from me!"

"Alexis." His voice was calm. "Get a hold of yourself. You were surfacing so fast I was afraid you'd get the bends."

"Oh!" Relief flooded through me. *"That's* why you grabbed me?"

"Of course. I was trying to help. What did you think?"

"I don't know! You grabbed me and I lost my head. There's a skeleton down there, Tom! I think it's Nan!"

"What did you think you were doing?" he demanded. "You're a novice diver. You shouldn't even be in the water without an experienced partner."

"I was looking for Josh!"

"Don't worry. He was here earlier with his scuba gear. But I talked him into going home."

Tom started toward the dock, and I followed him. On the pier, we peeled off our scuba suits. I shivered convulsively as I pictured the macabre sight beneath the lake. The sun had set. Night crept across the sky, drenching the clouds in a shadowy blue reflected by the water.

The lamppost flickered on. Its stark, white light painted the pier in an eerie glow. A cold gust coaxed goose bumps from my flesh as my thoughts tumbled about numbly.

Josh was all right! That was all that mattered.

"Thank God you're here," I said to Tom as I pulled my sweatpants on over my bathing suit. "I'm so glad you stopped Josh. When I got here earlier and saw his car and didn't see *him*—" I paused as I glanced at the parking area. "It's still here!" I gasped at the sight of the Fairlane, still parked in front of my car.

"I didn't think he should be driving." Tom briskly rubbed the towel through his hair. "I gave him a ride home."

"That's funny. I didn't pass you on the road."

"We took the long route," he mumbled. "As for *you, what* were you doing scuba diving in that death trap?"

"I would never have gone down if I didn't think Josh was in trouble. When I saw the bubbles I figured it was him, and then when I found the skeleton—! It was so awful!" I shuddered. "I can't believe Nan was under the lake all these years. It was like I was face-to-face with my own skeleton."

"Are you sure it was a human skeleton?" His tone was skeptical. "I seem to recall another false alarm involving the bones of a dog."

"This was *human*! And it was *Nan*!"

"Just because the skeleton had long blond hair doesn't mean it was Nan."

Had I mentioned the skeleton's hair?

I stared at Tom and his face seemed to distort. His mouth was the same as always—that tight little smile twitching on the round, tan face. His nose was still straight, the nostrils still flared. But his *eyes* . . .

Those small brown eyes gazing out from the familiar features had changed. They flashed with an intensity I had not seen before. They stared steadily into mine as he said, "You're wondering how I knew about the hair, right?"

"Well, I—"

He stooped down abruptly and pointed to my regulator. He grabbed the strands of golden hair tangled there and tore it out with a sickening rip. "When I saw this hair stuck in your regulator, I figured it was from the skeleton." He opened his fingers and the snarled locks fell to the dock.

I stared in horror at the knot of pale strands. This hair had once grown from the head of a smiling girl. She had brushed it each night—one hundred strokes so it sparkled like a new penny when the sunshine touched it.

"We've got to call the police," I said.

Tom's laugh was as sharp and cold as an icicle. His face was a mask of amusement.

A mask!

Sociopaths wear a mask, he had once said. That was what his face resembled now—a plastic, grinning mask with two dots of evil peering out from where the eyes should be.

Slow realization tiptoed over me with icy feet.

"What are you staring at?"

"Nothing," I said quickly. My voice sounded odd and high even to my own ears.

"Nan, Nan, Nan." He laughed again.

I edged away. His hand shot out and grabbed my arm. "I knew you were my Nan the first day you walked into class." His voice was strangely devoid of emotion. "I love you, Nan. I always have. Why can't you see that?"

"You're *hurting* me!" I tried to twist from his grasp. His fingers pinched deep into my flesh.

"At first I thought you had come back to me." Sudden rage curled the corners of his words. "Then you started fawning all over Josh—*just like you did with Scott*!"

"Please, Tom. Let me go!"

"Old Tommy was good enough for a friend when you wanted someone to drive you to work or help with your homework." His voice was raspy. "But you didn't want to be seen with him at the prom. Was it my turkey neck? Was I just Tom Turkey to you like I was to everyone else?"

"I don't know what you're talking about!"

"I don't have a turkey neck anymore. I gained weight and worked out. Women find me attractive now, Nan. Do *you* think I'm attractive, Nan?" He squeezed my arms so tightly I gasped out in pain. "Do you think I'm attractive?" he roared.

"Yes!" I sobbed.

"I've taken care of all the obstacles so we could be together again—just like I took care of them last time. Remember when I took care of Scott?"

"Oh, no!" I shrieked. "What have you done with Josh?" I fell to my knees and he yanked me roughly to my feet.

"Get a hold of yourself, Nan! I don't want to have to kill you again. I was sick with grief the first time. You don't know how bad that hurt me. But, Nan, if only you had returned my love, we would have had a wonderful life."

The face of death flashed before me like the sad skeleton dancing beneath the lake.

Tom was going to kill me.

He was going to kill me again.

If only you had returned my love . . .

It would never happen. I would never, ever love Tom. But my life was at stake. I drew on a strength I didn't know I had. "But I *do* love you!" I lied. My voice trembled like a thin blade of grass shivering in the breeze.

His face was an inch from mine and he squinted, as if scrutinizing my very soul.

Don't let the bad one stop you this time!

My words lost their tremor. They skipped off my tongue, sure and steady as I said, "It was always you, Tom." I forced my eyes to shine adoringly. "I remember that little bear you gave me."

"You remember *that?*" He was surprised.

"Of course. It was always special to me."

"Oh, Nan!" His powerful arms snaked around my shoulders as he embraced me. His breath was hot and oniony.

I wanted to run. He held me tight. The hint of a gag tickled my throat. I swallowed hard.

Lie, lie, lie. Lie to save your own life.

"I love you, Tom. That's why I came back." I willed myself to relax, to sag against him.

His fingers trailed through my hair and I thought of thick-legged spiders.

"It wasn't so bad killing the others," he said. "Judy laughed in my face when I asked her on a date. I wouldn't have asked, but she reminded me of you with that long blond hair. You'd been gone a couple of years and I missed you so much, you see.

"Judy was easy to kill. Early in the morning, before the picnic, I found her passed out on drugs and tossed her in the pond. She hit her head and it looked like an accident.

Her father was the police chief and called off the investigation because he didn't want it known his daughter was on drugs.

"I grew to like the killing. But I was afraid I'd end up in prison. So after I killed you and Scott and Judy, I swore off it. I thought I had it under control. Then you came back and I *remembered*. The instant I saw your pretty face, the pain came rushing back." He laughed—a frightening humorless sound. "Tawny—the little bitch—teased me all the time. She'd come to class in a tight dress and flirt with me so I wouldn't flunk her. I knew she was laughing at me. She got what was coming. Old Deke made the mistake of nosing into my business. I couldn't let him go to the police with what he suspected."

I wanted to scream, but amazingly I kept my voice calm as I asked, "What about Josh?"

"I'll get to that. Dottie would have been okay, but she found that damn tape. Scott left her a message, said he'd decided not to sell his car to me because we got in an argument over you. Scott said on the tape he was giving the car to his mother. She put two and two together and figured out I had not paid him for the car. I stopped by her trailer to see what she knew. I took one look at her face and it was obvious she had it all figured out. I didn't lay a finger on her, though. The problem took care of itself. She was so frightened to see me she had a stroke."

"What about Anita?"

"I thought she was going to be special. Thanks to your little poster prank, I found out she was running around behind my back. She learned her lesson."

"So it wasn't an accident?"

He laughed. "What do you think?"

"You seemed so worried about her," I said.

"I outsmarted you. You never suspected me, did you?"

"No."

"It was so easy fooling everyone. You got a phone threat in my office during one of our counseling sessions. You thought it was Deke, but I called you through my computer with a prerecorded message. It threw you off. Just like when I forged Nan's name on the postcard I sent to your family. They thought she'd run away."

"You hurt all those people—"

"Let's not worry about the others. Let's concentrate on you and me."

"You still haven't told me about Josh. What did you do to him?"

He stiffened. His hands slid around my shoulders then slowly crept up my neck. "I got rid of him," he snarled. "Why do you care?"

"I—"

"You said you loved me." His fingers tightened around my throat.

"I do!"

"Liar!"

I choked out a strangled plea. "Tom, *please!*"

"Do you remember the ride in the trunk of the Fairlane, Nan?"

"I don't know," I whispered.

"Right after I knocked your daddy out, I took you out to the Fairlane. We were going to be happy, you and I. I tried to tell you that, but you wouldn't believe me! You kept asking about Scott. So I opened the trunk and showed you he was no longer a problem. Instead of being happy, you got hysterical and tried to wake him up. But he wouldn't wake up. Remember what you said to me?"

"No."

"You said you hated me. You hurt me, Nan." The evil slits of his eyes spilled tears. He blinked them away. "I put you in the trunk beside Scott and I drove around like that for hours, wondering what to do. Finally, I drove out to the lake. I opened the trunk and asked you if you'd changed your mind. Do you remember what you said?" His fingers trailed menacingly around my neck. "You lied, Nan."

I shut my eyes, for I could not stand the sight of him an instant longer.

"Look at me!" he shouted. "I asked you if you changed your mind and you said yes, that you loved me. I let you out of the trunk and do you know what you did? You ran! But I caught you."

"You drowned me."

"Did you learn your lesson?"

"Yes!" I cried.

"So here we are again." His voice was as scratchy as sandpaper. "Your boyfriend is in the trunk and you are trying to decide if you want to join him."

Something stirred in the corner of my vision. I glanced over Tom's shoulder. My breath snagged in my throat.

Josh!

He was alive. Blood oozed down his forehead. He stumbled forward, careening awkwardly from side to side.

"So, Nan," Tom said. "What will it be?"

"You!" I shouted, trying to drown out the sound of Josh's approaching footsteps. "I want to be with you, Tom."

Josh bent and picked up Tom's scuba tank. He staggered toward us, his face contorting with the strain of lifting the heavy tank.

"I made a mistake last time, Tom," I babbled. "That's why I came back, to make things right between us."

Josh raised the tank up over Tom's head.

I held my breath, watching him.

"What are you looking at?" Tom asked.

"Nothing!"

He swung around. Josh's face froze in surprise as Tom plowed into him.

Josh's body hit the dock with a hollow thud.

"Leave him alone!" I shrieked.

Tom lunged. He straddled Josh as his powerful hands closed around his throat.

Sobbing, I dove toward the tank. I grabbed it. It was amazingly light in my hands. I swung my arms, swooping it into the air.

Don't let the bad one stop you this time.

I screamed as I brought the tank crashing down on the back of Tom's head.

38

The skeletons of Scott and Nan were positively identified by the county coroner. Tom had stashed the bodies in the Oxy Roxy eighteen years ago.

He'd gotten nervous when he realized Josh was planning to explore the old theater. Apparently, Tom was planning to move the skeletons to a new hiding place, but I found mine before he had the chance.

It was a strange feeling, attending my own funeral.

Grandpa picked out a white coffin decorated with carved roses. I tried to tell him that Nan's skeleton was just an empty shell—that it had no more meaning than snipped off fingernails. "Don't spend all that money on an expensive coffin," I said. "Nan's soul won't enjoy it."

Grandpa is stubborn. He will not accept that I am the reincarnation of his daughter. Neither will the rest of my family.

"If I'm not Nan's reincarnation, then how did I know what happened to her?" I demanded.

"You're psychic," Grandpa said. "That's the only explanation."

Perhaps he is right.

Perhaps I am so much like my aunt that her spirit sensed this and she communicated to me from the grave. Who is to say for sure?

Though he grieved for his daughter, Grandpa was comforted to learn she had not wanted to hurt him—that it was Tom who pushed him into the machine.

It took us a few days to piece the whole puzzle together.

Deke was little more than a bystander in the tragic tale. He suspected Tom was behind the murders of Nan and Judy and did not have the good sense to keep this fact from him. The police surmised Tom fixed the gas so it caused an explosion in the boiler room.

Tom himself could not verify this. He died instantly when I hit him with the tank.

Burrel had been on his way to see Deke when the explosion occurred. He was standing outside the back door of the basement when an orange ball of fire rolled out toward him. Frightened, he'd run away and hidden in an upstairs storage room in the Big Top.

He'd snuck down to the kitchen at night and eaten hamburger buns and cheese. He'd finally ventured out and was back to rummaging through garbage cans where I spotted him at the lake when I was looking for Josh.

Anita is engaged to Bruce Wingate. She'd been trying to break off with Tom for weeks before I moved to town, but he would not accept she did not return his feelings.

I was honored when Anita asked me to be a bridesmaid. She, of course, understands now that I had nothing to do with the threats against her.

Dottie is recuperating in a nursing home and has no

memory of the three months prior to her stroke. Josh and I went to see her and smuggled in one of her wiener dogs for a visit.

"I know she's kind of a strange woman, but I do feel something for her," Josh admitted to me. "If I *am* the reincarnation of Scott, then Dottie was my mother."

Josh and I have had endless conversation about our strange lives. "Remember when I told you about stealing the Fairlane?" he asked.

"Yes. You thought there was something precious in the trunk and you had to take it to the police."

"Now I know what was in the trunk. It was you."

"No wonder I've always been claustrophobic." I could not remember being locked in the trunk, but I could imagine it. I trembled, picturing the dark space squeezing around me. "It must have been awful for you, too," I said.

"It was. I've never liked being in tight spaces either. Good thing I found that scuba knife and tripped the trunk latch. Tom would have killed us both if I hadn't escaped."

A year has passed since Tom died. I guess I shouldn't be afraid any longer, but something bothers me. If *I* came back, does that mean that Tom could come back, too?

The idea makes me shiver.

I was in the grocery store the other day when I spotted a newborn riding in his mother's shopping cart. As I stopped to admire the baby, his eyes met mine—small brown eyes that stared back with an unwavering gaze that sent a chill through me.

Was it Tom?

Perhaps.

Or maybe it was simply a child with brown eyes like his.

That is probably the case, but for one terrifying moment, I felt as if I was looking into the eyes of a killer.